THESE FALLEN SWORDS

SONG OF THE FALLEN SWORDS
BOOK 1

RYAN KIRK

WATERSTONE
MEDIA

For my daughter
Light of my life

My daughter looked at me, tears welling in her eyes. "Why are we leaving?" she asked.

"Our home isn't safe any longer," I answered.

She was innocent then, unaware of the monsters that prowled the land and the sacrifices we'd made to live here. All she knew was that she would never walk the land again.

After today, her home was in the sky.

— SINGER WALLACE, *A SONG FOR THE SURFACE*

PROLOGUE

Radyn imagined his hoe was a maniblade and the soil a fallen enemy. He raised his weapon far above his head, then brought it down with a powerful shout. The edge of the hoe sank deep into the mix of fresh manure and old soil, spraying his ankles with fine debris. He pulled the hoe toward him, finishing his fallen enemy.

A chuckle behind him made him jump and spin around, holding the hoe before him as though he were a Sword of the clan preparing for his next opponent.

Father held up his hands in mock surrender, a wide smile on his face. He was lanky, nearly twice the height of his only child. Dirt stained his fingertips, and sweat carved small channels of dust from his cheeks, but his eyes twinkled with mirth. "Defeating villains again?" he asked.

Radyn's cheeks flushed, and he nodded. "Sorry, Father."

Andre put his hands down. "So long as this section of

the field is done by sundown, it doesn't matter how it gets done, so go right ahead. But the kitchen has brought food up for supper. Ready for a break?"

Radyn was. He'd woken up near the crack of dawn to help Father in the field. After nearly two hours of backbreaking work, he'd broken his fast with the other farmers, then hurried to the nearest school for his daily lessons. Those had lasted until about an hour ago when he'd returned to the fields. His stomach rumbled, and he nodded eagerly.

"Figured you might be. I'm grateful you came up to help, but you could have rested after school."

"You need the help. You're already behind, and I'm happy to lend a hand," Radyn said.

Father put his hand on Radyn's shoulder. "I'm proud to hear you say it."

They walked together to the tree where the kitchen staff were serving food. They'd brought up two large pots of porridge, and the men, women, and children who worked the fields queued for the food. Radyn and Father took their place, greeting familiar faces and trading stories about the day. Father spoke quietly with a couple, discussing his plans for the next day.

No one his age was nearby, but Radyn didn't mind. Andre liked to call him a "watcher," and he supposed the title fit well enough. He was naturally curious, and he found that by watching farmers at their work and asking questions, he could learn as much or more than he did in school. Today, he listened to two of his neighbors discussing Nuela's proposal to expand the population of Firestone.

Neither spoke out openly against the Blade of the city,

but they made no secret of their hesitation. More mouths to feed meant more work for the farmers, and they only had access to so much land. The Blade's proposal would cut into their annual reserves, leaving them at the mercy of a poor harvest.

Radyn had heard about the plan in school, where the teachers had presented it as something certain. More citizens meant more farmers, more craftspeople, and, most importantly, more young men and women who would aspire to join the clan. He'd not considered any downsides, but the farmer's complaints sounded reasonable. He made a note to consider the two sides of the argument when he had more time. For the moment, he withheld his judgment. Father always cautioned him about jumping to conclusions.

The queue moved quickly, and soon Radyn sat next to his father with a bowl of porridge in hand. Their dining room was nothing more than an open patch of wild grass, trampled flat over the course of hundreds of meals. One of Father's friends, a slim man named Otis, threw a question his way. "Radyn, you'll be finishing school in a year or two, won't you?"

Radyn nodded, his mouth full.

"What do you think you'll do after?"

The small circle of farmers all looked at him, and for the second time that hour, he felt his cheeks reddening. He stared down at the ground to avoid their gazes. "I'm not sure," he admitted.

He stirred the porridge in his bowl, then forced himself to look up. Father said it was important for young men to face the world. He didn't care so much about the world as he did Father, but it was as good a time as any to let Father know his thoughts.

"I might attempt to pass the trials to become a clan member. Otherwise, or if I fail, I'd be happy to work by Father's side in the fields."

They greeted his answer with several nods and a few grins.

"Both honorable paths," Otis said. He nudged Andre with his shoulder. "You must be proud."

Father studied his son with a careful eye, his expression revealing nothing of the thoughts no doubt churning behind his calm exterior. "I am."

The conversation moved on to other matters, and Radyn only halfway listened. Otis had asked the very question he'd been contemplating most of the day. A Dagger had come by his class this morning to speak about the process of joining the clan, answering questions until their instructor politely but firmly told the class they were abusing the Dagger's kindness.

Like a lot of his friends, Radyn sometimes dreamed about becoming one of the clan. Besides becoming a Singer, it was the most honorable role in the entire city of Firestone. But even Singers almost always were chosen from among the clan.

At times during this morning's talk, it had seemed to Radyn like the Dagger was trying to convince the children not to join the clan. He emphasized the brutal training and the never-ending menial duties initiates had to endure. If that had been the Dagger's purpose, it had been successful. At lunch, Radyn had heard a handful of his friends claiming that the clan was no longer for them.

Radyn hadn't decided. Becoming a Dagger, or even a

Sword, would ensure Father would never want for anything. But Radyn didn't mind farming, either. It was hard work, but just as essential to Firestone's survival as the clan's leadership. Farming would also allow him to stay close to Father.

He wasn't sure how Father would take his announcement, though. Father never spoke out openly against the clan, but he didn't seem to admire the Swords and Daggers the way others did. Radyn didn't understand why, but he'd also never had the courage to ask.

After they'd eaten and returned their bowls to the kitchen staff, Radyn asked Father about that morning's presentation. He mentioned it had felt like the Dagger had tried to turn initiates away.

"That's an astute observation," Father said. He chewed on a stalk of grass as they walked. "What do you think would happen if everyone in your class, who wanted to be a member of the clan, tried to take the trials?"

Radyn considered all the friends in his class who wanted to be Daggers. Until this morning, it had been almost everyone. "They'd be overwhelmed."

"Correct. And even if half passed the trials, they'd have too many initiates for the Daggers and Swords to handle. As they became overwhelmed, the quality of their training would suffer, and our clan wouldn't be as strong, even though their numbers grew."

Radyn shuddered at the thought. One part of Father's answer bothered him, though. "Why don't they just say that?"

"Often, people don't know exactly what they want.

Think of all your friends. If a Dagger had told them all I just told you, would it dissuade anyone?"

"Probably not."

"So instead, the Dagger tells you how hard it is. He or she reminds you of the countless hours of hard work you'll have to complete. It's a little like weeding the fields. Such talks dissuade those who aren't deeply rooted, clearing the way so that those who are can grow and thrive. I imagine you'll hear many such talks over the next year or two. Then those who remain will be excellent initiates."

Father's answer bothered Radyn, but it took him a moment to understand why. "If the clan can't handle so many initiates, why does the Blade want to expand the population?"

"Another good question. The difference lies in the speed of the change. The clan couldn't train a hundred additional initiates this year, but they could train ten more, and then an additional ten after that. They could prepare to handle a slow population increase. Raising children takes time, you know."

Radyn scowled at the humor in Father's tone. They were almost back to their field, though, and they hadn't exchanged so much as a word about his answer to Otis. He had to know, and the only way he'd find out was by asking. Father wasn't one to share his feelings otherwise. "Would you be upset if I tried to join the clan?"

Father didn't answer immediately. He thought for a few steps, then said, "No. I'm not sure the clan is the best place for you, but if that was what you truly wanted, I'd support you. That goes for any path you might choose."

Radyn offered his father a quick bow. "Thank you, Father."

He waved the bow away, but before he could say anything, the peal of bells filled the air. Both Radyn and Father looked to the sky. Radyn saw them first, and he pointed. At the moment, they were small, barely larger than a mosquito. They grew quickly, though. Dozens of them, flying in a loose formation.

Radyn's heart pounded, but he didn't move. Some part of his mind refused to believe the sight was real. Even as the bells rang and the farmers ran, he wondered if he was imagining it.

After a few more seconds, the figures were large enough Radyn could make out their wings. Then he saw the warriors riding atop the dragons.

That was when he realized how fast they were flying. It wouldn't be long before they were on top of Firestone. The realization woke up some older part of his mind. His eyes went wide, and he pulled on Father's arm.

Father stared up at the sky for a moment more, then shook his head. Radyn pulled again. The nearest stair was only two hundred yards away. Farmers had already yanked the door on the protective shed open and poured into the confined space, jostling one another as they disappeared beneath the surface. A queue formed, but it was nothing like the calm meal line. As farmers fought to reach the door, the entrance jammed up, keeping all from safety. Radyn pulled on Father's wrist. The sooner they reached the queue, the faster they could descend the stairs to safety. But Father wouldn't budge.

"There's too many," he muttered.

Too many what? Invaders? Farmers trying to escape? What was he talking about?

Father ran away from the stairs. Radyn, still trying to pull on Father's wrist, was instead pulled along. "Father!"

Radyn could do nothing but watch in growing horror as the shed and safety grew farther away. He reached out his free arm as if he could grab it, but Father's pull was too strong. Radyn struggled for a moment but was powerless against Father's greater strength. He nearly tripped and fell, then surrendered to Father's will and ran behind him.

They stopped suddenly near the middle of an unfamiliar field. Freshly tilled soil surrounded them, but the dirt they stood on was undisturbed. Father reached into the loose soil, then pulled on a thin chain hidden just below the surface.

"What's that?"

"A trapdoor used by the clan to ambush raiders. It leads to the lower levels, just like any other stairs or ladder."

"How do you know that?"

"No time to explain. Just get down there."

Radyn looked up at the sky, then swore.

The raiders had arrived. Several dragons had landed in fields behind Radyn. Warriors slid, jumped, and dropped off the enormous beasts like flies scattering off rotting food. Another dragon swooped close by, picking up two cows grazing nearby in its enormous claws. Their panicked *moos* were cut short as the dragon squeezed, shattering spines and ribs. Radyn stared, unable to look away.

Father pulled harder on the chain, and a square

appeared in the soil. With one last tug, the dirt slid off the door, exposing a square steel plate. It opened on oiled hinges, exposing an unlit drop beneath. Radyn saw the top few rungs of a ladder, then nothing but darkness.

"Get down there, now!" Father said.

Radyn forced his limbs into motion. He clambered down the ladder, then paused when he saw Father wasn't following him. "Aren't you coming?"

Father wasn't paying attention to Radyn. His gaze was on the developing battle.

"Where are all the Daggers?" Father asked.

A pair of maniblades flared to life against the setting sun. Two raiders advanced on the jammed stairway. They looked eager to cut their way through the bodies in their way.

Father looked around again. "They should be here by now."

"Let's hide," Radyn said. There was nothing they could do against the raiders.

Father shook his head. "Get below. I'll join you as soon as I can."

Without another word, he sprinted toward the raiders. Radyn almost cried out but pressed his lips shut so as not to warn the raiding Daggers. Father was only a farmer. What could he do against a Dagger?

Radyn knew he should retreat to the relative safety of the levels below, but he was frozen in place.

Father's long strides reached the raiders just as they cut down the first farmers scrambling to reach the stairwell. He drove his fist into the closest raider's face, who never saw the blow coming.

The raider crumpled. Before he could rise, Father

stomped hard on the man's neck. Radyn swore he could hear the crack from where stood half-hidden by the tunnel. The second raider turned and cut down, and Radyn's pent-up scream finally escaped from his throat.

The maniblade missed Father as he slid to the side. The raider looked as surprised as Radyn, but Father drove his elbow hard into the man's face. Blood gushed from the raider's nose, and his eyes rolled up in his head. His neck soon suffered the same fate as his companion's.

Radyn stared, wide-eyed, as Father reached down and stripped the shards off the bodies. He strapped them to his own wrists, then picked up the fallen hilts. He stuffed one into a pocket, but held the other in his hands. The maniblade extended from the hilt, the length of a sword.

"Get to safety!" Father yelled, his voice deeper and more authoritative than Radyn had ever heard.

The farmers used the opportunity to force themselves down the stairs. Father stood guard, a watchful sentinel.

Other raiders closed in on the stairwell. Radyn wasn't sure if it was because it was one of the central stairwells that led below or if Father's fight had drawn their attention, but it felt as if the majority of the raiders had closed upon Father.

The first reached him in less than a minute. The raiding Dagger swung his maniblade at Father, but Father's weapon was longer, and he avoided the cut easily. He snapped his wrists in response, and the Dagger fell, cut open from shoulder to torso.

Twice more single Daggers tried their skill against Father and were found wanting.

Those that came after were more cautious, but even then, Father defeated the pairs as they attacked. The last of the farmers made it down into the stairwell, and Radyn wanted to shout, to scream at his father to run, but there was no place for him to go. He was surrounded by raiders fighting to reach the same stairwell.

Radyn blinked, certain it would reveal that he imagined what he saw. Father was a farmer, so what chance did he have against even the lowliest of enemy Daggers?

Father slipped past another maniblade, stabbing it deep into a Dagger's stomach.

Then Radyn could see no more. Too many raiders had clustered around Father, and the only reason Radyn knew Father hadn't fallen was because the raiders weren't rushing down the stairs.

Radyn looked around, much like his father had minutes ago. Where were all the Daggers who would defend Firestone? They should have been here long ago, moments after the bells started sounding the alarm.

Radyn climbed one rung higher, looking for any sign of Father, but he was lost in the press of combatants.

The spell that had frozen him in place broke, and Radyn swore. He could do no good on the surface, and if Father knew he was still here, there would be hell to pay later. He took one last look for Father, then descended the ladder, closing the trapdoor above him.

The passage was unlit, so closing the door cast Radyn into a cave of perfect darkness. He didn't panic. He'd been climbing and descending ladders since he could walk, and he carefully planted each foot. Before long, his feet were on the solid steel decking of the level below. He gingerly reached out his hands, exploring the small space he found himself in.

It wasn't much more than the bottom of a long tube, but he found the handle for a door. He lifted the lever, opened the door, and emerged in an unfamiliar hallway. It was lit, though, so Radyn found a place to sit and waited for Father to return.

The deck underneath him shuddered, but Radyn didn't know why. He curled into a ball and waited.

The first sounds to reach his ears were those of boots slapping against the deck as they ran. Radyn looked up to see a squad of Daggers race around the corner, hilts in hand. They didn't stop until they reached Radyn.

One Dagger addressed him. "Who are you, and what are you doing here?"

Despite the fear that tightened his throat, Radyn spoke. "Radyn, son of Andre. We were farming when the raid started. Father didn't want to use the stairwell, so he sent me down here. But then he defeated a pair of raiders, and now he's fighting a lot more. You need to get up there!"

The Dagger frowned. "Andre, you said?"

"Yes!"

The Dagger glanced at one of his companions, who shrugged. The Dagger told Radyn. "Stay here. We'll see if we can find your father."

The Dagger pointed to the door Radyn had emerged from, and the squad climbed silently up the ladder like vengeful ghosts. Radyn waited, arms wrapped around his knees. The world shuddered again, and he looked up, halfway expecting a dragon to tear through the soil above and snatch him from the hallway.

He didn't know how long he waited in that hallway. He kept imagining his father running from an angry dragon. In every imagining, the dragon won. Radyn pulled his knees in tighter.

The Daggers had closed the hatch behind them, so no sound echoed down to Radyn's position. He couldn't guess if they were winning or losing, if the raid was close to over or just beginning.

Radyn jerked his head toward the open door when he heard the trapdoor open, and heavy footsteps descended the ladder. He strained his hearing, but the surface was silent.

The Dagger he'd spoken with earlier landed heavily on the deck. His once-clean uniform was covered in dirt and blood, and his eyes had a faraway look that hadn't been there before. He came over to Radyn and sat down beside him. They stared at the opposite wall together.

Radyn looked hopefully at the Dagger, who refused to meet his gaze. The Dagger gave a small shake of his head, and to Radyn, it felt like the deck had collapsed beneath him. He fell deeper and deeper into a hole that had no bottom.

"I'm sorry," the Dagger said.

He held his hands out and studied his palms, stained with blood.

"I'm sorry," the Dagger repeated, "but we'll do everything we can to take care of you. You have my word. Your father died a hero, and it's the very least we can do."

1

The Dagger's name was Viktor, and he remained glued to Radyn's side after the raid. At first, Radyn had wanted to return to the surface, but Viktor told him that wouldn't be possible. The clan had flooded the area and had all exits locked down. They wouldn't open again until they were certain they'd cleared the halls of the last of the raiders, but that was a process that would take most of the night, at least.

Radyn pressed, but Viktor didn't bend, and eventually Radyn relented. Viktor escorted him back to the apartment Radyn and Father had shared. The familiar hallways stretched on to infinity, but eventually, they reached Radyn's door. He bowed to the Dagger. "Thank you, but I'd rather go in alone."

Viktor returned the bow but didn't leave. He looked like he wanted to say something but wasn't certain how to say it. He rubbed at the back of his neck. "Your father. Was he tall, with dark hair?"

Radyn nodded.

Viktor swallowed hard. "He died a hero. He held off most of the raiders on his own, giving us the time to get there and catch the rest. I can't even guess how many lives he saved."

Radyn knew the story was supposed to make him feel better, but he only felt hollow inside. "Thank you for letting me know," he said, more out of politeness than gratitude.

"I'll speak to my commander tomorrow," Viktor said. "I'm sure a Shield would be here tomorrow regardless, but I'd like to request that the clan supervise your transition. Would that be acceptable?"

Again, Radyn knew he should have felt honored. A few hours ago, he would have bowed his forehead against the floor for such attention from the clan. Now, all he could perform was a small dip of his head. "I'd like that," he said.

"Good. Well, again, I am sorry for your loss. Firestone owes you and your father a debt we can never repay. Get some rest, and if you need anything between now and tomorrow, please come to the academy and ask for me by name."

Viktor didn't wait for Radyn to respond. He bowed again and hurried down the hallway, his footsteps nearly silent against the steel deck. Radyn pulled up the lever that unlocked his door and slipped into his apartment. He turned on the lamp beside the door, then closed the door and squeezed his eyes shut.

His apartment.

It wouldn't be his for long. The space was too valuable, and the city couldn't afford to let him remain in it alone. They would move him to a new apartment with roommates, most likely other young men without families.

He didn't care. A bed was a bed, no matter where it was. It wasn't like he and Father had spent much time at home.

He didn't want to leave, though. Not because he cared about the space itself, but because he didn't want to let go of anything that reminded him of Father. He wouldn't have a choice about it, though, so there was no point in complaining.

Radyn wandered around the rooms, picking up random objects, staring at them as though they held hidden meanings, then putting them down. Finally, a wave of exhaustion crashed over him. He stumbled to his bed, fell into it, and was asleep the moment he was horizontal.

Radyn woke the next morning to tears in his eyes. He wiped them away with the back of his hand and stared at the dull metallic ceiling above his bed. The clock in the room told him it was still a couple of hours to prime shift, but he didn't think he'd fall asleep again.

The apartment was too quiet. Father should have been up already, and it took Radyn a minute to remember Father would never wake him again.

The grief struck with unexpected suddenness, like a punch he didn't see until the very last moment. He rolled over, burying his face into his pillow and crying, just like he had after Mother had stepped through the gate after her long battle with sickness. He'd cried into his pillow so that Father wouldn't hear him and worry, and he did it now, even though Father had joined Mother on the other side of the gate and wouldn't hear him ever again.

The moment passed, and he was empty again. He rolled out of bed, washed himself with a rag and water from the sink, then dressed in clean clothes. The movements were habitual, without a single spark of life animating them. After he pulled the tunic over his head, completing his preparations, he looked down at himself and was surprised.

He didn't remember getting ready.

He wandered into the living room, where he sat down on their oldest chair and stared at the wall. He wasn't hungry, and there was no place to be. An hour passed without him noticing, and he was only startled from his reverie when someone knocked at the door. He opened it to find Viktor on the other side. The Dagger had changed into a fresh uniform. "I came to see how you were."

Radyn shrugged, unable to articulate a better response.

"My commander agreed the clan should handle your transition. Whatever you need, you just have to ask."

Radyn looked back at the apartment. It had been his home, but it didn't feel like it anymore. It had ceased to be his the moment his father's heart had ceased beating. Now it was just a few connected rooms.

"Will you help me move tonight?"

"Of course. What are you going to do today?"

The answer came fully formed into Radyn's thoughts. He'd never considered it, but it felt right the moment he said it. "I'm going to school."

He kept the same schedule he'd kept with Father. School during prime shift, then a stint on the surface after. Some of the other farmers gave him odd looks, and a few came forward to share their condolences, but mostly, they left him alone with his hoe and his field. There was even more work to be done than before, as much of their progress had been ruined by the raiders. Radyn worked until after the evening meal, then returned to the apartment, where he found Viktor and a handful of initiates.

They cleared the apartment in only a few hours, and by nightfall, Radyn was in a new place, a smaller apartment with two other roommates and one empty bed waiting for another abandoned youth.

Sunrise found Radyn in the fields again, followed by school, followed by the fields. Viktor found him in the evening and asked if he needed anything. Radyn couldn't think of anything, and Viktor left him alone.

So long as he kept himself busy, his mind didn't have to wander. He didn't have to think about what he'd seen or what the raid had taken from him. A successful day was one without thought, when he crashed into bed at the end of the day and slept until the morning bells woke Firestone for prime shift.

A few days later, Radyn heard the Blade was going to address the recent raid publicly. The night of the assembly, Radyn didn't travel to the surface. He joined the assembly, finding a quiet place near the back of the cavernous auditorium.

He'd only seen the 12th Blade of Firestone in person a

few times, and what little he knew of Nuela was through the legends told about her. She was a younger Blade—not even forty yet. She'd ascended to the position through a peaceful transition, the 11th Blade of Firestone having chosen her as his successor years before. It was a transition that had never been in doubt.

Nuela was a warrior of incredible skill, and in the raid before this one, had single-handedly held a stairwell against a veritable army of Daggers. She'd saved hundreds of lives that day and was widely considered among the best warriors and leaders the clan had ever created.

The first year of her rule had been a peaceful one, and she'd only recently begun exerting her newfound authority. Radyn supposed this raid was the first proper test of her leadership, and this assembly the first time she'd faced the public so directly.

As far as Radyn knew, her tenure to this point was fairly well regarded. She'd mostly continued the policies of her popular predecessor, and it was only in the last few months that she'd spoken publicly about her belief in growing Firestone.

He arrived well before the start, and people trickled into the auditorium in ones and twos. The ceiling was the same metallic ceiling found anywhere in Firestone, but when one entered from the rear of the auditorium, the deck dropped in increments; the ledges providing hundreds of people places to squeeze in. A wide raised platform stood at the very bottom of the auditorium. Often it was empty, but today there were five chairs positioned in a semi-circle facing the audience.

The auditorium filled in, and by the time the

designated hour struck, the room was packed. Radyn's quiet corner was no longer so quiet, the entire room bubbling with soft conversations between neighbors and friends. It only grew silent when a small group of people emerged from the front of the auditorium and climbed on the stage. Radyn recognized the Master of the Shields and two of the three members of the High Council, but his attention was drawn to the fifth individual.

His uniform and gait marked him as a Sword, but he exuded a palpable presence. The others onstage, leaders all, gave him space and deferred to him as he strode toward the chair on the far left end of the stage.

Radyn was so distracted by the Sword he didn't notice Nuela's entrance until she'd reached the stage and gestured for the other leaders to sit. She advanced to the front, ringed by the leaders of the city behind her and the people of the city before her. Though she was surrounded, she betrayed no hint of nervousness.

A scar ran down the side of her face from hairline almost to chin. She had a sharp nose and dark hair, but it was her eyes Radyn focused on. They were as dark as her hair, but something about them pulled him in. Her gaze struck him as one that took everything in but revealed nothing in return. She stood in front of hundreds, but none could guess what she thought.

Once the last of the audience's whispers had died down, she bowed. She spoke softly, but her voice had no problem carrying all the way to the back of the chamber. "Thank you for coming today, and thank you for your patience, as my Swords and Daggers have disrupted your daily routines. We are now convinced we have captured or killed all the raiders."

Radyn sensed a subtle wave of relief pass over the audience. The clan had locked Firestone down tight the last few days, meaning countless checkpoints for everyone to pass through. No one questioned the need for the disruptions, but they'd all be glad to see them end.

Nuela continued. "The raiders were from Whitehawk, a city we've never quarreled with. Based on the confessions of the prisoners before they died, we believe the purpose of the raid was to capture our Singers. None of the raiders could explain why they launched the raid, but their purpose was clear enough.

"The good news is that the raid was a disaster for Whitehawk. They lost three of their dragons, half a dozen Swords, and more than two dozen Daggers. I recognize this means little to those of you who lost friends and family in the raid, but know that Firestone is as strong as ever. I have decided we will not attack Whitehawk in retribution. Their attempt cost them almost a fourth of their entire clan, and I will not shed more blood than we already have. Whitehawk has nothing we need."

There was an outcry over the declaration, but Radyn paid no attention. It seemed like he should want vengeance for Father's death, but revenge wouldn't fill the emptiness that ate him up from the inside.

Angry objections from the crowd and calm responses from Nuela faded into a sort of drone, and Radyn's gaze lost its focus. He'd hoped to find some sort of closure here, but it turned out it didn't matter why Father had died.

He was still dead.

Radyn stood and left the auditorium, the debate still fierce within. He closed the door behind him and welcomed the quiet of the hallways. He hadn't made it far before someone called after him.

"Radyn!"

He turned to see Viktor behind him. The Dagger wasn't wearing his clan uniform, and it looked like he was coming from the auditorium as well.

"Sorry to bother you, but I saw you leave and wanted to check on you." He hesitated for a moment. "Are you upset that the Blade isn't going to attack Whitehawk?"

"No."

Viktor looked surprised.

"It doesn't matter. It won't bring back my father," Radyn said.

Viktor looked at him, studying him as though he suspected a lie. Eventually, though, he said, "I'm impressed. Most wouldn't realize that."

Viktor kept pace beside him for a minute, then asked, "I've heard that you've been working long hours in the field in addition to attending school."

Radyn exhaled sharply through his nose. "I'm fine. It's no more than I was doing before, and they need help more than ever."

Viktor nodded at the explanation, and Radyn hoped the Dagger would take the hint and leave. He didn't want to talk with anyone from the clan right now.

Viktor noticed, and he scratched at the back of his neck before saying, "If you need anything, just let me know. I'm always ready to help."

The Dagger returned to the auditorium, leaving Radyn alone and without a clue of what to do next.

2

The nightmares started a few days after Nuela's announcements. In them, Father was fighting off raiders as they emerged from the stairwell carrying Singers over their shoulders. The Singers' white robes were cast about by the wind, blocking Radyn from view of his father.

Every night, he was certain he was supposed to see something, but the billowing robes blocked Father from Radyn's sight. He ran toward them, only to get caught in a never-ending sea of white. He tore and clawed at the robes, only to wake in his bed, sweat pouring down his face, sheets wrapped tightly around him.

After the third night in a row, Radyn cursed the world and pressed his hands against his eyes. Rest became ever more elusive, and the days grew longer. He tried to fall back asleep, but sleep wouldn't come, and for the first time in weeks, he had no choice but to lie around with nothing to do.

Grief found him first. Radyn wished Father was around so that they could talk. Father had always had some piece of advice that had helped Radyn, and he desperately wished for that advice now. Unfortunately, the one man he trusted to give it was gone.

Radyn didn't know how to fill that absence. It lay deep within him, quiet so long as he kept busy but hungry whenever he stopped. Now that he was awake and still, memories of that night leaped to the front of his mind. Time and time again, Radyn found himself in the field, watching Father hold off an army of Daggers.

He tossed and turned in the bed, wishing sleep would take him away from the torment of memory.

It didn't, though, and Radyn was finally forced to confront the questions he'd been avoiding since that day. Viktor had recognized Father's name, and Father hadn't fought like a farmer, but Radyn had never known him as anything else.

Eventually, the bells rang to prepare the citizens for prime shift, and Radyn stumbled through his routine, staring bleary-eyed at his teachers at school as they tried to teach him writing, math, and history. Their voices were like bees buzzing around in his head. None of them had the answers to the only question that mattered.

When school let out, Radyn didn't go to the fields. The only thing that would banish his nightmares was knowledge, and there was only one place he could think of going for it. He climbed the ladders to the academy. The entrance was an enormous steel door guarded by two initiates. They took one look at Radyn and asked him what his business was.

"I'd like to speak to Senior Dagger Viktor, please," he said.

One initiate ran into the academy to find the Dagger, while the other continued to guard the door. Radyn sat on the bench close to the entrance and waited.

It didn't take Viktor long to appear. He bowed deeply to Radyn and asked how he could be of service.

"My father knew how to fight. When he picked up a maniblade, the blade was as long as a Sword's. Why?"

"You don't know?" Viktor looked genuinely surprised.

"For as long as I've known my father, he's been a farmer. He never gave me reason to believe anything different." Radyn was surprised by the bitterness in his voice, and it made him realize something.

He wasn't just sad that Father was gone. He was angry that Father had lied.

The realization hit him like a slap across the face. It seemed wrong to be angry with the dead, especially if the dead had died a hero of Firestone.

Wrong or not, he was angry, and now that he realized it, he recognized how fierce it burned. It was like hot coals buried near the bottom of a fire pit. Now that it had been exposed, it caught on fire with a roar.

Viktor wasn't aware of the fire now burning deep within Radyn, so he answered without hesitation. "Your Father used to be one of the clan. I'm not sure if he was a junior Sword or a senior Dagger when he left, but I know that many in the clan thought he had great promise. If the rumors I've heard are true, he and the Blade were close when they were younger."

Viktor's answer landed like heavy rain on Radyn's fire.

That his father had been part of the clan wasn't that surprising—after seeing him fight on the surface, there were few explanations that didn't involve the clan somehow. But to hear that he'd been friends with Nuela? What had happened?

"If Father was close to the Blade, how did he end up as a farmer?"

Viktor shrugged. "You'd have to ask somebody older to be sure. The rumor is that he and the Blade had a falling out, but that sounds like idle speculation to me. He might have also quit because of you. It's not unheard of. Some parents fear that remaining with the clan is too dangerous an occupation when there are children at home."

Radyn leaned back against the wall. Cold metal pressed against the back of his neck, easing some of his tension.

"Is something wrong?" Viktor asked.

Radyn snorted. "What isn't? My father was a liar, and here I find out he was a talented manirah. It's like I was living with a stranger for all these years, and now I can't even yell at him for lying because he's dead!"

His voice was louder than he meant for it to be, but there was no stopping the torrent now that it had been unblocked.

Thoughts of Father's death brought the memories to the fore once again, and he turned his anger on Viktor. "And where were you? Father fought for minutes by himself before any Daggers arrived."

The accusation broke Viktor's mask of equanimity. He bowed again. "The raid hit at the worst possible time.

Most Daggers and Swords were at a ceremony below, celebrating the graduation of a new group of initiates. The Blade left only a skeleton guard in place, and that was when Whitehawk struck. I'm sorry we couldn't be there when you needed us most."

Viktor's obvious distress cooled Radyn's temper. He hadn't meant to take it out on the clan, but Viktor was gracious in allowing himself to be the target of the outburst. Other clan members wouldn't be so tolerant of Radyn's disrespect.

Radyn's response was quieter. "No, I'm sorry. You did what you could, and you've shown me nothing but kindness." He looked down at his hands. "Just before he died, I'd told him I was thinking about joining the clan, and even then, he said nothing about his past."

"Are you still thinking about attempting the trials?"

"I don't know. I don't have the slightest idea what to do next."

Viktor thought for a moment, then asked, "Would you mind helping me with something?"

Radyn was already tired, and his instinct was to decline, but Viktor had been kind to him and an outright denial seemed rude. "With what?"

"The riders are bringing some fresh game tonight, and I volunteered to carry it down to the kitchens. Would you mind lending me your strength? It's hard work."

"Isn't that something the kitchen staff handles?"

"Normally, but everyone is short-staffed as Firestone recovers from the battle. The kitchens are no exception. They're barely able to make enough food for the evening meal, much less bring the game down for butchering."

Against his better judgment, Radyn agreed. If nothing

else, by the time they were done, he'd be so exhausted he'd have no trouble sleeping tonight. Maybe tonight the nightmares would leave him alone.

Viktor led the way to the surface, and the Daggers keeping watch over the Nest let them in without too much questioning.

Radyn had never been inside the Nest, but Viktor didn't give him a chance to look around. They made straight for the landing field, where a small hill of prey had already been created by the dragons. As they approached, a dragon and rider came in, dropped two more deer on the pile, and then rose back into the sky. Radyn couldn't help but stop and stare, and he didn't move again until Viktor nudged him in the side.

The work was as difficult as Viktor had promised. Sometimes he could pick up or drag a deer on his own, but some of the larger animals required two of them to move. Radyn and Viktor often worked together, hauling the animals to a slide that led far below. If Radyn had been younger and more irresponsible, he might have jumped on the slide himself, but tonight it was coated with blood from the animals, eliminating any last sliver of temptation.

They didn't finish until long after the sun had set. After they hauled the last animal, Radyn looked at where the pile had been and felt a sense of satisfaction at a hard job done well.

Viktor stood next to Radyn. "That was well done."

Radyn grunted, amused by the echo of his own thoughts.

"The food will go a long way toward helping Firestone recover from the raid."

Radyn's sense of satisfaction grew. He enjoyed farming, but it took months to go from planting to harvest, so it was rare to see so clearly the result of his effort.

Viktor turned so he was angled toward Radyn. "I've lost friends in battle, but my father is still alive, so I can't pretend that I know what you're going through. I know you're probably angry and sad, but I hope you never forget your father might have single-handedly prevented disaster. We don't know why, but the raiders from Whitehawk were going for our Singers, and if we'd lost them, we might not be able to control the Engine anymore. I wasn't exaggerating when I claimed the entire city owes you a debt."

"None of it brings him back."

"Sure, but his sacrifice might be what allows you to choose your future."

Radyn looked up and met his gaze, not sure where Viktor was going with this.

"I hope you'll attempt the trials. I think the clan could use a young man like you. If you're anything like your father, there's no telling what you'll accomplish."

Radyn didn't know what he planned, either, but he knew tonight was the first time since the raid he'd felt like he'd accomplished anything at all.

They'd done good work this evening.

His Father had been clan. He'd died a hero. Even his lies couldn't take that away from him.

Radyn was angry at his father, and still wasn't sure he'd ever figure out how to fill the hole his absence left, but he was proud, too. He'd served the city, just as Radyn had tonight, but his sacrifice had meant so much more.

Radyn would have been proud to follow in his father's footsteps as a farmer, but now a better opportunity rose before him.

He knew what he would do. He would join the clan.

To honor his father's memory and then surpass it.

3

Radyn tugged on his tunic one last time, took a deep breath, and knocked on the door to the academy. It was promptly opened by an initiate who looked only a year or two older than him. The gap in years was small, but the difference in their lives couldn't have been more obvious. The initiate was tall and lean, well-fed, and wearing a freshly laundered academy uniform. Radyn, in contrast, was short and too thin. He'd attempted to clean the stains from his shirt and pants before venturing here, but some stains never wiped clean.

"What do you want?" the initiate asked.

"To join the academy."

The initiate scoffed as he took Radyn in. "Are you serious?"

"I am."

The initiate shook his head. "Save yourself the embarrassment and time. Run back into whatever crack you crawled out of and stay there."

Radyn didn't retreat. "Anyone who desires admittance into the clan must be tried. Those are the rules."

The initiate stepped closer and sneered. "The academy takes only the best and most deserving. You're clearly neither."

Radyn fixed him with a stare but refused to respond.

After nearly half a minute of tense silence, the initiate swore and turned, leading him into the academy. Radyn wondered if the confrontation had been a last test to turn away those who weren't determined enough or if the initiate was simply an ass. The question only lingered for a moment, because he was in the academy, a place he'd dreamed about for years.

Radyn first noticed the cleanliness of the hallways. The main door to the academy opened into the basement level of the complex, four levels beneath the surface. The hallways and doors were the same design as most other hallways in Firestone, but every corner was free of the dust and grime that had built up over the years elsewhere. As they walked through the hallways, Radyn saw students of all ages cleaning.

He wondered if he witnessed a punishment or if cleaning was just part of daily life. Had he been on better terms with his guide, he might have asked, but he kept his mouth shut and his eyes open. That was usually the best practice, anyway.

Given the sheer number of initiates cleaning, Radyn assumed this was a normal practice. He remembered that day, a lifetime ago, when the Dagger had visited his class and talked about the endless chores. Perhaps he hadn't been exaggerating.

They stopped before a door that had the symbols for

"Admissions" painted upon it. The initiate gestured for him to enter. "Well, go on in," he said.

Radyn knocked on the door.

"Come in," answered a stern voice.

Radyn bowed quickly to his guide, which elicited a surprised look. He didn't bother explaining. After today, the guide would be a higher-ranked initiate than Radyn, and he deserved thanks for his reluctant efforts. Honoring elders was a pillar of the clan's code.

Radyn opened the door and bowed to those within. He left his shoes in the hallway and stepped inside.

The room was small but orderly. An older woman sat across a wide desk bolted securely to the deck. She studied him with the same intensity as he studied her. If the state of his dress bothered her, she didn't show any sign. When she spoke, her voice was firm and quick, making Radyn think of the hundreds, if not thousands, of hopeful students she'd had similar meetings with over the years. "And who might you be, young man?" she asked.

"Radyn, ma'am. I'd like to apply for the trials."

"You're in the right place, then. Can you read?"

"Yes, ma'am, I received high marks in school."

"I suppose we'll see soon enough. Why aren't your parents here?"

Radyn's breath caught. It had been almost a year, and the sorrow still caught him by surprise some days. He clenched his fists and focused on the desk in front of him. When he had control again, he said, "My mother died several years ago because of illness, so my father, Andre, raised me. He died in Whitehawk's raid last year."

The woman steepled her fingers and leaned forward. "You're Andre's son? All of Firestone owes him a debt."

Radyn hated that phrase, but he tried to keep his disgust off his face.

If the woman noticed, she gave no sign. "So why do you want to be here?"

There was no malice in the question. She was searching for something, but he couldn't guess what.

"My father gave his life to help others, and if I'm going to honor his memory, I need to do the same. Anything short of that seems meaningless."

The woman nodded again, apparently satisfied. She pulled some papers from a drawer in her desk and handed them over. "Then it's time for you to get started."

Radyn stared at the papers, realization slowly dawning. "Are these part of the trials?"

"They are." She pointed to a smaller writing desk in the opposite corner of the room. "You can work there."

Radyn hadn't come prepared to take the trials today. He'd assumed there would be time after he applied. But what else could he do? He nodded, reached out, grabbed the pile of papers, and brought them over to the small desk. All the tools he required were sitting there as though they'd been waiting for him. He settled in and began.

The breadth of the questions surprised him. History, mathematics, and shard lore made up most of the test, but there were questions about farming, other cities, and martial techniques. The test concluded with an exhaustive section on clan traditions. Radyn answered the questions as well as he was able, but the sheer number he knew nothing about disappointed him.

In those cases, he wrote as much as he could, explaining what he knew and what he didn't. No one had ever told him how the tests were scored, but a central pillar of the clan was honesty, so Radyn didn't claim knowledge that wasn't his.

By the time he finished, his hand ached. He'd never thought of writing as physically laborious, but he'd never written nearly so much in one sitting. The woman at the desk had made no mention of the time, so Radyn looked through what he'd written for mistakes. He added more to some of his answers and then stacked the papers neatly.

"I'm done," he said.

The woman looked up from the papers she'd been working on. "Bring them here."

He did, placing them like a treasure on her desk. She picked them up and read. Radyn watched her eyes, unable to believe how fast she read through what he'd written. He must have worked for hours, but it only took her minutes to judge the work.

She nodded once, then stood. "Follow me, please."

"Yes, ma'am."

They left her office and turned down the hallway. Radyn took heart when he noticed they turned away from the main door and walked deeper into the academy. The woman stopped outside a thick double door and knocked. It opened to reveal one of the larger rooms Radyn had ever seen in Firestone.

Students were arranged around the edge of the room. They trained martial techniques in pairs, supervised by a handful of Daggers and one old Sword. Some practiced kicking and punching. Others grappled on the ground.

The biggest and oldest students dueled with dull wooden weapons that simulated maniblades.

The woman grunted at him, and he realized he'd come to a stop as soon as he'd seen the room. This was what he dreamed about as he fell asleep every night. The clan training ground. He hurried forward to catch up, then saw the glowing training bracelets on the oldest students' arms. They had shards! Most in the room only had one-shard bands, but a few had two-shard bands. His dream had never seemed so close.

The woman walked him straight into the middle of the room, and the various trainings around the perimeter slowly came to a stop. The students lined up where they stood, forming an enormous square around Radyn and the woman. She bowed to the old Sword, who Radyn guessed was the chief instructor. Radyn followed suit.

"This is Radyn. He seeks admittance to the academy," his guide said.

The gray-haired Sword took Radyn in at a glance. "He seems like he has spirit. I have just the student to test him against."

He turned and gestured to a young man who was easily twice as heavy as Radyn. "Magni, approach."

The young man ran over, his footsteps impossibly quick and light for someone so large. Radyn knew little about fighting, but he knew fear, and his insides turned to ice when Magni fixed him with a stony stare.

The woman who'd given him the test explained. "The next part of our process is testing your ability to fight. Have you trained before?"

Radyn shook his head vehemently. The corner of the

woman's lips turned up in a smile. "Don't worry. Magni won't break anything."

That was hardly as reassuring as she seemed to think it was.

No one explained any rules. The two adults stepped back, and Magni took a fighting stance. Radyn attempted to mimic it, but the smirk on Magni's face told him he hadn't succeeded. Everyone around the edge of the room had formed a loose circle. Radyn thought the Sword should tell them to return to their training, but everything had ground to a halt to watch the trial. Radyn caught a few soft snickers as the initiates judged his form.

Radyn pushed the others out of his thoughts. He'd been in scuffles with other boys his age up at the farm. He didn't think he'd beat Magni, but he could at least show them he wasn't weak. If he could land a few solid punches, he'd consider the fight a success. The room quieted as the Sword raised his hand high. He glanced at both combatants, waiting for a sign they were ready.

After they'd both nodded, the old Sword brought his hand down like a knife. Magni advanced quickly and his foot flashed out.

One moment, Radyn thought he was prepared for the enormous initiate. The next, he was lying flat on the deck, staring up at the ceiling with an ache in his chest. The room was silent, and for a moment, he wondered if he'd been knocked unconscious and everyone had left. He let his head flop to the side, and he saw many of the students were watching and waiting. No one giggled or took any joy in his defeat.

Radyn groaned and pushed himself back to his feet. Magni stood a few paces away, bored. The Sword had his hand in the air, pausing the match as if what was happening even deserved the title.

Radyn again took his position across from Magni. He tried to slow the pounding in his heart but hadn't succeeded by the time the Sword brought his hand down again. This time, Magni struck him with a series of punches that lifted Radyn off the ground. He collapsed into a heap, his chest feeling like Magni had churned it into butter. Again, the room was silent.

He growled as he willed his body to move. What was any of this supposed to prove? Surely no one here thought he stood the slightest chance against this behemoth? What was he supposed to do?

He couldn't guess, but no one seemed inclined to give him any clue, and he wasn't about to surrender. Not even the lowest Dagger in the clan backed down from a challenge. Radyn hadn't thrown a punch yet, so Magni would be confident. Perhaps too confident. It was a slim hope, but considering how dark his thoughts were, it shone like a beacon calling the riders home in a storm. He returned to his feet, ignoring his body's protests.

The Sword's arm fell again, and this time, Radyn leaped at Magni, aiming a fist right for the giant's nose. Magni stepped back and Radyn's wild punch missed. He twisted in the air and landed off-balance. He kept spinning and launched a kick that connected solidly with Magni's side.

Radyn rejoiced, but only for a moment.

His kick hadn't even wiped the smirk off Magni's face. Magni's enormous fist came back, then blurred straight into Radyn's already battered chest. Radyn landed hard on his back and coughed. He didn't think anything was broken, but he couldn't remember ever hurting like this. Every breath lit a new fire up and down his chest.

The woman who'd tested him spoke. "You don't need to continue if you don't want."

Her voice was quiet and flat. Radyn couldn't tell if she wanted him to bow out or if she wanted him to continue.

He struggled back to his feet. It took him two attempts, but eventually, he stood across from Magni. "I'm not done yet," he said.

"Very well," the woman said.

The Sword's arm cut down once again, and Radyn threw himself at Magni. He had no plan except to overwhelm the giant with the sheer volume of his attacks.

Magni's spin was almost lazy, but when it finished, his leg snapped out and caught Radyn once again in the chest. The kick struck higher than the last, and Radyn's feet were yanked from underneath him. The back of his head struck the deck, and his world immediately went black.

When Radyn came to, he was still on his back in the practice hall of the academy. The training had resumed, which made him think he'd been out for at least a few minutes. The back of his head throbbed where he'd struck it against the deck, but a quick check of the rest of his body led him to believe the woman had spoken true. Magni hadn't broken anything, though he certainly could have.

The woman stood off to the side, speaking with the

senior Sword. When she noticed Radyn awake, she walked over to him. "Are you good to stand?"

Radyn sat up, and his eyes widened as the world twisted around him. Vomit rose in his throat, and he pushed it down. He closed his eyes until the dizziness passed. The bruises on his chest complained with every breath.

He opened his eyes a few seconds later. He nodded, then regretted the decision.

"Come, then. We can meet with the Blade before the end of the day."

The Blade? No one had said anything about meeting with the Blade. Radyn's heart pounded, and he returned quickly to his feet. He looked down at himself, bruised and bloody after spending most of his duel on the deck. "Like this?"

"She isn't concerned about your appearance. Especially not after a duel."

Radyn wished that was true and followed the woman. He took one last look at the practice room before he left. He hoped this wasn't the last time he saw it. As soon as the double doors closed behind them, he felt as if someone had carved out a piece of his heart.

They walked in silence; the woman giving Radyn no hint as to the outcome of his trials. Their journey took them to the very heart of the academy. It was quiet here. No one they passed spoke above a whisper. The woman left Radyn in an immaculately clean waiting area, filled with real wooden furniture, while she met with the Blade.

They didn't give him enough time to grow properly nervous. The door opened again, and the woman gestured him in. Radyn entered and found himself before the 12th Blade of Firestone.

She seemed more imposing up close than she had in the auditorium last year. Her expressionless gaze left him uncertain, and all he could think of was that he smelled like sweat and manure. He bowed deeply.

"Miriel says you've done well on the tests," Nuela said.

Radyn glanced at the woman he'd been following around for hours, feeling suddenly foolish that he'd never asked her name. He looked down at his shoes. "That's kind of her to say, but it doesn't feel like that. There were a lot of questions I didn't know, and I didn't stand a chance against Magni in the duel."

"Look at me when I'm speaking to you, Radyn," the Blade commanded.

Radyn gulped and lifted his head. He wanted to look anywhere except in those reflectionless eyes, but he had little choice. No one disobeyed the Blade.

"Good. If you become an initiate, you'll have to learn how to face difficult situations with your head held high. Best to get in the habit now." Nuela ran her hand over the papers that had become so familiar to Radyn earlier in the day. "To answer your unspoken question, *what* we test is only half the trial. The other half is *how* you test. Both the written portion and the duel are designed to push you hard. Miriel says you took quite the beating from Magni, and you certainly look like you did."

Radyn didn't know what to do besides nod. "Yes, ma'am."

"I don't care that you lost. I care that you kept rising after Magni knocked you down. That same attitude is visible in these papers, too. You didn't know the answers, but you wrote what you knew and didn't lie about what you didn't. Such is exactly what I'd expect from our best warriors."

"Thank you, ma'am."

"Only one question remains. What does it mean to you to be a manirah?"

"It means protecting Firestone. Fighting and dying for the people."

The answer did not satisfy Nuela. "That's what our pillars say, but what does it mean to *you*?"

Radyn only hesitated a moment. "It means the chance to find out what I'm capable of. To see if I'm worthy of using the shards. It means a chance to become as strong as my father was, and maybe find out more about him."

Nuela leaned back in her chair. "That's a much better answer."

She studied him for a moment. "I knew your father, you know, back when he was with the clan."

"You did?"

"We fought side by side for a long time."

Radyn knew the question was rude, but he couldn't help himself. "What was he like back then?"

"Reckless. Brilliant. Incisive." Nuela left a space between each of her answers. "He was one of our best, and I was sad to see him leave. But I was also glad he was on the surface that day. His fight might have saved us all."

Radyn was about to ask more questions, but Nuela cut him off with a wave of her hand. "If you want to find out more about him, if you want to *understand* him, then become a Dagger. Once you do, we can sit down and reminisce."

Nuela signed something on one of his papers and pushed it back to him.

"I approve your admission to the academy. Go home and pack your belongings. The clan will speak with the surface guild and inform them of your acceptance into the academy. Say whatever farewells you need to. As you probably know, you may not leave the academy for the first three months of your study, barring something extraordinary. Welcome to the clan."

Radyn bowed as deeply as he could while still standing. "Thank you, ma'am. I won't fail you."

Nuela dismissed him and Miriel led him back to the academy entrance. When he stepped through the thick doors, they shut behind him with a hollow boom. He stopped and stared. This morning, he'd been nothing more than a hopeful farmer. Now he was an initiate. It didn't seem real, like the last few hours had been a dream, and he'd just been standing outside the door, too scared to knock.

He shook his head to clear it. The Blade had given him a task, and he was dawdling. He hurried back toward the room he was already considering his former home.

There would be little farming for him anymore.

He was part of the clan.

4

Miriel told him to report to the academy by the beginning of prime shift the next day, and though the intervening hours were filled with tasks to complete, the time of his return couldn't come quickly enough. There were a handful of goodbyes to say and a bag to pack, but he hadn't been close to anyone since Father died, and he owned little. He understood most initiates found the first several months of clan training challenging, as it severed them from all that was familiar, but nothing outside the clan clung to him. Casting aside distractions would be a simple matter.

He packed quickly and never looked back when he left his old life behind.

Back at the academy, he was surprised to find Magni waiting outside the main doors for him. The giant carried himself differently now that they weren't in the training room. A nervous smile replaced the self-assuredness he'd maintained during their duel. "Miriel told me to meet you today and show you around. Hopefully, it makes up for the beating I gave you yesterday."

Radyn's chest still ached, but he bowed. "It's probably my fault for always standing back up."

That brought a hint of a genuine smile to the large man's face. "That you did. Couldn't tell if you were tough or just thick-headed."

"Maybe a bit of both."

"Well, come on in and I'll show you around."

Once they were inside the academy, Magni apologized. "Sorry about the trials. We all have instructions from the commanders to make the process as intimidating as possible."

The giant gestured to himself. "As you can imagine, that means that I often get stuck with the responsibility of dueling hopeful initiates."

"I don't know if you were the strongest initiate in that room, but you certainly were the most intimidating."

Magni grinned. "You would be surprised how many refuse to duel me. I'm probably responsible for a quarter of the failures we witness."

Radyn didn't have any trouble believing that at all. If anything, he was surprised the number was as low as it was. If he'd given himself more than a moment to think about it, he probably would have run the other way, too. But sometimes, there were benefits to being a little thick-headed.

Magni's tour was quick and efficient, with the initiate showing Radyn where he would eat, drink, study, and clean. The academy was, in most ways, a small city in and of itself, and everything Radyn could ask for was on the premises. There would be little reason to leave, even after his three months were up.

They stopped outside a room within the initiates' wing, and Magni entered without knocking. Compared to most rooms within Firestone, Radyn's new room was spacious. Twice as long as most bedrooms, it had space to fit a bunk bed along each of the long walls. On either side of the bunk beds was a small writing desk and a small chest for personal storage.

Magni spread his arms out wide, as though they gazed upon a magnificent vista. "This is where you'll be staying for as long as you're an initiate. There are four beds, but only two are taken at the moment. You'll be rooming with Bragen and Astram, who have both been initiates for less than a year. Bragen comes from a long line of clan Swords, which I'm sure you'll hear about before long. They're both decent guys once you get to know them."

Radyn frowned. If his guide had to convince him that his roommates were decent, they probably weren't.

Magni gestured toward the bunk on the right. "So drop off your stuff, get changed, and let's head to training. I'll wait outside."

Magni left him alone, and Radyn chose an unoccupied bottom bunk. He wasn't much interested in getting settled in, so he simply threw his bag on the bed and changed into the uniform waiting for him. It was a bit large, but Radyn figured he would grow into them. As soon as he was changed, he stepped out, and Magni looked up, surprised. "You're in a hurry to get started?"

Radyn nodded.

"Fair enough. I suppose I should warn you, though, that the first three months are hard for all new initiates."

"I'm not leaving much behind," Radyn said.

"Sure, but it's not just that. Training is hard, and older initiates like to make it even harder for the new arrivals. Makes their own training a little easier."

Magni paused outside the double doors that led to the training room. "You ready for this?"

Radyn shrugged. "Only one way to find out."

Magni opened the doors, and they stepped through together.

All eyes turned to them as they entered. Most of the initiates had been milling around, but as soon as Radyn and Magni entered, they became the center of attention. Magni introduced the initiates as they approached, and Radyn was soon lost in a sea of unfamiliar names and faces. He tried to remember all the names he could, but he was fighting a losing battle.

Eventually, though, two young men whose names Radyn did recognize came up to him. As usual, Magni did the introductions. "Radyn, this is Bragen and Astram, your two roommates."

His first impression of the two young men left him uneasy. Bragen was tall and broad-shouldered, and he wore a crooked smile that made Radyn think he was already the punchline of a malicious joke. Astram was nearly as tall but always stayed a step behind and to the side of Bragen, like he was afraid of what might happen if he stepped outside of the bigger man's shadow.

After they exchanged greetings, a strange stillness settled over the room. Initiates shuffled from one foot to another, glancing at each other with unspoken expectation.

Bragen stepped close as though he and Radyn were friends from long ago. "How long have you wanted to be a manirah?"

Radyn wasn't sure how to answer that question. He'd always dreamed of becoming a manirah, but for most of his young life, it had been the dream of a child who grew up on too many stories of epic battles and heroic last stands. He'd only seriously considered joining the clan within the last few years. Now, he decided the latter answer was the more sincere one. "I've been thinking about it seriously for two years now."

Bragen leaned in a little closer. "Normally, the clan doesn't allow anyone to touch a shard until they've passed the three-month mark, but there's another tradition among initiates. We always let the new arrivals have a brief opportunity to come in contact with the shards."

Bragen held out his hand and opened his fist to reveal his training band with one small shard glowing pale blue. "Give it a try before the instructors get here." Radyn looked to Magni for confirmation. The giant man's expression was blank, leaving the decision entirely up to Radyn. He couldn't deny the temptation, and he figured that if this was going to get him in any real trouble, Magni would stop him. So he took the band and strapped it to his wrist.

The effect was instantaneous, taking place the moment the shard embedded in the band touched his skin. All his senses became sharper. Colors were vivid, and the flat gray walls of the training room took on a variety of hues. He heard the bated breaths and hurried heartbeats of the other initiates and knew, without being told, that they were waiting for something. Most likely for something to happen to him.

Hearing their breaths reminded him to breathe, and the sharpness of the experience diminished. "Incredible," he said.

Bragen seemed disappointed but didn't let the expression show on his face for long. He turned back to Astram and made a sharp gesture. Astram backed up a step and gave the smallest shake of his head. Bragen thrust out his hand, and Astram relented, placing his own training band into Bragen's hand. Bragen held it out to Radyn. "Try two."

Radyn understood it was a trap whose snare he could not see, but right now, he didn't care. The strength coursing through his veins was incredible, and he thought that even if Magni attacked him now, the giant initiate wouldn't have a chance.

He reached out, took the band, and secured it around his wrist. He gasped as a fresh wave of power crashed over him. The sensations from the first band grew even more pronounced, and the heartbeats of his fellow initiates were like a chorus of drums pounding in his ears.

His attention wasn't on the drums, though, but on another sound. A soft, haunting melody ran beneath the cruder noises of his companions. His gaze became unfocused, and he stared into space as he sought to hear the song more clearly.

Besides its beauty, it possessed another quality he struggled to describe. It was unlike any song he had heard before. Most music was an attempt to fill a silence, something added by human hands and throats. This was different. This music was from within the silence, like it was part of the fabric of reality.

The sound of his name being called brought his attention back to the training room. He breathed in deeply, soaking in the sights and the sounds, reveling in the subtle textures he'd never noticed before.

"Radyn!" Bragen called.

Radyn smiled. "It's beautiful, isn't it?" The initiates looked at one another. Radyn saw confusion, excitement, and awe on most of their faces, but Bragen was an outlier.

Bragen was angry. He turned to one of the other initiates standing beside him. "Give me your band," he demanded angrily.

The initiate looked like she didn't want to, but she didn't even resist for the moment that Astram had. It was like Bragen had some power she couldn't fight. She handed her band over, and Bragen offered it to Radyn without a word.

The crowd murmured, which sounded like shouts to Radyn's sensitive ears, but he didn't care. All he wanted was to hear the song more clearly, and a third shard might allow him the opportunity. He grabbed the band before anyone could stop him and strapped it to his wrist.

The flood of power brought him to his knees, and he moaned as every sense was overwhelmed. The heartbeats of his fellow initiates made his head feel as though it were stuck in one of the bells that rang the alarms during a raid.

None of that mattered, though. He listened for the song beyond the limits of his physical senses. It was there, louder, clearer, and beautiful. The song of the universe, made just for him. He found his feet and smiled because, for the first time in years, it felt like everything was as exactly as it should be. He was right where he belonged, and all the tragedies in the world only seemed tragic because he didn't see deeply enough.

He noticed the hands on his wrists, but he was so lost in the bliss of the song that he didn't care.

Suddenly, it was all taken away from him. One moment, he was listening to the song of the stars, and the next, he was in a training room surrounded by concerned faces. His stomach churned, but the feeling passed quickly. He looked from face to face, wondering why they all looked like they were at a funeral.

"What?" he asked.

Then he recognized a familiar face, one that hadn't been in the room when he and Magni had entered. It was the old Sword from the day before. All the other initiates began looking down at their shoes, refusing to meet the angry gaze of their instructor.

They'd been caught.

If the sword was angry, he didn't show it. He looked Radyn up and down, then asked, "How do you feel?"

The song was gone, and the strength that had come with it was gone, too, but Radyn had experienced his first contact with the shards, and he was hooked.

There was no place else he'd rather be.

"I feel good," he said, and it wasn't a lie.

The Sword studied him for a moment longer, then gestured to the group, and Radyn's real training for the day began.

5

Radyn sat on his knees in a small room. He kept his back straight and his eyes locked forward. Nothing in the room helped him keep track of the passage of time, and he was no longer certain how long it had been. At times, he felt it hadn't been more than twenty or thirty minutes. Other times, he was sure it had been hours.

There was nothing obvious in the room to turn his attention to. It was an odd room, used, as far as he could tell, for one purpose only, which was for initiates to meet their masters for the first time. No art hung on the walls, and only one bare lantern lit the space. A small cushion sat unoccupied before him. Eventually, his new master would come and judge his worth. His expectation made every minute pass as though it were ten.

The sound of the door opening almost made his heart jump out of his chest. He fought the urge to twist and look, even though his instructions had been given in great detail. He bowed his head to the cold floor and pressed it there. "Welcome, master."

His master's footsteps were light but assured. Radyn opened his eyes, and though his forehead remained pressed to the floor, he glimpsed his master's feet out of the corner of his eye. They were smaller than he expected.

A soft rustling of cloth meant his master had kneeled on the cushion in front of him. "Welcome, initiate. Rise, and let us speak of your future."

The voice was that of a young woman. Radyn rose from his bow, and he found himself face to face with a junior Sword who couldn't have been more than ten years older than him. The first thing he noticed was that she was small. If they both got to their feet, he would stand significantly higher, and he was short for his age, a fact the tall Bragen and Astram never hesitated to remind him of.

Surprise twisted his tongue for a moment, but he soon remembered the words he'd been given. This meeting was a ritual, a rite of passage for all new initiates. "It is an honor to meet you for the first time, master. May my effort and my sacrifice satisfy your demands."

A hint of a smile passed across the Sword's face, leaving Radyn with the impression that she'd noticed his initial reaction and glimpsed his innermost thoughts. Shame rushed to his cheeks, but she continued the ritual without interruption. "It is an honor to serve as your guide. May my wisdom serve you well and steer you away from the mistakes I have made."

Radyn bowed again. "I've brought you an offering, a sign of my dedication."

His master gestured for him to begin. Radyn reached out and picked up the knife, waiting on the floor next to him. At first glance, it appeared to be an ordinary knife. The leather wrap around the handle was worn from frequent use. Radyn pulled the knife an inch from its sheath, revealing the clan inscription on the blade. His master nodded at the sight, and Radyn sheathed the blade. He let it rest in both hands, bowed, and held it out.

"This knife was given to my father, a farmer, by the clan as a token of gratitude for the service he provided as a farmer during his life. I have long cherished it, and now I offer it to you as a token of my gratitude for your service."

Her hands brushed against his as she took the knife. He rose from his bow and noticed she had a strange look on her face. She looked from the knife to him and back to the knife, and he feared that he had done something wrong already. She didn't speak when she accepted the gift, interrupting the rhythm of the ceremony.

As Radyn's concern grew into panic, she said, "Thank you for your gift. I'm moved by your selfless generosity. I shall care for it with the respect it deserves."

She reached her hand down to the floor beside her, then stopped. She brought her hand up, where it disappeared into a fold in her clan uniform. "For you, I gift to you one of the scales of Shriken. He has protected me since the first day I became a Sword, and I hope to offer you that same sense of safety."

Radyn reached out with a trembling hand. He hesitated, his hand frozen above hers. This was too valuable of a gift. Far too valuable. His father's knife, precious as it was to him, was nothing in comparison. He couldn't accept what she offered.

She nodded her head, though, encouraging him. He took the scale and pressed his forehead to the floor again. The ceremony didn't demand so much, but it was all he could do to express his appreciation. "Thank you, master. It will become my most treasured possession," he said.

"I trust you will keep it well. My name is Elora, and I am pleased to meet you."

Radyn completed the ceremony. "I am Radyn, and the pleasure is mine."

Elora relaxed, and Radyn did the same. "I have, of course, read all that was written about you during the admissions process, but written words alone can never do a person justice. Please, tell me about yourself."

Radyn did, recounting both his childhood and the series of events that led him to the clan. Elora was an attentive listener, and when he was done, she told him about herself.

Radyn hadn't heard of her before, but she quickly impressed him. She was one of the youngest Swords to earn the title. The clan recognized her both as one of their best riders and as a manirah with incredible potential. Radyn was her first initiate.

When she finished, she reached into the same fold where she'd put Radyn's father's knife and pulled out a small wooden box. Radyn guessed the wood was pine, but couldn't be sure. She set it between them, then slid the lid off. Radyn's breath caught when he saw the shard resting there.

The stone rested on a small bed of folded cloth. It was

half the size of the tip of his pinky finger, but it was the glow of the stone that consumed his attention. It filled the room with a pale blue light. Elora let him stare for several seconds before speaking.

"The clan is many things to many people. To some, it is the modern incarnation of the armies of old. When necessary, we raid other cities. We're the first defenders of Firestone when other clans attack us. To others, the clan is a keeper of order. Shields might keep the peace in the city, but they do so under the authority of the clan. And to a special few, the clan is something more transcendent, something more concerned with the refinement of the human spirit. Tell me, what is the clan to you?"

"An opportunity to see how much I am capable of," Radyn said.

Elora nodded. "I feel much the same. As you have already noticed, my stature is hardly intimidating. When I was young, life wasn't always easy. I didn't grow like the other students in school and was often picked on. When I first joined the clan, I did it because I wanted to prove how strong I was. That I was more than I appeared."

"And now?" Radyn asked.

"Now I no longer have to prove how strong I am, and when I look back, I realize I never did."

Radyn thought about that but wasn't sure what Elora meant.

She gestured toward the shardstone. "To me, becoming a Dagger or a Sword is about becoming the sort of person worthy of carrying a shardstone. And that is what I'll teach you, to the best of my ability."

"I'm honored."

"Understand this, though. I am only a guide. I can show you the way, but you are the one who has to walk the path, and it is not an easy one to walk. Are you ready to begin?"

Radyn didn't hesitate. "I am."

"Good. Then there is one last question I must ask. Masters and initiates are usually assigned randomly, but our case is different. They gave me permission to train you specifically, based on the information we've been given about you. I have in mind a unique style of training, one never attempted before. You are the best candidate for the training I've encountered since I've begun my search."

Radyn's heart beat faster. What plans did the clan have for him?

Elora continued. "It seems only right to me you enter this training with the full knowledge of what is coming. I seek to create a new breed of warrior molded in the path I have formed for myself."

She gestured at the shard. "Most in the clan are content to settle for crude manipulations of the shards. They rely on their own strength and speed, only using the shards as a means to increase those abilities. If you accept my offer, I will put you on a different path. One likely longer and harder, that will make you seem weaker than your peers for several months at the least. But if it's successful, I believe you may even surpass my record for becoming the youngest Sword."

She saw he was bursting with questions, so she gestured for him to ask them.

"What's the difference, and why me?"

"Those answers are related, actually. What I will train you to do is to forge a new type of connection with the shard, something more subtle and infinitely more powerful than the weak connections the others pursue. As to why I chose you? Because of the combination of a few traits. First, you proved during your admission that you were more than capable of persistence, which will be needed during the training. Second, you aren't a child of the clan, so you haven't been molded by the lessons many of our young learn. It's easier to teach a blank slate than to make you forget what you think you know. And finally, you must thank your fellow initiates for the prank they attempted to pull on you on your first day. That told me you have the necessary resistance to the stones to live through what I intend for you."

She spread her hands open wide, as though showing she had nothing left to prove. "So, what do you think? Will you join me?"

Radyn was a little intimidated, especially by the hint other students might not survive the training she intended to put him through. But he wouldn't be deterred, not after she'd told him what he might become.

"I will," he said.

Radyn returned to the room he shared with Bragen and Astram. He entered without knocking, barely aware of the grin on his face.

His two roommates were deep in the middle of a card game. They greeted him as he entered, then returned to their game. Radyn went to his writing desk and set down the small book Elora had given him to read that night. He turned the lantern on his desk up and read slowly through the pages. He'd never been a fast reader, and the words in the small volume were densely packed together.

Radyn jumped in his seat when Bragen clapped his hand on Radyn's shoulder. He hadn't even noticed that his companions' game had finished. "Who won?" he asked.

Astram's grin was answer enough.

Bragen seemed eager to talk about anything else. "How did meeting your master go? Who were you assigned to?"

"It was incredible. My master is Elora."

His two roommates shared a look, and their enthusiasm abruptly dampened. Radyn looked between the two of them. "What?"

Astram cleared his throat and suddenly seemed to find the ceiling the most interesting feature of the room. Bragen scratched the back of his neck and grimaced. Finally, he said, "Her skills are impressive, but you're going to have a hard time advancing in the clan with her as your master."

"Why?"

Bragen sighed and said, "The ways she does things is...strange. If you pick up her habits, people aren't going to trust you, and if they don't trust you, you'll never rise higher than junior Dagger, no matter how strong you are."

"Oh." Radyn leaned back in his chair.

He thought about Elora's promises that he might

become a Sword earlier than his peers, and he wondered who was being more honest with him. Bragen could be an ass, especially where his pride was concerned, but he wasn't one who outright lied.

Bragen sensed his indecision. "You should think about it, at least. It's unusual, but if you want, I can talk to my father and see if I can get you reassigned. Considering how well your trials went, I might be able to convince him."

Bragen came from a clan family, and his father was a senior Sword. Bragen never passed an opportunity up to let everyone know.

"You'd do that?" Radyn asked.

Bragen hesitated, then smiled widely. "Of course."

Astram, sensing Bragen's plight, came to the rescue and asked, "So, what did you give her?"

"A knife the 11th Blade gave my father. It's a family heirloom."

Astram's eyes went wide. "Truly?"

His roommate's reaction reminded Radyn of Elora's expression, and now he was certain he'd done something wrong. "Yes. Why?"

Astram laughed and shook his head. "Most initiates just write a short letter of thanks or give away some trinket."

"I thought the gift of admission was supposed to be something important to the initiate," Radyn said. He was sure of it. He'd read the instructions several times.

"Back in the old days, sure. But it's nothing more than a ceremony now. Master and student exchange some insignificant item neither of them values much, tradition is upheld, and then you start your training. No one actually cares anymore."

Radyn thought back to Elora's hand drifting to her side, where the gift she'd brought would have been, and how she'd given him something else instead. His right hand brushed against his pocket, where the scale was safely tucked away.

She'd given him something far more valuable than his meager gift. All because he hadn't understood the way things were. He felt the color rising in his cheeks, which made Bragen and Astram laugh.

"Is there any way to return the gifts?" he asked. He didn't care about getting the knife back, not now. He had to return the scale, though.

Bragen laughed some more and put his hand on Radyn's shoulder. "No. The ceremony is a binding agreement, so you're not getting your knife back until you become a Dagger."

Bragen squeezed Radyn's shoulder hard enough for it to be painful. "Don't worry, Radyn. From now on, Astram and I will look after you. We probably should have warned you about the gift traditions, but I forget you don't have a clan background. We'll tell you if there's anything coming up you need to know. And, if you want a different master, just let me know in a day or two, and I'll see what I can do."

Radyn bowed to both of them. They could be difficult, but they meant well, and this kindness was unexpected. "Thank you both very much."

Eager to hide his shame, Radyn returned to the book Elora had given him. He'd barely started reading when Bragen's hand landed on his shoulder again. The older initiate leaned down and whispered dramatically in his ear. "You know, you don't have to study, either."

"But Elora told me to."

Bragen shook his head. "There are no tests of knowledge for Daggers and Swords. All that matters is how well you can fight and how well you can bear the burden of a shard. Nothing else matters. Elora might ask you some questions about your reading, but you won't get in any trouble for not doing it."

Bragen and Astram announced they would be leaving for a while. They intended to spend some time in the girls' wing before it was time for the evening meal. "You want to come?" Astram asked.

They tempted Radyn. He was eager to meet more of his fellow initiates.

But Elora had given him a task. He trusted Bragen and Astram, but it seemed foolish to not finish the first task his master gave him.

"I think I'll stay here and finish this. I'll meet you for supper."

His two roommates looked exasperated but not surprised. "If you change your mind, you'll know where to find us," Astram said.

The other two left, their laughter echoing down the hallway. Radyn pushed himself away from the writing desk. He should chase after them. They knew the clan better than he did. Both had grown up in clan families. He should follow their example.

He felt the scale in his pocket and stopped.

Radyn hadn't joined the clan to meet girls. He'd come to push himself, to see what he was capable of. And he certainly knew he was capable of more than skipping his assignments and chasing after his roommates.

He returned to the writing desk and took a moment to compose himself. The laughter from the hallway faded, allowing him to focus on the text before him. Soon he was lost in his studies, Bragen and Astram's offer long forgotten.

6

Radyn knocked on the door harder than he meant to, then grimaced. Elora had given him the address for the training yesterday, and he thought he'd left himself plenty of time, but in his distracted excitement, he'd taken a wrong turn and not realized until a few minutes later. As such, he was late for his first full day of training with his master. He cursed and straightened his uniform, hoping it wouldn't be considered too terrible an infraction.

Radyn had been distracted because he had been wondering exactly what Elora's training would look like. He expected it would be unique, but how would it differ from training under a traditional master? He had quizzed both Bragen and Astram on their training, and their answers were so simple he suspected they were lying.

To hear them tell it, all they did was fight. They claimed training with a master was simply a more intense version of the same training they did every morning under the watchful eyes of the Swords and Daggers, but there had to be more they weren't sharing. He'd asked other initiates to be sure, and they had said much the same. A few had masters that made them read and study a bit more, but that was the extent of the exceptions.

Somehow, Radyn figured his training would be much different. Elora didn't strike him as someone set on following the methods of others. His biggest question was wondering just how different the day would be.

Elora called for him to enter, and he stepped into their training room with an apologetic bow. "I'm sorry I'm late, master. I took a wrong turn."

She waved away his apology. "Take a seat and catch your breath for a minute."

He did so, taking in the training room as he did. It was one of several the masters used to train privately with their initiates, so it lacked anything personal. The room appeared perfectly square with a high ceiling. A rack of wooden weapons stood along the wall to his right, and his heart beat faster at the thought of weapons training. To his left were several scrolls with the tenets of the clan written on them. The mat covering the floor was softer here than in the main training room, but there was little else to notice. Elora was seated on a small cushion much like his own.

She reached into a pocket, pulled out a training band, and tossed it toward him. Radyn caught it, wondering if this was a trick or a test. "Initiates aren't allowed to wear these until they've reached the three-month mark."

Elora stared hard at him, her expression unreadable. "Do you want to wait?"

Radyn didn't, and when he thought of that mysterious song he'd heard on his first day with the clan, he didn't care if this was a test. He strapped on the band and felt the same sharpening of sensation he'd experienced before. He remembered to breathe, and the power subsided until it became something he could handle. When he looked up, he saw that Elora's attention was tightly focused on him, noting every heartbeat and twitch. She arched an eyebrow. "Most at your stage would groan in agony right now."

Radyn shrugged. He wasn't sure what to say to that.

Elora said, "I've heard that when the initiates performed their usual prank, you ended up in contact with three shardstones. Is this true?"

Radyn confirmed it was.

"Tell me what that was like."

Radyn did, sparing no detail and spending most of his time describing the song he had heard and the impressions that had struck him. By the time he finished, Elora had a thoughtful look. After debating for a moment, she said, "This band will be given to you every day when you come to train, and you are not to take it off unless I specifically give you permission. Is that clear?"

Radyn nodded, even if he didn't understand the purpose of her instructions. He wasn't going to ask, but then she told him.

"You know that shardstones are fragments of the Engine, carefully collected for our use. You are probably also aware that every individual has a limit to the number of shardstones they can be in contact with at any time. A Dagger can handle two at most, and most Swords, junior and senior alike, can touch only three. There are a few unique souls that bear more, and this is my goal for you. To reach that stage, I'm going to put you in more contact with the shardstones than any of your peers. I will keep as close an eye on you as I can, but the strategy is not without risk. If it succeeds, though, you have the possibility of becoming one of the strongest Swords this clan has ever seen. Do you consent to this course of action?"

He found her promises intoxicating, but he couldn't bring himself to answer right away. A part of him screamed that all this was too much, that the life of a normal clan Dagger would be enough. But he dismissed that voice of reason. How would he live with himself if he didn't reach higher than everyone else? "I do."

Elora smiled, and they began their training in earnest.

It wasn't anything like he expected. Bragen and Astram might have spent their training being beaten up by their masters, but Elora never so much as raised a finger against him the whole day. In truth, he barely moved the entire time.

"Your first lesson is how to disconnect from the shardstone," she said.

"Don't I simply take it off?"

"Do you often see clan warriors without their shardstones?" she asked.

He bowed his head, surprised at his continued foolishness. Of course, they didn't go around without their shardstones. Everyone knew as much. It was how one could always identify a manirah. They might step out of their uniform after they completed their duty for the day, but they'd never be found without their stones.

"It's an honest mistake." As usual, Elora seemed able to look inside his head and see his thoughts. "Your fellow initiates don't wear their bands constantly, because you're right—the simplest way to disconnect from the shardstone is to take it off. To become a Dagger, though, means to never let the shardstone leave your side. So you must learn to disconnect even as it touches your skin."

"How?"

"Through a continued act of will. Some abilities granted to us by the shardstones occur without effort. You've already felt the sharpened senses and the stronger muscles. Other abilities are shaped by our will, such as the ability to form weapons and focus our attention. Cutting yourself off from the shardstone is the most basic of these abilities. It is where most initiates begin and end their training in this aspect of shardbearing, but for you, it will be the beginning of a very long journey."

"I still don't understand. It's against my skin. How do I disconnect?"

"Seek the answer yourself first."

Radyn blew out an exasperated breath. Then he closed his eyes and focused his attention on the connection between the shardstone and his skin. The training band kept one side of the shardstone pressed against his wrist. To his sense of touch, it was nothing more than the gentle pressure of a smooth stone lightly pressed against his skin. There was something else there, though. It wasn't the song he'd heard before, but something similar, a whisper of the Engine's strength flowing between him and the stone.

So how did he break it? If Elora called it an act of will, how did he impose his will on it? He imagined a thick door slamming shut between him and the stone.

The connection broke, and though he had the stone pressing against his skin, his senses were dull. The room seemed darker, Elora's expression less clear. He was back to normal, and he didn't think he liked it.

"Good. Now, reconnect," she said.

He almost asked how but figured Elora would tell him to find the answer himself. As she'd said before, she was his guide, but she couldn't walk the path for him. Connecting again was easier than he'd feared. The imagined door remained shut with little effort, but once he let it open to the stone's gentle knock, it turned into dust. His senses sharpened, and he felt whole again.

Elora made him repeat the process until he could perform it in his sleep. Then she had him do it again and again.

It was the only technique they practiced all day, and though he'd barely moved a muscle, by the time she finally let him leave, he was more exhausted than he had been after a long day in the fields with his father. He stumbled away from the training room, seeking the quiet of his quarters.

Elora hadn't asked for a single push-up or a single squat, but his body felt as though he'd been performing calisthenics for hours. His muscles ached, his step was slow, and his attention was unfocused. He understood now why the clan placed such an emphasis on the mastery of one's body. Connecting with a shardstone wasn't just the mental work he had expected; it was physical, too. The strength that rushed through his body when he connected was little different from flexing a muscle and holding the position. As powerful as he felt when connected with the shardstone, it wore him down more thoroughly than any exercise.

He was looking forward to a quick rest in his quarters,

followed by an enormous meal in the cafeteria, concluding with a quiet evening of study. Training with a master was much harder than the training he was already used to as an initiate.

The moment he opened the door to his quarter, he learned his wishes were a far cry from reality. Bragen and Astram were laughing loudly with one another, passing a flask back and forth as they entertained one another with outrageous tales. They had already changed out of their clan uniforms, which meant they didn't have any further duties tonight.

Radyn swore to himself. He must have had his days mixed up because he'd been sure they were on cleaning duty tonight. He wondered if there were any unoccupied quarters he could sleep in tonight to avoid their festivities.

Bragen grinned when Radyn stepped in. "Astram and I are taking a few of the women out to eat tonight. Apparently, the kitchens on the upper level have been baking some incredible desserts lately. Care to join us? We have room for one more."

Nothing sounded less appealing than an evening with Bragen and Astram. The two had only gotten more brash over the last few months. Bragen's success in training didn't help, either. Everyone knew well enough that he came from a clan family, but he took to the training well, and it was rumored that it wouldn't be long before he tested for Dagger and became an official part of the clan.

Radyn hated Bragen's loud demeanor, but he couldn't deny his roommate was a natural leader. Even Astram had developed considerable skills in the last few months. He'd always be Bragen's shadow, a relationship they'd developed back when they were kids, but he was also becoming a competent warrior in his own right.

Radyn attempted to be polite. "I appreciate the offer, but I'm exhausted after training. You two should have fun without me."

Astram swore softly, then said, "We always do."

Radyn was surprised by the obvious bitterness in Astram's response. Of his roommates, Astram was more polite than Bragen. Because it was Astram, the comment grated at him.

If he hadn't been so tired, he would have let the comment go like he had so often in the past. But he was irritated, and his own retort flew from his lips before he could decide on the wisdom of the response. "What's that supposed to mean?"

Bragen stood from his bunk and positioned himself halfway between Radyn and Astram. He spoke calmly, taking on the role of peacemaker. "You know what it means. We've been inviting you to join us since the day you got here. And you've almost never said yes."

"And? I'm here to train and become part of the clan."

Bragen shook his head, and his expression was one that a disappointed teacher might have used with a slow student. "Don't you get it, Radyn? We are the clan. There may come a day when the three of us are going to need to fight together. And we're going to need to trust that you'll have our backs. And you'll want to know that we have yours."

Radyn crossed his arms.

Bragen, undeterred, continued, "I know you look at us and see a pair of fools too distracted to amount to much. But when I look at you, I see a talented future Sword who is going to die alone because you trusted no one else in the clan. And because of that, we'll never be able to trust you, either."

"I've never done a thing to harm either of you! Why would you not trust me?" Radyn asked.

Behind Bragen, Astram snorted and shook his head. "You're a fool. Trust isn't about not harming one another. It's something that grows. It must be given in small things first, and only then can we trust each other with matters of life and death."

Astram stepped around Bragen and headed for the door. "Come on. Let's leave him to study in peace. He clearly doesn't need us." Astram shouldered past Radyn and stormed into the hallway. Bragen looked between the open door and Radyn, then shook his head and followed his friend.

Finally, the room was as quiet as he'd hoped, but Radyn wasn't pleased by the fact.

He stood in the empty room, not sure what had happened or why they'd argued. His roommate's arguments ran through his thoughts, and they left a bitter taste on his tongue. He turned and saw that Bragen had left the door open, as though leaving behind one last invitation to follow them.

Radyn looked at the door for a moment, then walked over and closed it, feeling more alone than he had on any day since he had joined the clan.

7

Months passed like they were days, and days passed like minutes. Radyn's training fell into a rhythm, a regular beat of exertion and study that shaped both his body and mind. Training consumed the lives of every initiate, but Elora had spoken truthfully about the demands she placed on him. She pushed him harder than any of his peers.

The world of the clan was a small one, but as he continued his training, he noticed the shifting patterns of time. Initiates that he had known since his first days with the clan either failed their training and left the academy or graduated and became the clan's newest junior Daggers.

Magni was among the first that Radyn saw graduate, and though he wouldn't admit as much to anyone, he was sorry to see the gentle giant go. Radyn had never forgotten the kindness Magni had shown him in his first days, and he'd found the giant to be one of his best sparring partners during the morning training sessions.

Because Radyn was smaller than many of the initiates, many took it easy on him, pulling their punches and not giving it their all.

Radyn detested the pity, and whenever he encountered it, it made him fight all the harder. But Magni had always been different. He'd understood, and he'd always gone hard against Radyn. Thanks to him, Radyn knew that if one of his techniques worked against Magni, it would work against anyone else.

He also made peace with his roommates. Bragen's words had cut deep the last time they'd argued, and Radyn made more of an effort to spend time with them when they invited him. He didn't agree to every one of their outings, but more than he had in the past. It was never as many as they wanted, but it resulted in a tenuous truce. They'd never put as much into their training, and he'd never put so much into making friends.

Sometimes it seemed like Elora was the only one who understood. She pushed him to his mental and physical limits, and he was grateful. As near as he could tell, he and Elora became closer than most masters did to their students. Some of it was no doubt due simply to the time they spent together, but there was also a sense of shared purpose that drew them together.

Still, he was surprised the first time she invited him to join her and her husband for a walk on the surface. For all the time they'd spent together, he knew little about her personal life. He readily agreed, and the date was set.

He met them on the surface outside the stairwell where Father had died. It was a common meeting spot for friends, couples, and families to gather for their time outdoors. With almost all of Firestone being buried in countless tons of rock and steel, getting outside was something most people treasured.

All evidence of his father's last stand had long since disappeared, and Radyn decided he was grateful he hadn't actually seen his father fall. Returning to the surface always reminded him of the raid, but because he'd never seen Father lying dead in the grass, the memories lacked the edge they might have possessed otherwise.

Elora was waiting with a man who stood about a head taller than her. His hair was going gray, though it looked like he was several years too early for the process to start. When he saw Radyn, he smiled easily, a remarkable contrast from Elora's resting frown. They bowed to one another.

"You must be Radyn. Elora has told me so much about you over the last few months."

"Jelrik, it's an honor to meet you," Radyn replied.

Radyn hadn't formed any specific ideas about what Jelrik might be like, but the man in front of him was certainly surprising. Elora spoke little of him during their training, but Radyn knew the man was a Singer, and a great one at that. He supposed he'd imagined someone more serious or perhaps more overbearing.

Jelrik was none of that and seemed to be an almost perfect contrast to Radyn's master. He spoke quickly, and his conversation veered from direction to direction like a dragon under the influence of a novice rider. He laughed easily and even elicited a smile or two from Elora.

At first, they spoke of nothing at all. Radyn answered Jelrik's questions about his training, heaping praise on Elora whenever he had an opportunity to do so. In return, Jelrik kindly answered Radyn's questions about what it was like to live as a Singer, though the answers weren't what Radyn expected.

"Truthfully, it's one of the most boring roles in all of Firestone," Jelrik said.

"That's surprising, considering how important it is," Radyn replied.

Jelrik grinned. "That's what most people say, but I think it's because they don't think too deeply about what our daily routine looks like. On a good day, we only sing to the Engine once, but even on a bad day, we only sing three or four times. Between songs, there isn't much for us to do, so it turns monotonous after a while."

"But you get to listen to the song of the Engine! I've only heard it briefly, but it's one of the most beautiful sounds I've ever heard. Isn't that a gift?"

Radyn noticed Elora tense at his words. Jelrik slowed for a moment, then resumed his pace.

"You're right that the song of the Engine is beautiful, but it's dangerous, too. When did you hear it?"

Radyn recognized the danger of the question, even if he didn't understand why it was dangerous. "The very first time I came in contact with a shardstone. It was a prank the other initiates played on me."

Jelrik glanced over to Elora, who elaborated. "When he didn't respond dramatically enough to one shardstone, they gave him three."

Jelrik looked horrified. He shot Elora a glare. "You're lucky word of that didn't reach the Singers. The Master of the Song would have had strong words for Nuela." He turned to Radyn. "I see now why Elora has been training you specifically. Few can endure three shardstones without hurting themselves. You're lucky you're as resistant to them as you are."

"Why is the song so dangerous?" Radyn asked.

"Because it draws you in, and if you aren't careful, it'll never let you go. Just as you in the clan train to disconnect from your shardstones, Singers train to disconnect from the song of the Engine. Shardstones can poison your body, but the song will steal your soul. It's also the reason we never sing alone. Even experienced Singers, if they dive too deep or for too long, can lose themselves without the help of others."

Radyn couldn't deny his morbid curiosity. "What happens if you lose yourself to the song?"

"We're not sure. As near as we can tell, the soul travels straight to the gate, and the body dies. So if Elora hasn't warned you enough, I'll do so now—stay away from the song unless you have a Singer guiding you."

Radyn dipped his head in acknowledgment of the wisdom. The conversation turned to less weighty matters, and Radyn was once again surprised by how lighthearted Jelrik was. The song was serious, but he was not. It stood in such stark contrast to Elora's taciturn demeanor, Radyn couldn't help but ask about it.

"You two seem so different, yet Elora says you two have been married for more than a decade. What's the secret?"

Jelrik looked to Elora, asking silently if she wanted to answer the question. She vehemently shook her head, which only made Jelrik chuckle.

When his mirth subsided, he said, "There's no real secret to it. We've been in love since the first time we laid eyes on each other—"

"*You* were in love the first time you saw me. I required a bit more convincing," Elora clarified.

"Sad but true," Jelrik admitted. "But the point remains that we knew we loved one another, and we knew it was something deeper than the youthful lust so many confuse with love."

Radyn was embarrassed to admit his interest, but Jelrik seemed open, and Elora was one of the people he respected most in the world. He and Father hadn't spoken often about love, mostly because Radyn hadn't been terribly interested back then. Now he found himself more interested in women, at least until he talked with them for a while.

It wasn't anything intrinsic to the young women he'd spoken to. It was just that they all lacked the ambition to be the best manirahs they could be. They were just like Bragen and Astram, content with becoming Daggers and rising slowly through the clan hierarchy.

"So, how do you know the difference between love and lust?" he asked.

Jelrik glanced again at Elora, and she fixed him with a glare that would have frightened a dragon away.

The Singer sighed and did his best to answer. "It's a connection, not that different from the one you and Elora are trying to forge with your shardstones. Lust is a powerful tempest that subsides quickly once it's satisfied. Love is a subtler force, a contentment that only grows stronger the more time two people spend together. It often puts me in mind of gardens,"—Jelrik gestured to some of the nearby plots—"because it requires patient tending to see results."

Radyn nodded along with the answer. He hadn't

experienced what Jelrik called love, but he could imagine it. "How did you two meet?"

Elora finally had a question she was willing to answer. "We were both in training to become Singers," she said.

Radyn almost tripped over his own feet. "You were in training to become a Singer? Why are you still with the clan?"

A cloud passed over Elora's face, and Radyn realized he'd stuck his foot deep in his mouth. "Sorry. You don't need to answer that if you don't want."

Elora looked to Jelrik for help, but her husband shook his head. She glared at him again, then said, "No, it's a fair question, and has an answer you've earned the right to hear. Not long after my initiation into the clan, I was on a path not much different from your own. I'd discovered these new ways of training, and I'd abandoned most of the traditions the clan kept trying to instill in me. The Swords were furious, but my rapid progress couldn't be argued with. Eventually, I became the youngest manirah in Firestone to become a Sword, and my progress attracted the attention of the Singers. I was invited to attempt their trials, which I passed without difficulty. They invited me to join the next training cadre, and I eagerly accepted."

Elora kept her face down, which was very unlike her. "I've told you I want to be stronger, but I've never told you why."

She looked at him as though begging him not to ask, but now he had to know. "Why?"

"Because I'm curious. Like you, I've heard the song, and I believe it represents something more than just the Engine. I think it's trying to tell us something about the nature of reality, and that's what I want to know. I want to know what's true."

She squeezed Jelrik's hand. "Despite everything, it brought the two of us together, so I'm grateful for that. But in all other regards, my training as a Singer went poorly."

"How so?"

Radyn hadn't meant anything pointed by the question, but Elora's face fell, and he felt as though he'd stabbed her unintentionally.

Jelrik answered the question. "As you've probably noticed, Elora isn't one for tradition and authority. Almost as soon as she was admitted, she was pushing the elders to let her experiment more, let her try more. She only trained as a Singer for about three months, but I'm reasonably confident she broke every rule and tradition they had. They ejected her after she tried to connect to the Engine by herself."

"You did *what*?" Radyn asked. He'd respected Elora before, but now he was ready to do anything she asked.

The combination of disbelief and awe brought a smile to her face. "It's true. It wasn't as good an idea as I thought. If not for Jelrik and a few others, I'm not sure I would have survived."

Radyn took a minute to absorb this new information. He'd always known Elora did what she thought was right, regardless of anyone else's opinion, but he'd never realized her rebellious streak ran so deep. He liked that about her. Their aims were different, but neither would be dissuaded.

"How did you two end up together, then?" Radyn asked.

Elora said, "Though it may not seem like it, Jelrik and I have a lot in common."

Radyn glanced between the pair. "I'll confess I don't see it."

"Both of us are obsessed with the song of the Engine. Jelrik will never break the rules like I did, but the same curiosity drives him. Someday, he wants to become the most skilled Singer in any city. Our obsessions manifest in different ways, but we're both trying to learn all we can. Jelrik keeps me from taking myself too seriously," Elora said.

Radyn looked at the couple in a new light. Of course, he'd respected Elora before, but this evening's walk had added to his list of reasons. Someday he hoped he would find someone who matched with him the way Jelrik and Elora did.

They returned to the stairwell before the sun dipped below the edge, and Radyn said his farewells. They went down first, and Radyn lingered for a while in the place where Father had given his life.

Radyn squatted and ran his hands through the grass as if he could stir up the remains of Father's ghost. He wondered if Father had felt about Mother the same way Elora felt about Jelrik, and he mourned the fact he would never know for sure.

When he stood, he felt something shift inside of him. He'd known, ever since Viktor had encouraged him to join the clan, that he wanted to be the strongest Sword in Firestone. That desire hadn't faded, but another had joined it tonight. He wanted to become as good a husband as a Sword, and when he eventually walked down the stairwell, it was with a smile on his face.

8

Radyn woke to the sound of the bells being rung by the overnight watch. Two of the four initiates on duty walked down the hall, ringing small hand bells to wake their sleeping peers. Radyn, like all initiates, had served that duty and found it distasteful. No one wanted to ring the bell that pulled friends from their peaceful slumber.

He rolled lightly out of bed and stretched. He pulled on clean training clothes, which were nothing more than a simple tunic and pants. Bragen and Astram, who'd stayed up far later than Radyn the night before, grumbled and rolled over in their bunks. They wouldn't rise until Radyn had left the room. Then they'd scramble and reach the training hall at the last possible moment, along with most of the other initiates.

Radyn had been an initiate for nearly six months now, and he still didn't understand his roommates' attitudes. The clan was supposed to promote honor and discipline, but the environment of the academy wasn't all that much different from the schools he'd attended when he'd been younger. The only difference was that there were far fewer books and far more sparring.

He walked calmly down the hallway, passing room after room of initiates just rising for the day. As usual, he was among the first to enter the training hall, where he went to his usual spot and began warming up. He jogged in place, jumped up and down, shadow-boxed, and threw a few easy kicks to loosen up his hips. A slow trickle of other initiates followed suit for the next few minutes, followed by a rush running in less than a minute before the morning bell rang.

Their instructors entered right on the bell, ignoring the obvious fact most of their initiates had arrived moments before. Without a word, the students lined up and began the routine that marked most of Radyn's mornings. They ran through the same movements and kept the same pace. The movement was light, designed to prepare those who'd just arrived for the more strenuous work to come. After all the initiates had worked up a light sweat, the Sword for the day demonstrated a specific martial technique. Today, it was a grappling move.

As usual, it was taught without words. Most instructors believed that language only impeded understanding of the heart of most techniques. They demonstrated, then had the initiates mirror their moves, guiding them physically if necessary.

Radyn paired up with another initiate, larger than him, then struggled to demonstrate even basic competence in the skill. Whenever his partner attempted the technique, Radyn ended up in a hold that threatened to break his arm. When he attempted the same technique, he still ended up in a hold that threatened to break his arm. Radyn swore under his breath, but he appreciated the lesson. Like Magni, his partner didn't take it easy on him and forced him to improve. The instructor guided Radyn a few more times, then moved on, disappointment written in his expression.

After, the initiates practiced some light sparring under the watchful eyes of their instructors. Radyn performed better here, as he could rely on the techniques Elora taught him. Still, two of his opponents forced Radyn to the ground, where he was next to useless. If he was going to pass the trials to become a Dagger, he would need to work on his grappling.

The training ended at a sign from the instructor, and the initiates hurried to clean themselves off and break their fast. Their porridge was basic but filling, and then Radyn walked to their training room for the day.

He found Elora pacing in the room instead of sitting. Radyn froze as soon as he noticed. She was always present and sitting by the time he arrived. "What's going on?" he asked.

Elora hesitated for a moment, then said, "Jyn has summoned me to his private study, and I think I'm going to bring you along."

Hesitation wasn't like her. More than once, she had reminded him of Bragen, in the sense that both of them possessed an unshakable confidence in their abilities. Every time he had the thought, he chastised himself because the expressions of their confidence couldn't have been more different. Elora's was quiet and internal, and she gave off this sense that she didn't need anyone or anything else to live well.

Bragen's, in contrast, was loud and borderline obnoxious.

She always encouraged his questions, though, so he asked her why she was unsure.

A mischievous grin turned the corner of her lips up, which made him smile. That grin told him they would both be risking trouble. Under other circumstances, it might have bothered him, but knowing that she would accept the brunt of any consequences gave him a willingness to openly bend the rules.

"Well, you weren't invited. And unless I'm misreading the message, Jyn is expecting this to be a private conversation," she said.

"So why do you want me with you?" Radyn asked, barely able to keep the disbelief from his voice.

"Mostly to irritate Jyn, but also because I think I have some inkling what he wants, and it might be beneficial to have you there."

Her answer was uncomfortably vague. "Are you sure it's wise to irritate Jyn?"

Of all the warriors in the clan, Radyn numbered Jyn among those he really didn't want to upset. Jyn had been the warrior accompanying the Blade at the assembly following the attack from Whitehawk. Radyn hadn't known him then, but since then, had learned plenty. Jyn was already a legend in the clan, and he had decades of service left to give. He was one of the unique souls that Elora had once spoken about, an individual capable of being in contact with more than three shardstones. His actual limit was a matter of great speculation among the initiates, and Radyn had heard guesses ranging from the barely impressive to the extraordinary.

He was also Nuela's right-hand man, responsible for much of the day-to-day ruling of the clan. It wasn't so much a rumor as a certainty that when Nuela stepped down, Jyn would become the 13th Blade of Firestone.

Elora shrugged at Radyn's question. "He and I go back a long way. You'll have nothing to worry about."

Radyn was convinced, so they left the training area together and walked toward the clan headquarters.

Though Radyn had been to headquarters before, it had only been a handful of times and not for several months. It was a small, contained wing tucked deep within the academy, like a peanut hidden within a shell. The only detail that marked headquarters from any other hallway was the set of enormous steel doors that kept it safe from raiders. Once inside, it could have been any other wing of Firestone, with doors at regular intervals and lamps spaced evenly down every hallway. Elora and Radyn had no problem passing through the layers of security, and before long, they ran into a familiar face guarding the door to Jyn's study.

"Magni!" Radyn said.

The giant glanced at once, then grinned when he saw who it was. "Radyn, what are you doing here?"

Radyn hesitated as he realized he wasn't sure what to tell Magni. He hadn't been invited. Thankfully, Elora answered the question for him. "We're here to see Jyn."

Magni looked between the two of them. "I was told to expect only one."

Radyn was ready to turn around and leave in peace, but Elora said, "There's been a change of plans. I think Jyn will want to meet Radyn. And if I'm wrong, I can assure you I'll take all the blame."

Magni looked at them, considered for a moment, and then shrugged. Elora was a Sword and above him in command. "Go on in, then."

They knocked, then stepped into Jyn's study, and Radyn was immediately taken aback. Most in the clan preferred to keep their spaces clean, almost to the point of barrenness. A scroll or two on a wall was considered lavish decoration, and Radyn had been within plenty of spaces where there was no ornamentation at all.

There was some rationale behind the decision: clan members moved frequently from place to place, so it made little sense to burden oneself with too many personal possessions. But Radyn felt it had also become something of a popular statement for clan members to make. It was yet another distinction that allowed them to stand apart from the rest of Firestone. The message was clear: let civilians consume the precious resources of our city. We manirahs will sacrifice even our own comfort in the name of our service.

It was a noble expression, though Radyn had never found it as sacrificial as other clan members seemed to believe. Swords and Daggers might not have scrolls and paintings on their walls, but they still ate better than anyone else in Firestone and never lacked any of the necessities that other citizens sometimes had to go without.

Still, he was surprised when he caught his first glimpse of Jyn's study. Two of the three walls were covered by enormous bookshelves, and those shelves were stacked from end to end and from floor to ceiling with books. Jyn's desk was simple, made of the same metal alloy that made up most of Firestone. But it, too, was covered with neatly organized papers and books. For a legendary warrior, he read a lot.

But then he thought of all the additional study Elora demanded of him, and he wondered if there wasn't a connection.

Jyn looked up as they entered. He smiled when he saw Elora, but the smile disappeared when he saw Radyn trailing in after. As soon as the door closed, he said, "I'm certain my message implied you should come alone."

"It did," Elora replied.

Jyn gave an amused snort and shook his head, surrendering the point. "Radyn, it's a pleasure to meet you. Elora has told me quite a bit about you over the past few months."

"Thank you, sir."

Elora rarely talked about herself, and Radyn never would have guessed that he was a subject of conversation between one of the most unique Swords in the clan and the most powerful. Why would they talk about him?

Jyn turned serious as he looked to Elora. "This is something I hoped to keep between us."

"I figured, but we're only two, and I trust him. He could be very useful."

Radyn sensed that there was more going on in this meeting than he knew, and he wished he could guess what it was.

Instinctively, he fell into the practices that had become second nature since he'd begun training with Elora. Radyn pretended to observe the scene from afar, like a ghost floating overhead. He was connected to his training shardstone but disconnected from his own body and emotions. He allowed his attention to float around the room, capturing details at will. The soft tapping of Jyn's foot against the floor echoed in his ears, and Jyn's heart beat a little faster than Radyn would have expected.

Radyn turned his attention to Jyn's desk and noticed a missive on top of it. From this angle, Radyn couldn't read the handwriting, but he could see the top half of the broken seal and recognized it immediately. The letter had come from Whitehawk.

Radyn's pulse beat faster, and he fought to keep his awareness separate from the emotions coursing through his body.

Jyn spoke as if Radyn wasn't present.

"I don't like it. He shouldn't be here," the senior Sword said.

Elora's eyes twinkled. "It's too late now. He's already figured out why I'm here."

Radyn hadn't, but Elora's confidence made him more certain of his own conclusions.

Jyn swore under his breath and pressed the palms of his hands against his eyes. "Why do you think your master is here?" he asked Radyn in a resigned voice.

Radyn put together what he knew and added a handful of educated guesses to the mix.

"The clan has recently received word from Whitehawk. They are asking for something from our clan, and there is disagreement among the High Council about what should be done. I do not know this for certain, but I suspect it has something to do with our Singers. You are hoping to use Elora to gather more information to help you decide what position to take on the matter."

Jyn shook his head and swore again. "It's frustrating

enough when you do that," he told Elora, "and now you've trained him to do it, too."

Elora grinned. "I seem to remember you telling me that was exactly what I was supposed to do."

Jyn sighed. "And now I'm regretting it. It seems training has gone well, at least." He looked to Radyn. "How did you know?"

"The letter from Whitehawk is on your desk. I can't read the writing, but I can see the top half of the broken seal. Thankfully, Elora has made me memorize the seals of all the remaining cities. The disagreement among the High Council is a guess, but you are known for your decisiveness, and there are few other reasons you'd want more information. The Singers were also a guess, but an educated one. Whitehawk wanted the Singers when it attacked a year and a half ago, and there's no reason to assume they wouldn't want them now. It also explains why you've summoned Elora. Besides her own abilities, she's married to Jelrik. You'd get more both from her own observations and those of her husband."

"It always seems so simple when you describe it," Jyn said. He took another deep breath and stared off into the distance behind Elora and Radyn.

Radyn observed that Elora's next question simply assumed that the matter of Radyn's participation was settled, though Jyn had said no such thing. "What happened? What do they want?"

Jyn handed the message to her. "They claim that their Engine is exhibiting strange behaviors, and they want our Singers to visit."

"What makes this any different from before?" Elora asked.

Radyn frowned and blurted out the question before he could stop himself. "What do you mean *before*?"

Jyn looked up from his desk with cold eyes. "Before the raid last year, they'd sent two messengers asking us to send Singers to them. We refused both, and then they attacked."

Radyn took half a step back as if someone had punched him. The clan had known. And if they'd known, why had they been so ill-prepared for the raid?

Jyn seemed oblivious to Radyn's agony as he turned to Elora. "This letter is far more desperate than anything I've heard before. Last time we thought it was some cheap ploy to reinforce a lack of Singers in their city, but now I'm not so sure. They're promising an enormous amount of wheat and unrestricted access to new hunting grounds. It's the sort of gift that would allow us to see Nuela's vision of a greater population become real. But it would also mean sending a handful of our senior Singers to a foreign city where there's no guarantee they'll return. All the food in the world doesn't matter if we can't maintain our own Engine."

Elora nodded along. "Just the fact that they would write at all makes them sound desperate. They can't imagine we'd agree after their raid."

Jyn shrugged. "It's one reason I'm inclined to accept the content of the letter as true. But it raises other questions."

"Such as?" Elora asked.

Jyn glanced at Radyn, identifying him as the source of his hesitation. Then he sighed and said, "Nuela's acting strangely about this. She's pushing hard to accept their offer. She's framing it as an act of mercy and an opportunity for us to grow. But it feels like there's something more going on. I'd give almost anything to get you in a room with her so you two can talk about it. I'm not sure I've ever seen her be so determined to follow a specific course of action."

Radyn saw Elora glance at him and stop herself from saying something that she would have otherwise. Instead, she said, "I understand. I'll look into it."

Jyn looked relieved. "Good. And you've done good work with Radyn. If he can help, let him. I feel like we're going to need every ally we can get as this develops."

9

After the visit with Jyn, Radyn had expected more dramatic changes in his life, so he was surprised when little changed. He asked Elora if there was anything he could do, but her answers were always the same: keep studying, keep training, and keep your eyes and ears open when people discuss the Engine.

He supposed he wasn't sure what more he'd expected, but the message from Whitehawk seemed more important than Elora treated it. He supposed Elora was following Jyn's orders, but he wouldn't guess that from their daily routine.

Radyn felt like he was being pushed to the side after Elora had risked censure to bring him to Jyn, but Elora didn't give his frustration time to build. Her training became more difficult than ever, and he quickly fell back to his typical activities. Radyn appreciated the structure of his days. He found he did well with the routine, and although his progress using Elora's techniques was slow, it was consistent. The meeting with Jyn had revealed to him just how far he'd come and reinforced his belief in Elora's training.

In his efforts to hear what people were saying about the Engine, Radyn began accepting all Bragen's invitations. The change in routine meant less time for rest, but Radyn judged the sacrifice worth it. He learned little about the Engine, but he enjoyed himself, and because he paid more attention on the outings than he usually did, he observed his roommates with a fresh perspective.

Bragen attracted friends no matter where he went. To Radyn, the skill seemed nearly magical. With a smile here and a whispered word there, Bragen always found the best tables and the best drinks. Radyn could never duplicate the feat, but his proximity to Bragen made him part of the group. He never felt close to anyone, so he appreciated walking the halls of the academy and exchanging smiles with familiar faces.

Six months to the day after the clan accepted him as an initiate, Elora invited him to meet her at her home.

She lived two levels above Radyn, among the other Swords, and only one level beneath the surface. He knocked on the door and Jelrik opened it. Radyn greeted him warmly, and while the greeting was returned, the Singer's smile seemed fake. He wore the pure white robes of a Singer, which he never wore unless he was on duty, but Radyn thought he wasn't supposed to sing today.

Jelrik invited him in before Radyn could ask. "Come on in. She's almost ready."

"I'm sorry for being a few minutes early. If you're about to leave, I can wait out here," Radyn said.

"Nonsense. You're essentially family now, so come on in. I'll let her know you're here."

Radyn didn't want to argue, so he stepped inside the small home. Old scrolls hung on the walls, written in script Radyn had trouble deciphering. A small bookshelf stood in a corner, packed with enough books to make Jyn jealous. He walked over to it and read the spines.

Jelrik went into their bedroom. Radyn heard the soft whispers that passed between the couple, though he couldn't make out the words. He sensed a tension in their voices, and he hoped he hadn't caused it. He and Elora rarely met here, but today was special.

When Jelrik emerged, he gave Radyn a tight-lipped smile. "Congratulations on six months. Elora's been impressed, and as you know, that's no easy feat."

"Thank you, sir."

Jelrik dipped his head, and Radyn returned the gesture. Then the Singer left, a whirlwind of white blowing through the open door.

Elora came out of the bedroom a few moments later. Radyn knew her well enough to recognize the signs of tension. "Is everything all right?"

"I'm not sure. He won't tell me what's happening, but he's worried about something."

"Is it about the message from Whitehawk?"

Elora chewed on her lower lip, considering her answer. "I don't know. I've pressed him about it, but he avoids the questions, which makes me think there is something happening with the Engine I don't know about."

"Have you told Jyn?"

"What would I tell him? I have nothing but half a

suspicion. I think Jelrik is upset because I agreed to take you today. He's worried I'm going to try something foolish."

"Are you?"

"I haven't decided yet."

Elora looked out the door Jelrik had just left through, then shrugged her shoulders. "But where are my manners? Congratulations are in order, I think."

"Thank you."

"I won't keep you in suspense. Based on my judgment, and supported by the evaluations of the other instructors, you are ready to advance to the next part of your training."

The news wasn't a surprise, exactly. The first graduation, as it was known, was the first rite of passage after acceptance into the academy. It typically happened after six months of training, though some students required a longer time to learn the basics. Radyn had expected to pass, but not by much. His martial skills were barely acceptable, but it was a relief that he wouldn't have to continue basic lessons with the newest initiates.

He bowed. "Thank you for letting me know."

The six-month graduation also opened up new possibilities. By passing him, Elora had granted him the ability to use the training band constantly. No longer would he need to remain under her strict supervision when he wore it. He'd expected something of a ceremony, but she simply reached into her pocket, pulled out his training band, and handed it to him.

"After today, I want you to wear the band as much as possible, but not so much you'll draw attention to yourself. Feel free to wear it around your ankle, if that will hide it from suspicious eyes," she said.

"Does it matter if others know?"

"Maybe not, but I fear we'll encounter problems if other initiates learn too much about your training. Nuela has only given me permission to train one person, and she'll withhold permission to train any more until she knows how you turn out. It'll be easier if the details of your training remain quiet for now."

They had descended several levels and were walking inward. Radyn had never been in this particular section of Firestone, but nothing about it attracted too much attention. The Makers had possessed a keen eye for symmetry, so navigation around Firestone was rarely much of a problem. Though they walked toward the heart of the city, it could have been a neighborhood like any other.

Elora stopped at a door. "Are you prepared?"

"I am."

She opened the door, and the hallway filled with the pale blue glow of the Engine. He saw Elora wince. She hid it quickly, but he'd been watching her for the reaction, so it was nearly impossible for her to hide it completely. It meant she'd been connected to her shardstones, though, which was dangerous this close to the Engine.

He ran his fingers along the band in his pocket. Tradition demanded that he not use the band today, and for good reason. This close to the Engine, it was more than possible that the song would capture his soul and carry it straight to the gate.

They entered the Engine Room, and Elora shut the

door behind her. They slid to the side, so they wouldn't be in the way of any other visitors. Then Elora allowed him to take the sight in, which he did with delight.

The room appeared to be a perfect sphere. There were no lamps and no doors except the one they'd entered through. The walls were the same metal found everywhere else in Firestone, but here they were almost as smooth as a mirror's surface. The platform they stood on was part of a walkway that bisected the room.

The Engine was both bigger and smaller than he'd imagined. When others spoke about it, it was with reverence, and so he'd come to think of it as something that stood many times his height. In person, it was smaller, but it had a presence that made it loom large.

Radyn couldn't help but stare. The enormous stone was clear, and if not for the blue glow lit from within, Radyn imagined he could have looked right through it. It floated in the air, connected to the city with a complex web of wires and tubes whose purposes Radyn couldn't guess. Even the Singers only knew a fraction of what the Makers had done to ignite and utilize the Engine.

The mundane worries of the world slipped away, and he thought about Elora and her brief time as a Singer.

"What was it like for you?" he asked.

"It was the most beautiful thing I've ever experienced. Even now, it feels like the song is deep in my bones, all the way down in the marrow." She paused, and Radyn had the sense she was wondering whether to share the next part. "It made me feel hopeful. It still does, actually."

"Why?"

"Everyone knows the shardstones connect us to the Engine, but no one seems to think too deeply about that.

The thing about a connection, though, is that it flows both ways. It's as connected to me as I am to it. It makes me a part of something larger than myself. That makes me feel hopeful."

Radyn nodded along. He didn't understand what she was trying to say, but he heard the awe in her voice. Everyone respected the Engine, revered it, even, but Elora's emotions ran deeper. If she believed there was more to the Engine than the clan taught, Radyn suspected it was true.

Elora surprised him when she continued. "There's also the nature of the song itself. I'm not sure if you felt the same when you heard it, but it feels so *right*, as if everything happening in the world is just fine."

"Do you believe that?"

"Some days."

"Do you ever regret not becoming a Singer?" he asked.

"Not really. Jelrik has taught me much of his daily routines, and the traditions of the Singers are even more rigid than those that guide the clan. My curiosity never would have been satisfied, and I would have gotten into more trouble. The truth is, the Singers barely know what it is they do. They treat the Engine like a machine. If they sing in one way, they get this result. They don't know why their songs work, they only know that they do."

If Elora had told him that at any other time, Radyn might have been more concerned, but in this room, it seemed right. The Engine was sublime, and any song paled in comparison.

They circled the Engine, following the walkway that ran

around the perimeter of the room. When they were about halfway around, the light from the stone flickered. It was subtle enough that, at first, Radyn thought he'd imagined it. But Elora straightened, and her eyes went wide.

"What's wrong?" he asked.

She held out a hand to quiet him. After a few tense moments, the light dimmed again. It was for less than a second, but Radyn was certain of what he'd seen.

Elora swore, the first time Radyn had heard a curse pass her lips. "We need to get out of here."

She ran toward the exit, and Radyn chased after her. Twenty feet from the door, the light of the Engine went out, and for the first time, Radyn realized they were in a completely sealed room with no other light. The darkness was absolute.

In that darkness was madness. Radyn no longer felt the deck beneath his feet. He took a step forward, but there was no resistance. Elora grunted.

The light of the Engine flickered, then flared back to life. Radyn found himself in the air, several feet above the floor. All of Firestone groaned as steel bent and warped under the incredible energies. The deck rose to meet him with surprising rapidity. His feet were no longer underneath him, so he crashed lengthwise against the steel grate.

Ahead of him, Elora landed lightly on her feet. "Are you hurt?"

Radyn shook his head. The first question that almost escaped was to ask if the Engine had ever done that before, but he knew the answer without asking. He'd experienced nothing like it and knew of no stories that were similar. Elora's trembling shoulders confirmed his guess.

"Is Firestone going to survive?" he asked instead.

She shook her head slowly as the door opened, and Singers poured through the door. Each one looked as frightened as Elora, and many were limping. Some of their faces were as pale as their white robes.

"I'm not sure," she said.

10

Trust, Radyn learned, was not so easily recovered after it was broken. That truth applied to cities as well as to people.

Every step he took was hesitant, as though his body halfway expected the deck to drop away again at any moment. He saw his own fear mirrored in the eyes and gazes of the manirahs working beside him. They all glanced around, waiting for the nightmare to resume.

What could they trust if they couldn't trust their own city? Hallways and rooms that had once felt like home now felt like prisons. Citizens flocked to the surface when they could, but any safety it inspired was illusory.

The event, whatever it was, had only lasted for a second or two, but it demanded weeks of effort to recover from. The entire clan halted their routines, leaving only a skeleton crew on the surface to stand guard against raiders. The rest of the clan's might was turned toward the effort of repairing Firestone, and Radyn was caught up in a whirlwind of activity.

The amount of work that needed to be done after the disaster meant that there was little time for questions. At first, many called those few moments of terror "The Fall," but it wasn't long before he heard the senior Swords calling it "The Little Fall" as loudly and as often as they could. The lie seemed so obvious and so crude that Radyn couldn't believe the gambit would work.

But it didn't take long for the new designation to spread, and Radyn took note. So long as the clan spread the lie, no one questioned it openly. It was a minor change, but it bolstered people's courage and gave them the strength to press forward. Friends could laugh about "The Little Fall," whereas they couldn't laugh about "The Fall."

Changing what those few seconds had been called might have changed Firestone's attitude, but it didn't change the magnitude of the damage. For the most part, people hadn't suffered major injuries. Several people had died, caught in unfortunate positions in the disaster. Bruises and sprained ankles were common, and a fair number of broken bones needed to be set. Daggers and Swords helped as best they could, using their shardstones to heal that which could be healed.

The devastation was no laughing matter, though. Anything fragile that hadn't been secured was broken, and Radyn spent most of his time helping citizens pack up their belongings to bring to the recyclers. He couldn't guess how many thousands of pounds of materials were being dumped into the ancient machines, but they hadn't worked so hard so long as he'd been alive.

If he wasn't busy hauling debris to the recyclers, he was carrying replacements throughout the city. He delivered plates, cups, chairs, and bedframes, the small necessities that had suddenly become so much more important than before.

All classes within the academy were canceled. Masters and instructors worked side-by-side with the initiates. Radyn didn't care about the interruption to his studies. He'd never really doubted his decision to become an initiate, but he'd never been more certain he'd made the right choice than he was in the aftermath of The Little Fall.

He pushed himself harder than anyone else. From the moment he woke to the moment he stumbled, exhausted, into his bunk, he was helping in any way he could. No furniture was too heavy, no destination too far away, and no task too small. He lost himself in the work as the days blended into one another.

In time, the sense of urgency faded. There were no further falls, and life returned to normal with surprising rapidity. Radyn searched high and low for other ways to contribute, but it became harder to find anything that he was qualified to do. After two weeks, he resumed his daily training with Elora, and three days after that, he had completely returned to the familiar routine and rhythms of the academy. The Little Fall became little more than a bad memory.

The story of The Little Fall came to an official conclusion a week later. The Blade announced that Firestone had been attacked by a nearby city using some sort of new weapon. Beneath Nuela's declaration was another message explaining that they were still investigating the details but that they were sure they were safe from other attacks. That declaration, sprinkled on top of the last three weeks of normalcy, eased most worries.

Radyn turned his full attention to his own development. He attacked his training with renewed vigor. The brief crisis had made him realize he could push himself harder than he thought and that he had more to give. Elora encouraged this new dedication, even as Bragen and Astram complained he made them look bad.

Radyn didn't care. If they were concerned, they could always work harder.

The tenor of their training changed, too. Elora began focusing more on combat, showing ways for Radyn to use his newfound abilities to his advantage. Much of their time was spent with maniblades, but she didn't neglect grappling and striking, either.

Radyn wondered at the change but never inquired. The timing might have been a coincidence, or perhaps Elora sensed something he didn't. Either way, he appreciated the change, and it made him appreciate Elora's methods even more. Because his basic skills were so refined, it seemed easier to pick up new ones. He was certain he was catching up with his peers, if not surpassing them.

Just as Elora had promised when they'd first started training.

Three and a half weeks after The Little Fall, Radyn woke to the sound of whispers in his room.

"Should we wake him?" Bragen asked.

"I'm worried that if we don't, and he wakes up while we're gone, he'll report us," Astram said.

"But we aren't breaking any rules! No one said we couldn't."

"What are you two arguing about?" Radyn asked.

The other two went silent. Then Astram said, "We were going to visit the observation deck, and were debating whether you would want to join us."

Radyn had never been, and his curiosity was immediately piqued. But he was also tired, and his roommates were acting suspiciously. "Why at night?"

His roommates stared at each other, and Astram shrugged. Bragen sighed. "I've heard word that Firestone is approaching something important. The riders have called their dragons, and they're planning on visiting tonight. The clan is trying to keep it quiet, though."

Radyn sat up. Bragen's father served directly under Nuela. If any initiate would know about a secret plan, it would be his roommate. All initiates were supposed to be in bed, but as Bragen had argued earlier, the rules were more implied than written in stone. There was no punishment for wandering the halls late.

"Sure. I'll join you."

He didn't miss the look his roommates gave one another, and it stung. He knew they viewed him as someone who studied too long and trained too hard, but he wasn't that different from them. If Bragen's rumors were true, he wanted to see whatever it was the clan was trying to keep quiet.

They turned up the lantern in their room and threw on clothes. When they were ready, Bragen turned the light back down, and Astram slowly opened their door. Bragen led the way.

It was strange walking the halls of the academy after dark. All the lights were turned down low, barely giving off enough light to see by. When Radyn looked up and down the hallway, he saw no one else. Given how busy the academy usually was, it made him feel like he'd stepped into a dream.

They climbed a ladder that led to the floor where the Daggers lived.

"What are we doing?" Radyn whispered.

"No guards on the doors at the upper levels right now," Bragen whispered.

This was news to Radyn, who only ever entered and exited the academy through the main door. Bragen's words proved true a few minutes later as they left the academy grounds without being challenged.

The journey took them at least twenty minutes. Part of the problem was their desire to avoid others, which kept them in residential districts. But part of the problem was simply that they were a long way from the observation deck. They wandered inward and down, dropping level after level.

Most of Firestone was as quiet as the academy, though Radyn and his roommates passed a few random citizens. Corridors were dark and the markets were silent. At times, the only sounds Radyn heard were those of his breath and their footsteps against the decks. He rarely wandered the city at night, and he didn't like it. During the day, he thought of Firestone as the people who lived and worked here. It was lively and filled with warmth. With everyone asleep, he saw only decks, walls, and ladders. Firestone became a place humans lived, but it wasn't a home.

They finally reached the lowest levels of the city.

Doors here led to large storage rooms where many raw materials were held. The three roommates followed the hallway to its end. Bragen opened the door, and they stepped through into a small chamber with a hole in the floor. The hole was covered by a steel hatch, which Bragen opened. Below was a ladder and the observation deck.

Radyn's entire body tensed at the sight below. Living in Firestone, he'd never had to contend with the idea of heights, but he did now. He backed up to the edge of the wall, as far away from the hole as he could. Astram laughed. "First time?"

Radyn nodded. He couldn't bring himself to speak.

Astram stepped over the hole and dropped through, not even bothering to use the ladder. He laughed as he fell. Bragen did the same, and their voices carried up from the open hole, reassuring Radyn it was safe.

Radyn breathed deeply. If he was to serve the clan, this was a fear that would need to be faced. What better time than the present?

He forced himself to inch forward. His body protested, but he ignored its complaints. His heart pounded so hard it felt as if it was trying to escape his ribcage.

He stared down into the abyss, only to realize it wasn't an abyss at all. The observation deck was a steel grate, just like hundreds of others Radyn had trusted his life upon. Radyn wiped his palms against his pants and descended the ladder. The feel of the steel in his hands was familiar, the ladder no different from any other around Firestone. He didn't look down, and before long, his feet were on the deck.

He couldn't convince his body to let go of the ladder, but he turned so he could take in the incredible view. His eyes went wide.

He'd heard the stories, of course, and seen the drawings and paintings scattered throughout Firestone. But nothing came close to seeing the world below for the first time. Even though it was covered in darkness, its brutal majesty was apparent. The ground below was grassy, undulating waves of silvery hair swept this way and that by the wind.

Dangerous as that land was, longing seized Radyn's heart, squeezing it until he thought it might burst. One reason he'd been willing to follow in Father's footsteps, at least until Whitehawk's raid, had been the opportunity to spend most of his days on the surface with the endless sky overhead. It was where he felt most at ease, where he most often felt like he belonged.

It hadn't been enough, but the land below was. He let his eyes travel across the vast scene, lit by the dual moons that hung like dim suns in the sky.

His reverie was interrupted by Bragen and Astram pointing excitedly at something in the distance. Radyn followed the direction of their fingers and saw a glow on the horizon growing closer. Firestone drifted toward the light, powered by the Engine that not even the Singers fully understood.

Radyn tore his eyes from the glow to the mass above. If he pressed his face against the bars, he could see the shape of Firestone, the weight of the city balanced above his head. If the Engine was to fail now, all he'd have was a moment of flight, and then nothing. An incomprehensible mass of stone and steel would crush him in an instant.

In drawings, Firestone looked a little like a misshapen top. The surface was mostly flat, with small channels running throughout to catch and filter rainwater. The top levels of the city, just beneath the surface, were the most expansive, with each lower level a little smaller than the one above. From his position at the bottom, Radyn could just about imagine the entire city as the bottom curved away from his sight.

The glow on the horizon became a fire, pulling all of Radyn's attention away from Firestone. From this distance, it looked like a mountain in flames. Not a volcano, which was something Radyn had learned about when he was in school. More like a jagged peak, ejecting bursts of fire in random directions. Some flames were sustained, but others sputtered and died like a candle at the end of its wick.

Radyn stared with his roommates, trying to decide what it was he was staring at. If his roommates knew, they didn't say. Wind blew their hair back and made Radyn squint.

Dark shadows appeared in the air between Firestone and the flaming mountain.

The sight never failed to instill a sense of awe in Radyn. He'd recognize the silhouette of a dragon anywhere, and he knew they'd taken off from Firestone. They flew in a loose formation, and Radyn imagined he could see the small shadows of the riders on their necks. He pointed up at the riders, and his roommates nodded. The dragons also headed toward the mountain, scouting ahead for Firestone.

Though Radyn couldn't say for sure, he was almost certain Elora rode among them. She was one of the best riders in the city and wouldn't miss this opportunity to take to the sky.

Bragen's rumors had all been true.

"Do you have any idea what we're flying toward?" Radyn asked.

Bragen shook his head. "I only overheard a bit of a conversation I wasn't supposed to. It sounded serious, though."

For a time, there was nothing more for them to do than stand and watch. Radyn couldn't tear his eyes away from the flames for long. In time, some riders returned and others left.

It couldn't have been more than twenty minutes, but it felt like Radyn had been waiting for a lifetime, a slow sense of dread creeping up from his fingers and toes until his whole body felt cold.

The mountain seemed far away until the moment it wasn't, as Firestone slowed to a stop outside the range of the most intense bursts of fire. Even up close, it took Radyn several minutes to understand what he was seeing. Flares lit up the side of the mountain, but it was no mountain. Twisted steel jutted from the stone, and human debris littered the slopes. Radyn saw broken furniture and shattered doors. Riders circled the mountain, careful to avoid the flames.

The lower reaches of the mountain were crawling with activity. Radyn recognized several of the creatures from his academy lessons. Predators that roamed the land, eager for the taste of human flesh. They sniffed around the base of the mountain, climbing over shifting debris and digging with claws and tusks.

The hunting appeared to be good.

As Radyn watched, he understood what had summoned the predators. He understood what he was looking at.

When Radyn spoke, his voice was barely above a whisper. "That's not a mountain. That's a city."

11

"Single file, initiates! Stay close to your assigned partners."

A dozen commands were shouted and echoed by the senior Swords as they wrangled the entire might of the clan. Overhead, the sky was dull and gray. The water that fell from the sky was too heavy to be called a mist but too light to be a proper rainstorm. Radyn stood with Bragen and Astram in a line that stretched almost thirty initiates deep.

He'd rarely visited this part of the surface before, thanks mostly to the imposing wall that separated it from the farmland. It was controlled by the clan, and it was where riders and their dragons met.

He was in the middle of the Nest, waiting for his turn to ride a dragon for the first time.

The dragon serving the line next to Radyn's landed, the beating of its enormous wings spraying the gathered initiates with water and wind. Two initiates in the front of the line followed a Dagger's instructions, climbing gingerly onto the neck of the beast. The rider showed them where to sit, and both initiates held on tight. At a command from the rider, the dragon beat its wings again and jumped off the side of Firestone.

Radyn thought he heard a scream as the dragon took flight.

Everywhere he looked, the scene was repeated. Dragons landed, loaded, and dove as quickly as their riders could urge them forward. Off to one side, dragons landed with enormous baskets that could hold half a dozen warriors.

The morning after he and his roommates had witnessed the fallen city, an announcement had traveled throughout Firestone. The fallen city was Whitehawk, and the announcement claimed it had been attacked. Firestone would remain in the area for a time, both to search for survivors and to raid the ruins for supplies. Tragic as the loss of a city was, the materials needed to survive were precious and couldn't be wasted. Other cities would soon arrive, but as the first on the scene, Firestone had a unique opportunity to improve the lives of every soul on board.

No doubt, Nuela also saw an opportunity to push her own agenda. With the supplies from Whitehawk, there would be less opposition to growing the population.

Radyn watched the scene quietly, but his thoughts churned within. Perhaps Whitehawk had fallen to an attack, but he was skeptical. He thought of the letter the High Council had received, the difficulties Whitehawk claimed to be having with their Engine. He couldn't help but think of The Little Fall and of Firestone's own future.

Radyn kept his thoughts to himself. He desperately

wished for Elora's guidance, but she was one of the many Swords who'd taken to the air to keep both Firestone and Whitehawk's ruins safe. He watched the happenings but reserved his judgments for when he had more time.

By noon, the entire clan had gathered to listen to the Blade issue her commands. That afternoon, they would launch the largest rescue and salvage mission they'd ever attempted. Every initiate who had acquired their training shard would be ferried to Whitehawk's ruins. Each of them wore the band on their wrist, glowing with the soft blue light of the Engine.

"Glad we aren't with them," Bragen muttered. He tilted his head toward a group of younger initiates preparing for an incoming dragon.

The beast approached with an enormous basket in its claws. It dropped the basket, then circled around and landed in front of another line. The younger initiates unloaded the basket and sorted the new material. Once that was done, the initiates would carry it throughout Firestone, delivering it to where it would be best used. It was backbreaking work.

Radyn didn't think they'd have it much easier in Whitehawk, but at least they'd be able to claim the benefit of having traveled to another city. Outside of Gatherings, such occasions were rare.

A dragon landed in front of their line, and the three initiates ahead of Radyn and his roommates climbed on. Everyone else shuffled forward under the watchful eyes of the supervising Dagger.

Radyn had never stepped off of Firestone. Until today, when he'd not only leave the city of his birth, he'd travel down to the surface. Part of him couldn't wait for the dragon to return, but a part hoped it never did. He remembered the predators circling the edges of the fallen city, and he didn't care to meet them anytime soon. Humans no longer ruled this world.

The dragon and rider returned, lashing Radyn and his roommates with water. This close, Radyn felt something more than the wind and rain. It felt almost like an invisible blanket pressing against him.

The Dagger ushered them forward, and the force increased. Radyn struggled with each step. The Dagger noticed Radyn's trouble and hurried over. "Disconnect from your shardstone," he said.

Radyn frowned. He hadn't even thought he'd been using it, but now that the Dagger drew his attention to his wrist, he realized that he'd connected. His stomach turned to ice. Elora would be furious if she discovered he'd been so sloppy. He cut the connection and the force pressing against him vanished.

Bragen and Astram had already taken their positions on the dragon's neck and glared at him impatiently. He hurried up the dragon, following the Dagger's instructions to the letter.

The dragon's scales were warm to the touch but not hot. Even though he wasn't connected to his shard, Radyn could feel the power of the creature as he clambered up the neck. He positioned himself where the rider pointed, but he'd barely had time to settle in before the dragon spread its wings and lumbered forward.

None of Radyn's childhood imaginings came close to the reality of riding a dragon. How many times had he sat backwards on a chair, clutching the back and pretending it was a dragon's neck as he rode into battle?

But a chair was stable, and a dragon was not. It was scale and muscle in constant motion. Radyn squeezed his thighs and tightened his grip. He fought to keep his balance.

"Relax!" the rider called.

Radyn tried, but the next moment, the dragon casually dove off the edge of Firestone. Radyn screamed, but he took solace in the fact he wasn't alone.

He was falling toward a ground that seemed impossibly far below. His stomach leaped into his throat. Tears streamed from his eyes as the wind whipped past his face.

Then the dragon spread its wings, and Radyn no longer fell. His stomach did somersaults as the dragon settled into level flight. Radyn looked down as the ground passed beneath him.

He was flying!

An obvious fact, perhaps, but it hit him with a physical force. He'd never once felt a lack of anything growing up in Firestone, but that was only because he'd never experienced this. As a child, Firestone had been his whole world, but as a rider, the whole world was his.

The dragon banked and dropped toward Whitehawk. It landed near the top of the ruin, where a staging area had been created. Radyn scrambled off first, followed by Astram and Bragen. As soon as they were a safe distance away, the dragon and rider took off, rising back toward Firestone. Radyn watched them for a minute. From down here, Firestone hung in the sky like a dirty diamond. It seemed so small.

Bragen pulled him away from the staging area. A

Dagger intercepted them, taking in their training bracelets with a glance. "Initiates?" she asked.

Bragen nodded.

"Follow the yellow markings." The Dagger pointed to a slash of paint on a nearby wall. "They'll eventually lead you to another Dagger, who will assign you a specific task."

They bowed and followed the markings. The fires they'd seen the night before had largely burned out, but evidence of the flames remained. The yellow markers guided them through a maze of twisted steel, eventually leading them to a hatch that led deeper into the ruin. Bragen went first. He was halfway down when he slipped on the ladder and cursed. He dropped the rest of the way. "Careful, it's bent and slippery from the rain."

Astram and Radyn descended without a problem, thanks to the warning. They searched for the yellow marker that would guide them deeper, and Astram grunted. "Weird," he said.

Radyn swallowed hard and nodded. On one hand, the hallways of Whitehawk were eerily similar to those of Firestone. Everything from the lanterns to the spacing of the doors was the same.

Except here, the hallway had been bent and twisted as though the structure had been made of clay instead of steel. Bragen found the first marking and followed it. The deck twisted, making walking difficult. Using their hands to steady themselves, they navigated the twisting passage. Soon they were walking on a wall, which made Radyn think that at any moment, he was going to fall to the side.

Some doors they passed were open, meaning they had to jump across. Those that weren't appeared sealed shut by the twisting of the passage, likely never to open again. After passing a few open doors, Radyn wished none would open again. Each opened door was a portal to a unique nightmare. Most of the broken furniture had been raided, sent on a long journey that would end in Firestone's recyclers. The bodies were left where they fell, many in grotesque positions. Limbs lay at unnatural angles, and skulls had been crushed as entire homes had been twisted into new arrangements.

Radyn was no stranger to death. His family hadn't been the only one killed in the raid that had made him one of Firestone's wards. Even so, the sights made his stomach churn.

He closed his eyes. Elora's lessons echoed in his thoughts. He imagined stepping out of his body and witnessing everything as a dispassionate observer.

When he opened his eyes again, his stomach had settled. He studied the scenes, trying to understand the story the details told.

"It must have fallen at night," he said.

"Why do you think that?" Bragen asked.

"Everybody was in their homes. If this had happened during the day, there wouldn't be so many bodies here."

Another revelation quickly followed the first. A certainty that he'd been lied to. "This wasn't an attack. Or, at least, it wasn't a raid."

Astram put his hands on his hips. "You can't possibly know that."

"Think about it. Even if the raid happened on a stormy night, there would have been at least a few minutes of warning."

Bragen could pick up the thread. "And if they'd had warning, they wouldn't be in their homes."

"The Blade told us it was an attack, so it was an attack," Astram said.

"Maybe it wasn't a raid, but something else?" Bragen offered.

Radyn shrugged. For the moment, all he knew was what hadn't happened. He didn't yet know enough to say what did. But he sensed he was approaching dangerous territory with his roommates, so he didn't press the matter.

They returned to the hallway and followed the markings. They emerged at what had once been a market space. A Dagger sat in the center, using a broken plank as a makeshift writing desk. He looked up as the three initiates approached. "New arrivals?"

Bragen nodded.

Radyn peeked over Bragen's shoulder and saw the paper before the Dagger was a rough map of the surrounding area. The Dagger consulted the map and pointed down a dark hallway. "Explore that hallway. Test all the doors and open as many as you can. We've found a handful of survivors in this area, so keep an ear open, too. Go as far as you can, but use your best judgment. If the way isn't blocked after a thousand paces, come back and let me know."

They acknowledged the orders, grabbed two lanterns next to the Dagger, and then went down the hallway. Bragen and Astram held the lanterns, leaving Radyn to test the doors.

The first few were sealed shut, too twisted by the force of the impact to open.

The fourth door they tried was at their feet, and it opened without a problem. Radyn pulled it open and held out his hand for a lantern. Astram handed his over, and Radyn squatted down next to the door and dangled the lantern in the room.

Blood covered the walls, and a sickening smell rose from the open door. "Is anybody alive?" Radyn asked.

He wasn't surprised when there was no answer. He waited a moment, listening for anything, but nothing moved within the home.

"Let's keep going," Bragen said.

Radyn returned the lantern to Astram. Of the next six doors, two opened, revealing similar scenes to the ones they'd already seen.

The next door was over their heads, and when Radyn tried it, the door refused to budge. He was about to move on to the next one when he thought he heard something. He held up a hand for quiet.

"Someone's calling for help," he said.

Bragen shook his head. "I don't hear anything."

"Me neither," Astram added.

Radyn pointed up. "I think it's there."

His two roommates looked at each other. "You sure, or is this just you imagining things again?" Bragen asked.

"I'm sure of it. Help me with this door."

Astram, the tallest of the three, shrugged at Bragen and pulled at the latch. When it didn't move, he repositioned himself so he could exert more force on the handle. The veins on his neck bulged, but the door refused to cooperate. It had bent too much in the crash. He let go and shook out his hands.

The cry from above came again, this time loud enough for both of Radyn's roommates to hear it.

"We should break down the door," Radyn said.

Bragen shot him a dubious look. "How?"

Radyn held up his wrist with the training bracelet. "Form a blade. Then either cut a hole or attack the hinges and the latch."

"I can't form a blade without a hilt," Astram said.

"Me neither," Bragen added.

"Really?" Radyn asked. Both had been initiates longer than him, and both were closer to testing for Dagger. Bragen was expecting the test almost any day now.

Bragen glanced at his feet. "It was never something we had to master."

It didn't matter. "Then I'll need you two to lift me up so I can work. I should be able to form a blade long enough."

Bragen might have been ashamed of his lack of ability, but he still stepped up and took command of the situation. "We can do that, but I think you should cut a hole in the door. Even if you destroyed the latch and the hinges, I don't think the door would come free. The frame is too twisted."

Radyn agreed, and after a few moments of scrambling, was perched awkwardly on his roommates' shoulders. He was by far the lightest of the three, but the other two kept shifting underneath him. He ignored them and focused on his shard. The training band pressed it against his wrist, and he connected to it.

No matter how many times he repeated the technique, the connection always surprised him. Elora described it as opening a door to a dragon, and the description seemed apt. Once a shard was in contact with a body, it wanted to connect. Becoming a manirah was less about learning how to connect with the shard than it was about learning how to shut the door and keep it under control. Using the small stones conferred speed, strength, and mental acuity on the user, but too much use poisoned the body.

Or at least, that was what the clan believed. Radyn wasn't so sure anymore. He'd been wearing his band day and night since Elora had given it to him at the six-month mark, and he felt fine.

Radyn dropped his defenses against the shard and basked in the cool rush of strength that spread through his limbs. Then, as he'd practiced with Elora, he imagined a small dagger in his hand, sharper than steel. He channeled the strength of the shard into the form, and the construct appeared in his hand, glowing with the same pale blue light of the shard.

In his hand, it felt like any other dagger, but it wasn't. Radyn gazed upon it for a moment, then thrust it into the door as though it were the heart of a mortal enemy. The dagger slipped through the steel as though it were paper. Radyn worked carefully but quickly, cutting a hole big enough for them to climb through. The steel door put up some resistance, but Elora had trained him well. When the hole was nearly complete, Radyn braced it with his left hand.

The hole slid free of the rest of the door, and Radyn pushed it away so it clattered several feet away from them. He stopped channeling the power of the shard to the dagger and it vanished. He put a hand on each of his roommates' heads, then braced so he could get his feet on their shoulders. When he stood, most of his head and shoulders were through the hole he'd made. "Is anyone here? We've come to help."

"We're trapped in the bedroom!" said a voice.

Radyn pulled himself through the door. He had to push aside a broken part of a chair to slip through. He cleared a bit of space around the door, then reached down through the hole. "Lanterns," he said. A moment later, he had light in the devastated room.

Furniture lay everywhere against the wall he was standing on. Most of it was a few steps away, in the direction of the kitchen. He saw no blood or bodies, for which he was grateful.

He reached down and helped pull Astram up through the hole. Together, they pulled Bragen up.

The three roommates then began the process of reaching the bedroom door. The geometry of the room made it difficult to access, but Bragen cleverly suggested piling some of the furniture together to create a makeshift staircase. After a few minutes of labor, Radyn clambered up the furniture to reach the door. As expected, the latch didn't work.

Once again, he created a dagger, and this time he carved an even wider hole. He warned the survivors on the other side of the door to stand back, then kicked the hole open.

Three young women emerged, all about Radyn's age. They were dirty and covered in bruises, and they moved slowly. Their lips were cracked and bleeding. Radyn helped them down the shaky tower they'd built. They moved carefully, returning to the hole in the first door that Radyn had cut.

Astram and Bragen dropped to help the women while Radyn stayed up top to lower them slowly. While everyone got into position, Radyn asked the women what had happened.

A young woman with pale hair answered. "There was no warning. One moment, the three of us were together. We'd finished supper and were relaxing in my bedroom. Then the city fell. We floated for a few seconds, and then everything got confusing. When we came to, we were trapped in the room. We've been shouting for what feels like days."

Radyn dipped his head. "You'll be safe now. We'll take you with us to Firestone, where you'll be cared for."

The women said thanks, and as Radyn helped them down through the hole, he was proud of his decision to join the clan. He could serve, helping those the same way the clan had helped him after the raid.

He couldn't ask for anything more.

"My name is Radyn," he said, forgetting he hadn't introduced himself yet.

The woman who'd answered his question bowed. "Aria. It's a pleasure to meet you."

"Let's get you out of here," Radyn said.

She bowed to him. "I think I'd like that very much."

12

Radyn followed Elora up the stairs toward the surface, hounding her with questions. She ignored them all until Radyn reached out and grabbed her wrist. "Why won't you tell me anything about Whitehawk?" he demanded.

"I've already told you," she answered.

"You didn't tell me anything!"

She finally turned and faced him. She was two stairs above him, so she looked down at him like he was a child. "I don't *know* anything more about Whitehawk than you, but I'm sure we've come to the same conclusions."

Radyn wasn't satisfied, and he continued to press. "Whitehawk's Engine failed, didn't it?"

"You've seen and heard as much as I have. What do you think?"

He wasn't in the mood to have his questions turned back on him. It was fine during training, but a city had fallen from the sky, and the tension in Firestone was simmering. "Why won't you just tell me?"

Elora put her hands on her hips. "Because I don't know and because I'm trying to train you to rely only on yourself. If I told you Whitehawk was raided, would you believe me?"

"No."

"So you've already reached your conclusion based on what you've seen and heard. What else is there for me to add?"

"But what if I'm wrong?"

"Then you'll make poor choices, and hopefully, you'll learn from them. It's good to keep questioning, but don't rely on any authority, including mine, to provide your answers. As soon as you do, you've given up one of your greatest strengths."

Elora pulled away from him and finished climbing the stairs to the surface. Two Daggers stood guard at the door, and they bowed as Elora passed. Radyn hurried after her.

The last few days had been difficult. Radyn had returned to the ruins of Whitehawk several times, not to look for more survivors but to strip the city of all that Firestone could use. Everyone in the clan had worked themselves to the bone, but Whitehawk's demise was Firestone's greatest prize in the past decade.

When he wasn't busy hauling materials and food out of Whitehawk, he was in his room studying the proclamations the Blade had made regarding the fallen city. They were, as far as Radyn was concerned, outright lies. The story was that Whitehawk had been attacked by the same type of weapons responsible for The Little Fall months ago, but Whitehawk's Singers hadn't been up to the challenge. Every message ended with an assurance that Firestone was as safe as ever.

Reading the proclamations angered Radyn. He could well understand the desire to reassure the citizens, but such a blatant lie couldn't do anything but come back to bite the Blade. Eventually, someone outside the clan's High Council would learn that Whitehawk had requested aid for their Engine weeks before they fell from the sky.

And as far as Radyn knew, the High Council had done nothing.

If the word spread, panic would follow. It wouldn't take long for people to connect the events surrounding Whitehawk with the Little Fall, and then they'd doubt their own safety.

Radyn certainly did.

As Elora strode across the grounds, he asked, "What does Jelrik say?"

"That, as far as he can tell, our Engine is fine. He's been frustrated because his schedule has lost its normalcy and he's not been singing as much."

Radyn kicked at a clump of dirt. "Jyn wanted our help, but I feel useless."

"You won't for long." Elora stopped outside the thick wall surrounding the Nest and signed the papers, which gave her and Radyn access. The guard examined the papers and then waved them through. A small door in the wall opened and Radyn walked into the realm of dragons.

Some of the area's mystique had worn off over the past few days. He'd been working in and around the Nest often now, and although he wouldn't say he was comfortable around dragons yet, they were at least familiar. Elora led him toward the command building, where she went in and spoke with Macken, the Sword who commanded the Nest. She emerged not long after, waving for him to follow. "Macken's not pleased that we're letting an initiate train with a dragon, but the last few days have made it clear we need more riders, and Jyn wants you in the air."

"Do you know why?"

"Because he thinks you're going to be valuable to the clan, and I think he sees trouble on the horizon. He wants you ready for when it arrives."

They came to a large area where several dragons rested, protected by enormous roofs that sheltered most of their powerful bodies from the elements. Elora stopped in front of a sleek young dragon with scales that reflected the light differently, depending on the angle. Mostly they seemed black, but if the light struck just right, a rainbow-colored ripple would pass through the scales. The dragon cracked one eye open as they approached, and Radyn sensed a deep intellect in that gaze.

"Radyn, this is Tanwen. He's young, but already one of our fastest dragons. Today, you're going to become one of his riders."

Radyn's heart beat faster at the thought. Under normal circumstances, only Swords were allowed to become riders. The link with a dragon required a powerful connection with one's shardstone, and those that earned the badge on their uniform displayed it proudly. Radyn had long dreamed of flight but had never imagined his time would come so soon.

Elora gestured for him to approach Tanwen. "Connect to your shardstone and reach out to him."

Radyn frowned. "Won't that push me away?"

"Only if he's already working with another rider. Now, when he's at rest, there's nothing to worry about."

Radyn did as she commanded. After his first experience, he'd always been careful not to connect with his shard near a dragon. Today, though, there was no wall of force pushing against him. He reached out with his will.

The bond with the dragon flashed brightly in his mind, leaving stars in his vision and a physical sense of being pulled out of his body. He blinked and stumbled, and though Elora no doubt noticed, she didn't panic.

"It's normal to feel some disorientation. The bond with the dragon, like your connection with your shardstone, goes both ways. Your awareness will be split between your senses and Tanwen's. Take some time to get used to it."

Radyn began to understand why only Swords were allowed to become riders. The strength of the sensations that assaulted him was incredible, almost as if he was connected to multiple shardstones. The breadth of the dragon's senses was far greater than his own, and if not for Elora's training, he would have been lost in a moment.

When his breathing evened out, and he could control the vast amount of information flowing through his mind, Elora encouraged him to climb onto Tanwen. Radyn did so, blinking as he fought to make sense of the paired awarenesses dancing in his skull.

"Relax," Elora said, "a dragon isn't something to control. They're a force that must be ridden. We don't command them so much as work with them. We suggest what we want, and if Tanwen agrees with you, it will happen. The stronger your will, the more likely they are to agree. I expect Tanwen here will test you thoroughly on this flight."

"You won't be with me?"

"I can do no good riding with you. I'll be riding Shriken, but you should know I can only be of limited help. You and Tanwen are bonded now, meaning there's little I can do except try to keep you safe. Continue getting used to each other, and I'll meet you here soon."

Elora left to mount Shriken, and Radyn did as she asked. He felt Tanwen's strength as though it was his own, and it seemed as though the dragon's mighty heart beat in time with his much smaller one. The longer they remained bonded, the better Radyn could separate what was him and what was Tanwen, though the boundary between them remained fuzzy.

Elora returned, mounted on a small dragon with burnt red scales. She gestured them forward, and Radyn gave Tanwen a tug.

Tanwen didn't budge.

Radyn tried again, this time imagining them walking toward the lip of Firestone. Tanwen rumbled underneath him, then rose with a surprising grace. They followed Elora and came to a stop at the edge of the city.

Thanks to the missions in Whitehawk, Radyn had flown before, but always in the confident hands of a more experienced rider. Now that he was alone, icy tendrils of fear crept around his heart. Tanwen rumbled again, but this rumble struck Radyn as being dissatisfied. Tanwen sat down, in no hurry to go anywhere.

"Don't give in to the fear," Elora advised.

"Easier said than done."

"True enough, but don't forget the power of the bonding. Your confidence will feed Tanwen, just as your fears will sap his strength. Find your courage."

Radyn imagined all the times he'd dropped off the edge of Firestone with other riders, the incomparable feeling of flying as a dragon's wings caught the air for the first time. If a junior Sword could ride a dragon, so could he. He imagined jumping off the edge with Tanwen, and no sooner had the thought crossed his mind than it had become a reality. Tanwen practically leaped off the edge, and Radyn and his dragon plummeted through the sky.

Radyn didn't need to suggest anything to Tanwen. The dragon opened its wings and caught the wind. Radyn whooped with delight. Granted, Tanwen wasn't carrying any of the weight Radyn was used to dragons carrying between Whitehawk's ruins and Firestone, but Tanwen flew faster than Radyn had thought was possible. Wind pulled his hair back, and his joy mixed with Tanwen's.

They banked both left and right at Radyn's suggestion, but it was Tanwen who suggested more dramatic maneuvers. Radyn felt the dragon's idea like a temptation in the back of his mind. Drunk on their early success, Radyn agreed, and Tanwen rose, twisted, and dove. As Elora had said, Radyn wasn't so much controlling Tanwen as he was riding alongside him.

He found Elora in the sky and swooped down to fly beside her. She was watching him with a grin on her face. "It looks like you're getting the hang of it," she said, her words barely carrying over the wind.

He nodded enthusiastically.

She gestured for him to follow, and he passed the suggestion along to Tanwen, who was happy to obey. They flew together for several minutes until a familiar sight appeared ahead of them.

Elora slowly bled altitude, and Tanwen followed suit. They landed gently upon the small landing zone that had been cleared from the top of the ruins of Whitehawk. Elora hopped off her dragon and Radyn did the same. The area, which had once been crawling with people, was empty.

"Let Tanwen go find some food."

Tanwen didn't need to be told twice, and the dragons flew off together, searching for their next meal. The surface might not be safe for humans, but it was a rich hunting ground for dragons.

Radyn tracked Tanwen as he flew, less with his eyes and more through their bond. A part of him still felt like he was flying, and he wondered if, when Tanwen ate, if he would feel satiated.

"I'm sorry if I seemed short with you," Elora said.

Radyn shook his head. "I was asking questions I could have answered for myself."

"Sure, but that's not what caused me to be short. The truth is, I'm worried, and I don't know what to do. Whitehawk was having trouble with their Engine and they crashed, and as you well know, we've had trouble with ours, too. We've enjoyed the Engines and their gifts for so long, I fear we've become complacent."

Elora's confession unsettled Radyn more than he cared to admit. He'd always relied on her calm approach to solving problems, always expected there was nothing she couldn't do. He knew she wasn't perfect, but she was one of the most competent people he'd ever known.

"Is there anything we can do?" he asked.

"For now, not really. The best we can do is keep our eyes and ears open. Whitehawk fell, but maybe one of the survivors knows something that can help us prevent another disaster. I'll keep talking to Jelrik, too."

"I can talk with those we rescued from the bedroom. I've been meaning to check on them anyway, but I haven't had much time," Radyn said.

"A good idea." Elora paused. "I know it can feel difficult sometimes, but don't forget your training. Pay attention, now more than ever, because there's no telling what detail might mean the difference between Firestone flying for countless more generations and it falling from the sky."

Radyn supposed it was as good advice as any, and soon they called their dragons back. After they mounted, they began the climb back to Firestone, and although Radyn still thrilled at the thought of flight, his thoughts about the future were dark.

13

Finding the women he and his roommates had rescued from Whitehawk turned out to be a challenging task. Firestone had the space to accommodate the refugees, but it wasn't prepared for so many new arrivals at once, and in the rush to save lives, any effort to keep track of people was abandoned.

Radyn had heard rumors that the Shields planned a new census once the situation settled, but for now, people were living in whatever spaces were ready for them. Many generous families had opened up their homes, and neighborhoods had banded together, donating spare beds and furniture to prepare empty homes for new neighbors.

In theory, the Shields were supposed to track the addresses of the refugees, but the task had overwhelmed them. Radyn checked with the Shields first at their headquarters, but the staff there had no record of any Aria arriving from Whitehawk. The Shields helped, though, by suggesting a few places in Firestone where new arrivals had congregated. Radyn visited them one at a time, asking after Aria.

In the third neighborhood he checked, he had success. A woman there knew Aria and knew what neighborhood she'd ended up in. It wasn't one on the list the Shields had given him, but Radyn followed the clue and asked after the new arrivals in the suggested neighborhood.

The entire process took him more than a day, but eventually, he knocked on a door and saw Aria once again.

Her eyes went wide when she saw him. "Oh, it's you."

Radyn supposed he was glad that she recognized him, but the tone of her greeting left him uncertain of her feelings toward him being here. He also realized, as he stared awkwardly at her, that he hadn't planned on what to say to her once he found her.

For maybe the first time ever, he wished Bragen was here. His roommate always knew what to say to start a conversation.

Radyn bowed to cover his embarrassment. "I'm sorry to interrupt, but I came to see how you and the others were doing."

Aria studied him for a moment, then stepped out into the hallway and shut the door behind her. She took his arm and started walking.

Radyn stumbled after her, his thoughts trying to catch up to this sudden and unexpected turn of events. After a few awkward steps, he matched her stride, but he didn't know what to say. All he could do was steal quick glances at her. Without facing her straight on, he couldn't see her face well, so he couldn't even guess her thoughts. Her grip was firm and her step was steady, though. She moved like a woman with a plan.

As they walked, she answered his question. "Physically, my roommates and I are fine. Firestone has been more than generous with food and water, and we've all recovered from the time we spent trapped in the room."

Radyn noted what she didn't say, and the way her voice quavered when she spoke about being trapped in the room told him plenty. She might be unhurt, but that didn't mean she was well.

Any sympathy he might have uttered seemed inane, so he focused on what he could do. "Is there anything I can do to help?"

She'd been waiting for the question. He was certain of it. "You're a manirah, aren't you?"

He shook his head. "An initiate, though I expect I'll take the tests to become a Dagger within the next month or so."

She leaned close to him, and he almost pulled away. He didn't even know her, but here she was, pressed against him as though he were her closest friend.

Or maybe more.

He would have pulled away but couldn't bring himself to do so. Her arms around his made him feel like he was needed.

"Has anyone in the clan explained what happened to Whitehawk?" she asked.

The question trapped Radyn and brought him to a

stop. The clan story remained a lie, and he knew it, but his standing in the clan would be endangered if he said anything else to her.

She noticed his hesitation and pulled him down a narrow corridor connecting two larger hallways. Suddenly, he felt less like he was escorting her and more like he was being dragged away. She spun him by his elbow and pushed him gently against a wall so that she could face him. Any trace of meekness was gone, and Radyn slowly came to understand how completely he'd been fooled.

Apparently, the best training in Firestone meant nothing the moment a woman took his arm.

"I know it wasn't a weapon that brought my home down," she said. Her voice was low but confident.

Radyn swallowed and wondered what he could say that wasn't a lie but didn't put him in trouble with the clan.

"You know something, so what is it?" she demanded.

Radyn looked up and down the corridor, but there was no one to save him. When passersby in the main hallways saw him and Aria, they assumed it was a quiet liaison and hurried past.

She slammed her palms against the wall on either side of his head. "What do you know?"

"Nothing," he said.

She stared into his eyes, then snarled. "Pathetic." She stormed down the corridor.

He watched her go, his heart sinking. Not because she had called him pathetic but because he'd let himself down. The clan's pillar of honesty loomed large in his thoughts. The Blade may have lied, but that didn't mean he had to. Still, it was a risk.

She didn't give him much time to decide. She was almost back to the main hallways when he said, "Wait."

She stopped, and he joined her. "Can we talk somewhere more private?"

She tilted her head as she studied him, then nodded. "Where do you have in mind?"

"There's a maintenance corridor a few levels down. It has a bench we could sit on."

"Lead the way."

Radyn did, painfully aware that her arms were no longer wrapped around his. She followed a step behind and to his side, as though she was afraid he'd pounce on her if she wasn't careful. He felt like he should say something, but nothing seemed fitting, so he chose silence.

Eventually, they reached the small corridor Radyn had known about, and as he'd promised, a bench waited for them. He sat first and she joined him after a brief hesitation. Again, he glanced up and down the corridor. The hallway it intersected was a quiet one, so they were about as alone as they could be. He swore that when he became a Dagger, he would ask for private quarters.

"When you asked me what I know, I wasn't lying," he began.

She pressed her palms against the bench, preparing to stand and walk away.

Radyn hurried to explain. "I don't *know* anything, but I believe you're right. It wasn't a weapon that brought down Whitehawk."

Aria settled back on the bench and fixed him with a

stare. "Why do you believe that, if you don't *know* anything?"

Her mocking tone stung, but it was no more than he deserved. Radyn took a deep breath, too aware he needed to tread lightly. "The things I've heard and seen, they aren't supposed to leave the clan. Hell, most of the clan doesn't even know any of this. What are you going to do with what I want to tell you?"

She shrugged. "I don't know. I suppose it depends on what it is."

It wasn't enough of a reassurance to calm Radyn's jittery nerves. His pulse was racing, and he didn't think it was just because he was alone in a corridor with her. She shook, and it took him a moment to realize she was tearing up. He reached out to comfort her, then held back.

"Everyone says they're sorry, and everyone's been more than kind, but no one understands."

Her voice was low, so much so that Radyn had to focus to listen.

"We don't even think about these miracles the Makers built for us. How they keep us alive and away from the terrors of the surface. We take our mandated time on the surface, but these hallways and corridors are all we know. All we've ever known."

She wiped her eyes with the back of her hand. "And then one day it falls. Your world goes black and your stomach presses into the back of your throat. It's impossible to describe, because it's *everything*. Your entire world, twisted beyond recognition in the blink of an eye."

Radyn wanted to claim that he understood, but

comparing The Little Fall to Whitehawk was like comparing a scratch to an amputation.

"Somehow, you live through it, but when you emerge on the other side, no one will tell the truth. They lie to your face, and you know it's a lie, but if you say anything, people will look at you like you're mad."

She looked up at him with red-rimmed eyes. "All I want is to know the truth, no matter what it takes."

Radyn looked into those eyes and there was only one thing he could do. Her determination was the same as Elora's. The same as his own. "Your Engine failed," he said.

Her sharp intake of breath betrayed her surprise. Then she swallowed and asked, "How do you know?"

"I don't, but I'm reasonably sure. More than a year ago, Whitehawk raided Firestone to kidnap our Singers. That raid failed, but a few weeks ago, a messenger arrived, pleading for Firestone to send our Singers to you. The High Council was still debating the best course of action when your home fell."

They sat in silence for a minute as Aria absorbed all that she'd learned. "How did it fail? Why?"

"I don't know, but I worry about Firestone. Several months ago, our Engine went dark for a couple of seconds. It's nothing compared to Whitehawk, but I think it's a good part of the reason the Blade is lying about what happened to your city. She claimed our Little Fall was an attack, so to prevent a panic, she needed to say the same about Whitehawk."

Aria stood, and for a heartbeat, Radyn worried she was going to run away and shout what he'd told her to the world, but she paced back and forth in front of the bench. "Does everyone in the clan know this?"

"No. Only the High Council and a few others."

She glanced at him. "Why you, then? If you're only an initiate?"

"Because of who my master is. It's mostly coincidence I know any of this."

"Can you learn more?"

"What do you want to know?"

Aria considered that before answering. "I want to know why Whitehawk's Engine failed, and I want to know if Firestone might face a similar fate."

"I want to know the same."

Aria sat down next to him. "Then let's compare what we know so we can figure out what we need to learn."

The afternoon passed in a blur. Radyn told Aria about his training, the Little Fall, and everything he knew about the Engine. In return, Aria told him about the days leading up to the fall of Whitehawk. Her memories were bitter, but she filled in as much detail as she remembered.

When they finished, they weren't any further ahead than earlier. Aria agreed she would seek out any manirahs from Whitehawk and ask them if they had felt anything unusual before the fall, and Radyn promised to keep her abreast of anything he learned.

They ate supper together that night, pestering one another with endless questions. Radyn had never met anyone as curious as her, nor had he ever met anyone who had the same clarity about what they wanted to learn and do. Most of his fellow initiates drifted through their days, and Aria was a welcome contrast.

After the meal, Radyn escorted her back to her

apartment, and as they walked, she took his arm again. This time, it felt far less manipulative, and he bowed deeply to her when he dropped her off.

There was a spring in his step as he left her apartment behind. He hadn't found the answers he sought, but he was thinking he'd found something much more valuable instead.

14

It seemed impossible to believe, but the urgency that surrounded the fall of Whitehawk faded, and life returned to its normal rhythms. Whitehawk's citizens became Firestone's, and they went about establishing their families. In his more cynical moments, Radyn wondered if the unexpected developments overjoyed Nuela. She'd gotten her population increase without the decades of effort she'd been planning for.

He knew that was unfair. The additional citizens had placed a burden on Firestone that would trouble them for years to come. Food reserves would dip incredibly low this year, and even though the riders hunted throughout Whitehawk's hunting grounds, food would be scarce for a year or two. Farmers were complaining loudly, even as their numbers swelled with additional help.

Still, life went on. Aria couldn't find any manirahs from Whitehawk with useful information, and Elora and Radyn hit a wall, too. According to Elora, Jelrik was still anxious, but not as worried as he once had been. Their only clue, slim as it was, came when Jelrik mentioned in passing that the Engine sounded healthy "again." Elora had quizzed him relentlessly, and all he admitted was that for a time after The Little Fall, some of the more sensitive Singers had noticed a discordant note in the Engine's song. But it was gone now.

Neither Radyn, Elora, nor Aria knew what to believe, but their daily routines sanded away their fears, leaving them uneasy and uncertain, but with no specific course of action to follow.

Bragen and Astram completed their Dagger trials and wasted no opportunity to rub their advancement in Radyn's face.

Elora held him back for another month, then submitted his name for the trials. He'd been nervous, but they ended up being no more than a demonstration and a sparring test. He became a junior Dagger and moved to his own private room, as he'd sworn to himself.

Elora had feared that his advancement would weaken his ambition for training, but her worry was groundless. Although he had more tasks now than before, he continued to arrange for training at every opportunity, which was why he was here again today.

Radyn sat on his knees before Elora, his perception so sharp it almost hurt. The soft sound of the fans circulating the air in the room was as loud as an angry infant wailing in his ear. The trickle of sweat down his arm felt like a river carving its way into a valley. Though he sat ten paces away, he saw the way Elora's nose expanded and contracted as she breathed.

"Enough," she whispered.

Radyn shifted the cycle of energy through his body,

dulling his senses. Connected to the two training shards on the band, his senses were still sharper than any civilian's, but compared to the agony he'd just experienced, they seemed like nothing at all. Most of his peers would have struggled to maintain focus, but thanks to Elora's training, it came naturally to him.

After allowing him a few minutes to recover, she asked if he was ready. The question was rhetorical. She'd been watching him like a hungry dragon circling above wounded prey. He wanted to rest his aching limbs, to ease the pounding in his head, but he'd learned over the months of training to trust her more than he trusted himself. She'd proven, time and time again, that she would push him right to the edge of breaking, but she'd never shove him over. So he bowed, and a blade appeared in her hand.

As usual, she didn't use the hilt that was at her hip. She believed the hilt was unnecessary for training, a crutch too many initiates relied upon. After Whitehawk, Radyn was also convinced. If not for her insistence he learn to control the strength of the shards without a hilt, who knew what would have happened to Aria or her friends?

Radyn stood. He opened himself to the stones, sharpened his senses, and formed his own blade. With only two shards, he couldn't form a maniblade as long as Elora's, but he wasn't expected to.

She advanced, and they met in the middle of the room, their glowing blades crossing and crossing again. He saw the way her weight shifted as she prepared to strike and heard the sharp intake of breath. Her speed gave him no time to think, forcing him to rely on the techniques driven deep into his muscles after hundreds of hours of training.

The silent beat they danced to grew faster as Elora's blade cut and cut again. The last shreds of Radyn's thoughts were banished, replaced by pure awareness and instinctive reaction. His mind grew more weary than his arms. Finally, she slipped past his defense. Her blade turned into a club and she tapped him on the forehead.

Radyn cursed softly as he let his own blade vanish. Whenever he believed he neared his master in skill, she reminded him how much farther there was left to travel. He knew he improved every day, but it never felt like enough.

"Don't be so hard on yourself," Elora said. As usual, her sharp gaze and knowledge of Radyn's attitudes allowed her an almost frightening insight into his thoughts. She'd taught him to do the same, but he hadn't yet mastered her methods of observation. Though he'd spent more time with Elora than anyone else, she remained opaque to him.

"You beat me easily."

"Not so easily. I have more experience than you, which matters, but the greatest separator is our shards. Once you become used to the strength of a Sword, our duels will be determined by the slimmest of margins."

She gestured to his wrist. He closed himself off from the shardstones, bracing against the loss. It didn't hit as hard as it had when he'd first started training, but it wasn't a pleasant experience. A wave of lethargy crashed over him and he fought back a yawn. He bowed and handed the band to her. Then he dug in his pocket for the band he wore as a junior Dagger. It was only one shardstone, but it still filled his limbs with strength.

"How have the last few days been?" Elora asked.

"Wonderful."

"And when you close yourself off from the shardstone?"

Radyn wanted to lie, but Elora would notice. "I haven't disconnected often."

Elora sighed, but Radyn got the impression his answer wasn't wholly unexpected. "You know my worries, and I think if you're going to continue along this path, you should at least have yourself checked by a healer. But what are your thoughts?"

"Now that I've had a taste, I don't want to live as others do."

"Despite the risks?"

Radyn nodded.

Elora considered for a moment, then said, "Very well. Before you leave today, there is something else we need to talk about."

Radyn could guess well enough. Elora's tone of voice said it all. "Aria?"

"Aria."

"What did she do this time?"

"She stole a second-level training band."

Terrible as the crime was, Radyn chuckled. Of course she had. "If I can return it, will she be left alone?"

"She stole a second-level training band," Elora repeated, her eyes hard.

Radyn held his tongue, and finally, Elora nodded. "If you can retrieve it by tomorrow, I'll make the problem disappear, but she needs to stop with this nonsense. She's drawing more attention to herself than I can deflect."

Radyn bowed deeply. "I understand. Thank you, master."

Elora dismissed him, and he hurried out of the room before she changed her mind. He went first to his room, where he cleaned off and changed his clothes. Then he left in search of Aria.

The first place he checked was the home she shared with her friends from Whitehawk, though he didn't hold out much hope. When he turned the last corner, he saw a Shield standing outside her door. Radyn walked by without stopping, offering the Shield a curt nod as he passed. Because he wasn't in uniform, the Shield didn't pay him any attention.

If Aria wasn't at home and couldn't return, there was one place she was most likely to be. Radyn descended through the levels of Firestone. He passed through all the residential levels, most of which were located closer to the surface. The lower levels were filled with spaces for storage, the ancient machinery that kept Firestone alive, and ventilated workshops.

One of those workshops, long since abandoned, was his destination. He knocked on the door, three knocks followed by two, and waited.

He listened to several latches being undone before the door swung open, and Aria peeked out. She scowled when she saw him. "Elora sent you, didn't she?"

Radyn nodded. "Are you going to let me in?"

She glanced down at his wrist where his band was. Her scowl deepened. "I couldn't stop you if I wanted to."

"If you said no, I'd leave you be."

Her scowl broke. "Sorry. But it wasn't easy to snatch the band. I didn't think they would figure out it was me so quickly."

"They've already put a Shield outside your home."

Aria groaned, then opened the door and let him in. She checked the hallway behind him, then closed the door and latched it up tight. "My roommates are going to be furious."

"It's not like it's the first time you've done something that resulted in the Shields looking for you."

"That's exactly their problem," Aria said.

The workroom was a little larger than the average living room, with a powerful vent dominating the center of the ceiling. Beneath the vent was a steel table, bolted to the floor, covered in tools. The missing training band was under a light with several tools surrounding it. Both shardstones had been removed from the leather.

"What are you hoping to learn?" he asked.

"Anything and everything. How they work, why they work, and what else they do."

"Why not ask a Singer? They know more about the Engine and the shardstones than anyone."

"I have, and they're useless. All they know is what they've been taught, which isn't much more than a combination of old superstitions and traditions that they can't explain. They're trained to maintain the Engine, not to understand it."

It was always the same with Aria, and her problems were just one flavor of the challenges that had faced many of the Whitehawk survivors. Radyn understood in his head, but not in his heart. They'd seen their entire world collapse one evening. Everything they'd known, everything that had been solid and real, destroyed.

Their reactions were varied. Some survivors had become farmers. They spent every possible moment on the surface, descending only to sleep. Thoughts of being trapped in rooms and hallways brought them to their knees. Others pretended it had never happened, that they'd moved to Firestone from Whitehawk during a Gathering, and that all was well.

Aria made knowledge her shield. Though she wouldn't say as much, all the trouble she had caused over the last few months was in the pursuit of answering a single question: why had Whitehawk's Engine failed? She'd broken into administrative rooms, searching for secret documents. Then she tried to join the clan to gain access to shardstones, but as soon as someone had strapped a training band to her wrist, she had ended up on the floor, crying silently while attempting to pull the band off.

Then she'd tried to work with the Singers, but they only recruited from the clan, and her fear of shardstones prevented her from making any progress there.

So, she'd pursued the problem on her own. Radyn wasn't clear exactly what she did with all her time, but her determination was evident. He couldn't condone her methods but found himself attracted to the fire that burned in her spirit.

At least, that was what he told himself. He also found her easy to talk with, quick to understand, intelligent, and beautiful. He'd never taken as much interest in women as his old roommates had, but Aria changed his mind. She interested him in a way no one had before. He sought out opportunities to see her, and they'd become friends. The relationship caused him no end of trouble, but he'd come to appreciate the chaos she brought to his otherwise orderly life.

Most days. Some days he wished she would obey the rules of Firestone, even if by accident.

"You'll need to give them back. Elora promised she'd keep you out of trouble if I could return them by tomorrow."

Aria's grin stretched from ear to ear. "So, you're saying that so long as I return them by tomorrow, there won't be any consequences?"

Radyn groaned. "That's not what she meant."

"But it is what she said."

Radyn buried his head in his hands. "One of these days, you're going to get me in a lot of trouble."

When he dropped his hands, she was beside him, a mischievous grin on her face. "I think you like it."

"Mostly, I just like you."

The words slipped off his tongue before he could stop them. Though they'd spent entire days together, he'd been careful not to say anything about his feelings. He didn't want to risk what they already had.

Her grin never faltered. She kissed him on the cheek. "I know."

She took a step back, leaving him confused. "If you want to be useful, there's something else happening tonight that I meant to attend, but I can't be in two places at once, and apparently my time with this band is limited. Care to go instead?"

Radyn was immediately suspicious. "Where and why?"

"I just want you to visit a tavern."

Radyn didn't believe for a moment that was all she wanted. "Why?"

"I heard a rumor there might be some people meeting there tonight. So go, relax, and use those senses you've been developing with Elora. If you hear anything interesting, let me know."

Her brief kiss instilled a boldness he didn't know he'd possessed. "It would be less suspicious if we went together."

Aria laughed. "Nice try. If we went together, a fight between Daggers could break out, and you'd not notice. Besides, I already have plans for the evening." She gestured at the shardstones. "So you should go in my stead."

He didn't have anywhere else to be tonight, and he always had a hard time saying no to her, so he bowed. "Fine."

She gave him the address, so Radyn left the workroom and started toward the tavern, curious what mystery Aria was throwing him in the middle of.

15

Radyn stared at the tavern Aria's address had led him to and cursed himself for his foolishness. Experience had already taught him that following Aria too closely would only get him in trouble, but it didn't seem to stop him from making the same mistake over and over. Offhand, he could think of three or four better uses of his time, from reading some of the histories Elora had assigned to him to training some of her techniques he hadn't yet mastered.

Somehow, they all became meaningless as soon as Aria requested that he do something for her.

He understood his reasons, but he didn't like the fact that she held him in such effortless thrall. It spoke poorly of his own discipline. If he was going to become the strongest Sword Firestone had ever seen, he couldn't afford to be so easily swayed.

The tavern was in a section of Firestone he rarely walked through. He wasn't a complete stranger, of course. Part of Elora's training demanded that he become exquisitely familiar with the city. Such study was an outgrowth of her belief that it was vitally important to be aware of one's surroundings at all times, and that meant knowing the city he lived in as well as he knew the tenets of the clan. When he'd been an initiate, she'd ordered him to spend an hour every night wandering parts of the city he didn't know.

So he'd been through here, though not for some time. Not because there was anything wrong with it but because his own haunts were closer to the academy and closer to the surface. All the taverns in Firestone served the same ale, so there wasn't any point in wandering far beyond the steel doors of the academy. This market was nearly a perfect mirror of the market he frequented, at least in terms of design. It was a large open space, two levels high, with several buildings within. Most of the shops offered the necessities - clothes, soap, and the like. A small teahouse sat near the edge of the market, an island of calm in the otherwise active space.

Unfortunately, his destination was the tavern that sat at the very heart of the market. From the outside, it didn't seem like anything special, but a steady flow of people went in and out the front door, far more than any other shop in the market. Far more than went in and out of the one closest to the academy, for that matter.

Radyn watched for a few minutes. Aria had said nothing about a specific time, and a glance through the windows revealed nothing out of the ordinary. He wandered around the building, noting the entrances, exits, and windows. After one slow circle around the building, he stopped and frowned. He walked around again, then nodded to himself.

The tavern had a back room, which wasn't immediately obvious from his glance through the front windows. It had to be a decent-sized space, but there were no windows to give him a sense of what was within.

When he felt there was nothing left for him to learn from wandering around the building, he went inside, found an unoccupied stool at the bar, and ordered an ale. He wore his civilian clothes, and after he left Aria's, he'd moved his band so it was around his ankle, covered nicely by both his socks and pants. He'd left his hilt back at the academy when he'd went searching for Aria, as he'd not assumed he'd have any need for it. No one had any reason to assume he was clan, so his arrival attracted no particular attention.

He nodded to his neighbors, but huddled close around his ale, inviting no conversation. He sipped at the drink and let his awareness spread through the boisterous room. His first impressions were reinforced. The tavern had nearly two dozen tables and booths, and almost all were filled with patrons enjoying various levels of inebriation. The harvest had been strong this year, even after accommodating for Firestone's increased population, and the taverns had been allotted more ale than usual, an accomplishment everyone was eager to celebrate. Most tables held two or three, although some booths were crowded with up to six customers. Radyn listened to one conversation after another.

"I'm going to propose!" one man exclaimed to his friends, his cheeks flushed with drink.

"We're thinking about asking administration for permission for a third child," whispered one woman to her confidant.

One father bemoaned, "My daughter has been a nightmare since she failed her clan trials."

And so on. They were interesting stories, and Radyn was tempted to follow the thread of a few, but none were the reason he was here. If Aria said something interesting was happening, she meant something very different. He sipped at his ale until it was gone, looked longingly at the front door, then sighed and ordered one more. If nothing had happened by the time he sipped a second one into oblivion, he would leave.

Halfway through his second, he noticed an unusual pattern. People began trickling into the tavern, one after the other. Unlike most customers, the new arrivals came alone. They walked around the bar into a small alcove Radyn had noticed but had paid little attention to. They slid aside a curtain, revealing a narrow, dark door. The first group that entered stationed two burly men outside the door, then went in. After, everyone who entered spoke briefly with the guards before being allowed entrance. Radyn connected with his shardstone and listened in.

A short woman was the next to meet the guard's challenge. The guard on the right of the door, who seemed in charge, asked, "Why are you here?"

The woman had little patience for the delay. "I'm here for the meeting, you giant buffoon."

The large man, understandably, was not perturbed. "We can't let anyone in who hasn't been invited."

She sighed. "Song of the Engine."

The guards let her pass.

Radyn listened to another exchange, which also ended in the same phrase. He stared at his rapidly shrinking ale. The wise decision would be to leave, return to his room in the academy, wake up early, and retrieve the training band from Aria before reporting to Elora. He considered for a moment, then tossed the last of his ale back and walked over to where the two guards stood. They looked him up and down but without malice.

"What do you want?" the guard on his left asked.

Radyn offered a small bow. "I'm here for the meeting."

"Have you been invited?" the guard on the right asked.

"Song of the Engine," Radyn replied as nonchalantly as possible.

The guard gestured for him to enter, and he did.

The back room of the tavern was larger than he'd imagined. Today, the tables had been pushed to the sides and all the chairs had been lined up to face the front. From the looks of it, the arrangements had been made hastily. Seven people were already here, and there were chairs for about a half-dozen more. Most of the chairs at the back had already been taken, so Radyn took one near the middle, hoping he would blend in with the crowd.

Others arrived after him, and soon the room was comfortably full, with only a few chairs remaining. A few of the crowd seemed to know each other and spoke in quiet whispers, but for the most part, people sat in expectant silence.

Radyn studied them, searching for clues that might tell him more about who he shared the room with. He looked at hands, clothes, and shoes, absorbing the details like he'd been trained. He didn't think there were many farmers or craftspeople here. Hands were too clean and too soft.

The door opened again, and Radyn's awareness perked up. While most arrivals hadn't resulted in much notice, everyone turned together, responding to some deep impulse few could name.

The woman who entered certainly caught Radyn's eye. She was taller than average and thin as a stick. Radyn would have called most people with her build weak, but her confidence and gait said otherwise. She radiated strength, drawing the eye and attention of every person in the room without so much as a word. She walked down the aisle and stood in front of the small gathering. For a long moment, she stood there, commanding their focus with an ease Nuela would have been jealous of. She made direct eye contact with several of the crowd, dipping her head in acknowledgment. When her gaze rested on him, he swore he saw a spark of recognition.

He bowed toward her and received a slight dip of her head in return.

Finally, she spoke. Though the room was nearly filled with people, she didn't raise her voice. Radyn heard every word clearly.

"It seems to me, as I look out on this gathering, that it would be easy to divide us based on our differences. We have scholars, leaders, and shopkeepers among us. At least one of us is an honored Singer, and one is a clan Dagger." She looked at Radyn as she spoke, and his blood went cold. There was no way she should have known. Yet she had, with only a glance. Or had she known who he was before?

His mind spun and he tried to disentangle his

awareness from his emotions. It was a lesson Elora drove into him repeatedly. The more crowded his mind became, the less aware he was. A single mention of Aria's name in a duel was enough to let Elora slip past his defenses without a problem, and this felt much the same.

The woman continued, and he forced his attention to her words. "But when I look upon this crowd, I don't see what divides us. I see what brings us together. Some in positions of power might call it needless worry at best or paranoia at worst. I call it discerning wisdom, the ability to see the truth, even as so many seek to distract us with lies. All of us are here today because of one simple truth, terrifying at its core."

She paused, and Radyn was certain not a single soul breathed. Many of those sitting next to him leaned forward with expectant looks, as though they guessed what she was about to say.

"The Engine is dying," she said.

Radyn blinked. In his darkest thoughts, he'd feared as much, but he'd never dared speak them out loud, as though saying anything would make the nightmare real. And there was no evidence. Hadn't Jelrik just claimed the Engine was fine? He leaned forward with the others, hanging onto the woman's every word.

"The evidence surrounds any with the eyes to see," the woman said, once again casting her gaze around the room. "From the Fall last year to the destruction of Whitehawk several months ago. The Blade tells us we have been under attack, but there have been no attacks. Speak to the survivors of Whitehawk. There was no raid and no warning. Their Engine died and they fell from the sky. Today, our Singers tell me that the Song of the

Engine has changed, but they aren't allowed to speak of it. Our leaders are in a panic, but they hide the truth from the very people who might save them."

Radyn sat still, stunned by the enormity of the accusations this woman was leveling. Did Nuela know about this meeting? Radyn glanced at the windows, wishing he could see outside them to see if Daggers had surrounded this meeting to end it prematurely.

Several people nodded along. If they were shocked by the accusations, they didn't show it. She paused, allowing her claims to fester like an open wound. Then she said, "Few of you are here today to be convinced. You've seen with your own eyes, and you've asked the questions no one else dares to ask. You're here because you don't know what to do against the terror of the truth, and I'm here to tell you that my allies and I are searching for a way to survive. I won't lie to you like our leaders. I don't have an answer yet, but there are two promising directions of study."

Radyn, like every person in that room, hung on to every word.

The woman held up a single finger. "The first is an idea most would dismiss as ridiculous. It is that we survive on the surface."

She held up her hand to stall any objections. "Although this is a tantalizing possibility, I understand it's a difficult solution to accept, and I won't try to convince you tonight. There are only two facts I would bring to your attention. The first is that our clan is strong. We have Swords, Daggers, and riders to spare, and there are those, more well-versed in clan matters, that believe we have the strength and the skill to hold land on the surface. Second, I would ask you this: why do you believe the Blade when she tells you the surface is so dangerous? If Nuela will lie to you about the Engine, what can we trust?"

Radyn found that line of questioning deeply unsatisfying. Nuela might be lying about the current situation, but claiming the surface was safe was foolish. The surface had been uninhabitable for centuries. Radyn had seen the nightmarish creatures surrounding the ruins of Whitehawk with his own eyes. Unfortunately, the woman's question seemed to connect with the others.

"The second line of study is the one that I've placed most of my hopes on," the woman said.

Again she paused, allowing the audience to come down from the agitation she'd stirred by mentioning the surface.

"It is possible that our Engine is sick, for lack of a better term, and that we can heal it," she said.

"How?" someone in the crowd asked.

"The details are beyond me, but it is a discussion that I'm having with the Singers. The best way I can explain it is this: our Singers are trained on how to maintain the Engine and keep it in tune. There is a small but growing group of senior Singers who believe that they are capable of more, of creating a new, healing song. I don't know how likely it is, as I'm not a Singer, but those among our movement who are believe it's possible."

There were several questions, which the woman answered calmly, but Radyn noticed many lacked substance. Competent as the woman was, the group didn't strike him as being mature. They were still finding their way, a truth the woman was more than willing to acknowledge.

Before long, she brought the meeting to a close. "Today, I ask only for your pledge. If you find my argument compelling, please join us."

Radyn wondered what would happen if he refused. Though the men at the door were larger than him, he didn't recognize them as clan, so if it came to a fight, he'd have the upper hand.

The back room grew louder as people stood from their chairs and shuffled forward to offer their pledges of loyalty. Radyn considered it. What did it matter what he pledged?

Elora's teachings were lodged too deeply in him, though. A lie, or a false promise, had a way of circling around and haunting a person. The woman hadn't issued any threats about not joining, and the worst case was a fight against the two outside, which didn't concern him.

While the others worked their way forward, eager to press their foreheads to her hand, Radyn walked to the door without looking back. He felt the woman's gaze on the back of his neck but ignored it.

He opened the door, stepped through, then closed it quickly behind him. The guards glanced at him but gave him no trouble as he left. He exited the tavern quickly and hurried through the market, quieter now because of the late hour. He kept looking behind him, but no one followed.

Once the market was safely behind him, he clambered up several ladders, eager to put several levels between him and the meeting. The more he thought about it, the more it concerned him. He needed to report to someone at the academy.

Radyn kept his head down and nearly bumped into several people as he hurried toward the safety of the clan. Elora would know what to do.

He didn't sense the presence behind him until it was too late. Either their footfalls had been completely silent, or he'd become so distracted he hadn't noticed. Before he could turn, he felt a cool hand against the back of his neck.

"Sorry," a soft voice said.

The sensation was unlike anything he'd experienced before. It felt like someone had pulled all the strength from his body, and he wanted nothing more than to take a long nap. His legs lost their strength, and he was asleep before his body hit the deck.

16

When Radyn woke up, his world was dark, and it took him a few moments to understand why. A blindfold had been tied tightly around his eyes. He was sitting upright, and a pair of manacles had been fastened around his wrists. A brief tug pulled the chain taut and told him they were connected to an anchor on the floor.

So, he was a prisoner of the clan.

He hadn't had the privilege of witnessing an interrogation firsthand, but they'd studied the practice enough in his lessons. It also made sense. Only a supremely skilled manirah could have executed that technique in the hallway against him. It was another skill he'd heard of, but had no firsthand experience of before tonight. A shardstone normally granted strength, but a sufficiently skilled healer also knew how to take strength away.

Knowing he was held by the clan stilled his pounding heart. They were all on the same side here. He would simply need to prove it to them. He calmed his breath and found his center. Either they hadn't searched him, or they'd completely missed the band around his ankle. He connected to the shardstone, not to cause trouble, but to sharpen his senses.

His sight was still useless, but he heard footsteps approaching through a closed door. A few moments later, the door opened and three people stepped in. Radyn sniffed the air. At least one visitor was a woman, her scent more floral than that of the others. But one scent was distinct enough for him to recognize, even with the blindfold.

They took chairs, but Radyn decided to lead the interrogation for them.

"Senior Sword Jyn, I'm glad to have you here," he said.

The woman cursed under her breath, but Jyn laughed. "If any of you think Elora's training isn't a unique weapon in our armory, I'll present to you her star apprentice, junior Dagger Radyn." The volume of Jyn's voice changed, and Radyn realized Jyn was speaking to him. "Radyn, tell us about your surroundings."

Radyn suppressed a smile. It was quite the bold move, expecting him to impress them when he'd only seen Radyn's skills in action once. Jyn's reputation for decisive moves extended beyond just his skill with a maniblade, then.

Radyn thought quickly. It was said Jyn rarely did anything with a single purpose. If he was here, it meant he hoped Radyn could help him to some mysterious end. Who would Jyn have brought along, given the circumstances?

Radyn's first guess was Jyn's own advisors, but Radyn dismissed the idea quickly. Given what he'd just heard at the meeting, Aria had shoved him headfirst into something big, which meant Jyn would have more important people with him, people whose opinions would shape the course of the clan.

Radyn stabbed into the dark, reasonably certain he was correct. "Senior Sword Jyn, you're here today with Senior Swords Anetta and Malvin. I'm currently being held in one of the interrogation cells at the academy."

Anetta swore again, but Jyn's laughter drowned her out. Once the scene had settled down, Jyn said, "Take the blindfold off. There's obviously no point in it."

Senior Sword Malvin did so, and Radyn blinked as the light hit his eyes for the first time in several minutes. Once his vision cleared, he bowed toward the three senior Swords as far as his bonds allowed. Of the three, only Jyn seemed pleased to be there. But of the three, Jyn was also the one with the most power in the clan, so Radyn took heart. He observed, as Elora had taught him.

Most would look at Malvin and dismiss him out of hand. He was of average size and strength, and age had stolen most of the hair from the top of his head. Anyone who thought so little of him, though, would pay the price. His eyes were dark and calm, and Elora spoke highly of him. She'd modeled much of her training after lessons he'd given her years before, though she'd pushed beyond him in skill.

Anetta paced the room with quick strides, her grey hair almost white under the bright lanterns in the interrogation room. Everything about her spoke of impatience and speed, but she accomplished more in a day than most did in a week.

Together, they were three of Nuela's most trusted

advisors, and they rarely had occasion to be by each other's side unless the Blade was near.

Anetta questioned him first. "What were you doing at that meeting tonight?"

Jyn held up a hand. He met Radyn's gaze. "I take it you understand the importance of this meeting?"

"I do, sir."

"We may lack the extent of the abilities Elora has trained you with, but we have both time and resources on our side, and everything you say will be judged carefully. Please answer our questions completely and truthfully. If you hesitate out of fear of punishment, I can assure you that any inconvenient truths will be punished less harshly than the smallest lie. Am I clear?"

"Very much so, sir."

"Good. Please answer senior Sword Anetta's question."

Radyn had been tempted to protect Aria, but there was little point. Elora would guess why Radyn had gone to the meeting and shared the information willingly, so protecting her would only bring more trouble to them both. So he told the senior Swords about Aria's quest to discover what had caused Whitehawk's Engine to fail and about her request to attend the meeting tonight. He left out any mention of the training band Aria had stolen, hoping it was beyond the scope of their inquiry.

Malvin wasn't satisfied. "Why did she ask you to go instead of going herself?"

"Partly because she was busy with a project, sir, but partly because she's aware of the abilities I've developed thanks to my training. I believe she assumed my presence would reveal more than hers would."

They allowed him to continue his story, though he was frequently interrupted by Malvin and Anette, who had questions about who was in attendance and what, exactly, had been implied by the speaker. Jyn sat behind the other two, watching the exchanges without a word.

Eventually, Radyn reached the end of the story, when he'd been captured and brought here. He took a deep breath and sealed his lips.

Jyn spoke for the first time in a while. "What do you think?"

Radyn knew the question wasn't directed at him.

Anette glanced at Radyn, gave a small shrug, then said, "Sure. Do what you will."

Then, without another word, she stood up and left.

Malvin thought for longer, the silence stretching in the room until it was almost uncomfortable. Finally, he said, "He's only a junior Dagger, but he shows considerable promise. Elora is also overly fond of him. His loss might cause problems for your other plans."

Radyn tensed at the phrase "his loss" but said nothing.

"That would be for me to worry about," Jyn said. "I want to know if you think it is worth the risk and if you'll support me when we speak to Nuela."

Malvin thought again, but it wasn't for nearly as long as before. "Yes, to both."

He also stood to leave. Radyn bowed, but Malvin exited the room without returning it. Radyn turned to Jyn. He'd never been in a room alone with the senior Sword before, but he couldn't deny the excitement of the moment.

He was face to face with Jyn, the strongest Sword in

the clan. The one man Radyn would have to surpass if he wanted the title for himself. Just being in his presence was a gift, a chance to observe the habits and manners of the strongest warrior alive.

Jyn gestured at Radyn's hands. "There's no need for those."

Radyn needed a moment to understand, then his eyes went wide. Jyn watched him, and Radyn knew even this was a test. He couldn't guess the correct answer, so he trusted his instinct. He was already connected to the shardstone around his ankle, so he formed a dagger in his hand and sliced through the manacles and chains with a single cut. They fell to the floor with a clang and he let the dagger vanish.

"Impressive. Even among those capable of the old ways, I've never seen anyone form a dagger with such ease."

Radyn wished he could claim credit, but it wasn't his to claim. "Elora has been quite diligent with my training. She deserves thanks for anything I can do."

Jyn nodded. "I've always prided myself on judging people, and I like you. A bit too clever for your own good, perhaps, but that's not the worst fault in a person by far."

Radyn wasn't sure what to say to that, so he said, "Thank you, sir."

"I'd like to recruit you for a task."

"Whatever you want."

"Normally, I'd be happy to simply issue the order, but the nature of this task requires more than blind obedience. What would you say if I told you the clan has been lying to the people of Firestone for years, not just about Whitehawk, but about much more?"

"I'd say that you're lying."

Jyn grunted and shook his head. He scratched at the back of his neck, then said. "Radyn, we have been lying."

Radyn felt like the deck had disappeared from beneath his feet, and he was suddenly falling, as if someone had pushed him off the edge of the city and he was plummeting to the surface. Everything in Jyn's demeanor told Radyn the senior Sword spoke the truth. Given the nature of their meeting, only one explanation made sense.

"There *is* something wrong with the Engine," Radyn said. Why would Jelrik lie? Or did he not know?

Jyn nodded. "As far as we can tell, it isn't dying, but that's not saying as much as I wish it did. Only a few of the senior Singers have noticed, as the changes have been subtle, but the Engine's song isn't the same as it has been in the past. The Master of the Song, Haden, and Nuela have tried to keep the news quiet, but it's a secret that's hard to keep."

"What does that mean for Firestone?"

Jyn shrugged. "Truthfully? Nobody has any idea. The Singers are trained to maintain the Engine, but too much of the knowledge of the Makers was lost in the exodus from the surface. It's possible, though not likely, that the Makers designed the song to change. But given what happened to Whitehawk, the few of us who know the truth are, of course, worried that the Engine might fail."

Jyn's revelations felt like a wet, heavy blanket had been thrown over Radyn. The interrogation room shrank, and he found it hard to breathe.

Elora's practices provided him some slight relief. She'd trained him to step outside himself, to observe like he was a stranger in his own body. Radyn did so now, imagining he was watching the scene from above. He saw his own face, eyes wide with shock. Not just because the Engine was dying but because the clan had betrayed him.

Betrayed them all.

What was the point of becoming the strongest if the clan you served didn't trust its own strength?

"Why lie?" he asked.

Jyn's face turned hard. "You're not a child. You understand why."

Anger anchored Radyn back in his body and centered him against the existential terror of the Engine's failure. "The clan's code demands honesty."

"It also demands we protect the city. You're a rational person, and Elora has trained you to separate yourself from your emotions. But you can guess the reactions of people if we told them the Engine was sick. And what else can we do? We certainly can't land on the surface, despite this woman's mad ideas. You can judge, if you like, but what choice would you make if our positions were reversed?"

Radyn's silence was answer enough. It felt like Jyn had ripped a veil from his eyes. Radyn clenched his fist, not because he was upset with Jyn, but because he was angry at himself. Elora taught him to *see*, but even after all these years, he was still blinded by his beliefs. He was supposed to be better than this.

"What would you have of me?" he asked.

"First, I would know what you expect of yourself. Young as you are, you've already developed a reputation as someone who works hard. You're not disliked by your fellow Daggers, exactly, but you aren't popular among them either. Elora loves you like you were her child, and there's no doubt you've taken to her techniques. But I know little about you. What do you want? Why did you join the clan?"

Radyn grinned. He wasn't sure where this boldness came from, but he wasn't scared of offending Jyn. "I want to take your place as the strongest Sword."

Jyn grunted at that. "I see now why Elora likes you. She's never gotten over the fact I can bear more shardstones than her, even though she's the only Sword in Firestone who has a chance of beating me in a duel."

Jyn's offhand comment made Radyn grateful for all the choices he'd made over the past two years. Elora was the master he needed, and surpassing Jyn was a worthy goal.

"To answer your question, I would have you join those who plot against the clan," Jyn said.

Radyn shook his head. "They're despicable."

"No, they're not. They're driven by a deep belief that what they do is right. They've brushed up against parts of the truth, and it's led them to believe the clan is their enemy. It's unfortunate, because they've turned some of the best minds in the city against us. If you join them, you can keep us informed so we can all work together to save the city."

"Why me? As you've just said, I'm only a junior Dagger."

The corner of Jyn's mouth turned up in a smile. "*Because* you're only a junior Dagger. They'll never believe I met with you, even if you tell them. Mostly, though, it's because of Elora's training. If they'd let her in, I'd send her instead, but her loyalty to me is too well known, which makes you the best candidate I have left. You don't have her experience, but you're nearly as observant as she is. This isn't about trying to destroy the group. Hopefully, you'll never have to so much as swing a fist. This is about talking, about noticing, and about deducing. From everything I've heard, and from what I've witnessed firsthand, that means you."

Radyn opened his mouth to accept, but Jyn held up a hand to stop him.

"Before you say 'yes,' you need to understand. You can tell Elora, because she'll figure it out anyway, and I trust her, but you can't tell Aria or anyone else. You can't even tell anyone else in the clan. If you do this, you do it alone, and you report only to me. Will you do it?"

There wasn't much of a choice. Not for Radyn. "Of course."

Jyn stood and offered a bow, honoring Radyn's decision. "One last thing, and please, bring all your skills to bear for a moment."

Radyn was confused by the request, but he obeyed. He focused his shardstone-enhanced senses on Jyn.

Jyn looked him in the eye and said, "Whatever I have done, and whatever I will do, will always be for the benefit of Firestone and for the clan. My life means nothing, but my service means everything."

The words moved Radyn, but the delivery moved him even more. He understood why Jyn had asked for his full attention, because there was no doubting what he'd just witnessed.

The man who dreamed of becoming the Blade of the clan had just bared his soul to a junior Dagger, and in so doing, had earned Radyn's undying loyalty.

17

The healer's name was Maisie, and her stare was cold enough to freeze a dragon's breath. She looked between Radyn and Elora, as though deciding which to attack first. Her face was wrinkled and her hair was gray, but of the two women in the room, Radyn was definitely more frightened of the healer than his master.

"Are you mad, girl?" Maisie asked.

If not for the edge in her voice, Radyn would have smiled. If anyone else had called his master "girl," she would have had her maniblade out in a moment. But the two of them clearly had history, so he kept his lips sealed and his gaze down.

Before Elora could squeeze in a reply, Maisie unleashed another tirade.

"Ever since you were little, you've had strange ideas. Thought the clan would knock most of them out of you, but it seems I was wrong."

Elora weathered the berating with equanimity. "I could order you to do it."

"If you tried, I'd give you a beating that would make you think you were a misbehaving child."

Radyn didn't understand how Elora kept her composure in front of such disrespect. Instead of raising her voice or arguing, Elora just smiled and asked, "So, are you going to do it or not? You're the only one I trust."

Maisie waved an arm in the air like she was shooing a bug away. "No need for flattery, girl. Of course I'll do it. Just had to make sure you understood how poor an idea it is."

The old healer turned her eyes toward Radyn then, and there was an unsatisfied hunger in her look.

When Elora had first made the suggestion, she'd said the only healer in Firestone who would dare such a thing was Maisie, and Radyn was beginning to see why. She didn't heal because the act brought her joy. She healed people because it allowed her to study bodies in more detail. Illnesses taught her as much as health, and Radyn had just volunteered to become her next subject.

"Well, no time to waste. Why don't you lie down on the table and we'll get to work," Maisie said.

Radyn obeyed, rolling onto the table and holding out his arm. Maisie took out her healing kit, selecting a small blade that looked so sharp it could shave the hairs off a spider's leg. She dipped the blade in alcohol and stared at his arm. "Where do you want it?"

"Somewhere it won't be seen and where it won't get in the way."

"How small is it?"

Elora took a handkerchief out of a pocket and unwrapped it. A soft blue glow filled the room. Maisie arched an eyebrow. "Smaller than I expected."

"These aren't exactly easy to come by, and he doesn't need that much yet."

Maisie grunted. "Planning on doing this again, if this one works?"

Elora nodded.

Maisie didn't seem displeased by the answer. She turned her full attention to Radyn. "You want something to drink?"

"No, ma'am."

"Brave and stupid. How I miss my youth."

With that, Maisie bent to the task. She cut open his arm, the incision no bigger than it needed to be. Radyn gritted his teeth, but the pain wasn't as terrible as he'd expected. Maisie slipped the shard into his right arm, then closed her eyes. Radyn felt the strength of the Engine passing between them, and his arm grew suddenly warm. As he watched, the incision closed around the shardstone, leaving nothing more than the faintest hint of a scar.

Maisie wiped away the blood and *tsk*ed. She shook her head. "Next time, there won't be any evidence at all. The power flowed differently with the shardstone so close."

She stood. "Anything else?"

"Don't tell anyone," Elora said.

Maisie snorted. "Obviously. Well, Elora, always a pleasure when you're involved. Take care and say hello to Jelrik for me."

"I will. You could come over sometime."

Maisie put her hands against her back and stretched. "Jelrik is fine to look at, dear, but he's a bit boring for my tastes."

With that, she was out the door, leaving Radyn and Elora alone. After all the discussion that had gone into this moment, Radyn felt a little let down by the event itself. Maisie had turned out to be easy to convince, and the experiment only took a few minutes. Radyn flexed his arm.

"How does it feel?"

"I can barely tell that it's there. It's different than the bands, but not much."

"That's good. Ready to connect?"

"Not really."

"I don't care. Connect with it now."

Radyn obeyed, opening himself up to the shardstone. The strength of the Engine flowed through his limbs.

Elora watched with a close eye. "How does it feel now?"

"Stronger than I would have guessed. Closer to wearing two shardstones on my band than one."

They'd wondered if that would happen. Shardstones were usually worn pressed against the skin, although they'd found examples in historical texts of Daggers and Swords having the shards embedded into flesh. The accounts claimed the benefit was greater than mere contact, and Elora had guessed Radyn would draw more strength from the Engine. Even she seemed surprised by how much, though.

"I suppose that's good, then. Makes me feel a little better about you agreeing to Jyn's madness."

They'd argued about it when Radyn had first told Elora. She'd threatened to march straight to the senior Sword's home and beat him half to death. Her reaction had surprised Radyn. She had little choice but to agree, though, but it had been her idea to embed a shardstone within him.

"You've been training to be in contact with shards for longer than most. You'll never get relief, but you'll also never be without a shardstone. If the people you're seeking to find are careful, they'll search you before every meeting. This way, you won't have to worry."

Radyn had agreed, and she'd been the one to find Maisie. Radyn didn't know where she'd found a shardstone and decided it was better not to ask.

He formed a large dagger and admired his work.

"You're right. A small shardstone like that would never create a blade so long," Elora said. "You're making me think I should get one."

Radyn let the blade vanish, then disconnected. The feeling wasn't like it was with a band. There, the disconnection was complete, but now some fragment of the shardstone's power lingered in his limbs. He'd prepared his body for something like this over the last few months, but it still seemed weird to have the shard's power always trickling through him.

"Maybe see how I take to this before you jump to talk to Maisie again," he said.

Elora nodded. "I suppose that's wise."

For a month, he waited. Twice more Maisie came to him with her sharp blades and her healing touch, and now he constantly felt his body resonating with the Engine's power. He welcomed the strength, but the cult that Jyn feared gave him no opportunity to channel that strength to a constructive end. After the meeting, no one contacted him, and he began to assume he'd simply been forgotten.

He stewed in his helplessness. It felt like history was being made all around him, but he had no part to play. Every week Radyn wrote a report for his commanding Sword, including a small, coded section that made its way to Jyn's study, Unfortunately, every week he could do nothing but say that he hadn't yet been contacted. He hated disappointing Jyn, but he couldn't think of a way to reconnect with the group. Aria didn't hear any more rumors, and although Radyn visited the tavern several more times, he saw no sign of another meeting.

To combat the feeling of helplessness, he threw himself into training. It took time to get used to the new shardstones, not just in combat, but in daily tasks, too. He had to be careful not to move too fast or squeeze too hard. Even when he was "disconnected," the strength still ran through his limbs.

His duels with Elora became more even, to the point where he even started winning a few. Elora welcomed the losses with a grin, then fought harder to beat him.

And in the evenings, there was always his time with Aria. Whenever he wasn't on duty he sought her out, usually finding her in the abandoned workroom. During the day, she apprenticed for a craftsman who traded his wares a level below the academy, but as soon as prime shift was over, she returned to her true passion.

Radyn knocked on the door to her workroom, following this week's code, and waited for her to unbolt the door. When she let him in, he had to pick his way through piles of junk to find a place to sit. "What is all of this?"

"I'm trying to build tools that will help me study the shardstones without damaging them. I have a whole set of experiments I'm hoping to run the next time you let me borrow your band."

Radyn groaned. He'd let her borrow his band a few weeks before, as he didn't need it anymore, but it seemed that wasn't enough for her. "If either the clan or the Singers find out what you're doing, I'm not sure what they'll do."

"Then I'll just have to make sure I don't get caught."

Radyn helped her work for a while, which mostly meant he held things while she hammered, screwed, and glued them together. They worked mostly in silence, which Radyn didn't mind. He enjoyed seeing the change that would come over Aria as she fell into a trance-like focus. The rest of the world fell away. She would mutter to herself and sometimes sing songs he didn't recognize.

It was a joy to watch. There was something about watching someone else lose themselves in an activity that inspired him to train harder.

Sometime later, long after the kitchens had stopped serving supper, she looked up from her work and stretched. "Thanks for the help. Want to join me on the surface?"

"It's past dark."

"The best time. It won't be crowded."

Radyn took note of Aria's pale skin. "You should try going up during the day."

"I know, but I get distracted."

Radyn agreed, and they started the long climb to the surface. The Dagger on duty gave them a questioning look but let them pass without too much question. Once they were out of hearing, Aria asked, "I take it you didn't hear from them today?"

Radyn shook his head. Jyn had told him not to share the nature of his task with Aria, but she'd pulled it out of him the next day. He couldn't lie to her, and she wouldn't settle for him withholding information.

"Any luck finding the woman leading the meeting?"

That had been another frustrating part of the last few weeks. When he wasn't training, he'd asked his commander for patrol duty, which gave him the chance to wander far and wide around Firestone. He'd caught sight of a few of the members of the meeting, and he'd passed on their information to Jyn, but he'd yet to see a glimpse of the woman.

At one point, he'd even enlisted the Shields, giving them a detailed description, but nothing had come of it. In his more frustrating moods, he wondered if he'd met with a charismatic ghost. He'd spent his morning patrol today looking for her but with no success.

"I'm not sure what to do. I've tracked down every lead I can think of, but it feels like I'm stuck until someone else acts first."

"You've identified some of the people at the meeting. Are there any connections between them that might lead you to the woman?"

Radyn had also thought that, but he couldn't find the thread that linked the people at the meeting together. As the woman had said, they were a diverse group of people. "How did you find out about it?"

"My master was invited. He didn't tell me about it, but I saw the open invitation on his desk."

"Does he worry about the Engine?"

"He's from Whitehawk. Of course he worries about the Engine, but he didn't go to the meeting."

"I still can't figure out what they hoped to accomplish. I'm beginning to regret I didn't pledge my loyalty back then. At least then I'd be involved."

She led him into a small grove of woods. "You did what you thought was best. Just like you did when you risked your life to put those shardstones in your body. Just like what you did when you chose to keep Elora as your master. It's good to learn from the past, but don't doubt yourself."

Aria leaned back against a tree and pulled him close. "Besides, it's not a very attractive trait. Just keep fighting. You'll find a way."

As they often did, her words encouraged him. He leaned toward her and, for a while, forgot his worries.

18

Radyn never gave up, but it wasn't his own efforts that brought him closer to the conspiracy. One morning, he was on patrol when he received orders from his commanding Sword to report to the Nest immediately. The orders had come from another junior Dagger, who knew nothing more about the orders than what they said. It was unusual to be pulled from duty, but orders were orders, so he let the junior Dagger finish his patrol while he found the nearest ladder that would lead him toward the surface.

Up top, a bright blue sky greeted Radyn. Firestone had been slowly moving south as winter encroached upon the northern hemisphere, ensuring that the surface continued to receive enough sunlight to support the crops. They'd passed through a turbulent storm system a few days ago, which had required the Singers to raise Firestone higher than it normally flew. Now they were back at a normal altitude, floating about a thousand feet above the surface. A few puddles remained, but most evidence of the storm had already disappeared.

He reported to the officer at the Nest's gate, who checked his name against the day's allowed list, then let him in with directions to visit with Macken. Radyn bowed and walked toward the command building. It had been a few weeks since he and Tanwen had flown, and their last task had been a brief hunting trip to help top off Firestone's game reserves.

With any luck, he'd be in the air again today, but he couldn't guess at what was so important he would be pulled from regular duty.

It was a quiet day within the Nest. Several of the dragons were gone, and most of the rest were napping in the sun. Radyn watched a pair of dragons lounge for a minute, jealous of the ease of their day. He knocked on the door of the command building and stepped inside.

Senior Sword Macken was a giant of a man, nearly as large and intimidating as some of the dragons he treated more tenderly than his own children. Rumor among the initiates was that he was some sort of offspring between dragon and woman, and there'd been times Radyn almost believed it. The man's shouts could strip armor from a warrior, and Radyn had little difficulty imagining his enormous hands ripping prey apart. If a manirah treated dragons well, they had a friend for life in Macken. But if anyone was foolish enough to harm a dragon, well, then an angry dragon was the least of their worries.

Macken fixed Radyn with a stare as soon as he entered. "Junior Dagger. Thank you for coming on such short notice. You've been requested for a mission."

"Sir?"

"Someone wants a ride to the surface, and somehow, they've pulled enough strings to get the council to approve it. You're taking her down, escorting her while you're there, and returning as quickly as you can. Do you understand?"

Radyn followed every word of the Sword's commands, but they made no sense. "No, sir?"

"Good. Then it's not just me."

Macken looked like the Blade had just ordered him to send the dragons on a suicidal charge. "I don't know what's happening, but I guarantee there will be hell to pay. Tanwen is currently well-rested, and I imagine he'll be eager to see you, but I don't want any stupid stunts from the two of you. Not today."

Radyn held up a hand before Macken could ramble on for longer. "Sir? I've never been to the surface. Unless you count Whitehawk."

"I don't, and I'm well aware you've never been. I made my concerns clear both to my superiors and the lady, but I might as well have been speaking to a wall. Whatever's happening, some people are bound and determined to make this happen."

Macken leaned in close, and Radyn thought he smelled ale on the man's breath. "So, I'm going to make myself as clear as possible to you, because Elora tells me you're not as dense as I think you are. Bring the woman down, let her see whatever it is she needs to see, then get her right back. Don't linger for a second more than you need to. We're not that far from the territory of the Makers, and the land is practically crawling with predators, at least according to our most recent reports.

Not a second longer than needed! Am I making myself clear?"

Radyn gulped and nodded.

"Good. Now get out of here before I change my mind and risk the wrath of every important person in Firestone."

Radyn left the office, more confused than he'd been before he'd received his orders. He found Tanwen in his nest, but he wasn't alone. A woman stood there.

The speaker from the meeting, whom he'd been hunting since that day.

He failed at hiding his surprise, which elicited a hint of a smile from her. "Radyn, it's been too long."

"What do you want?"

She played coy. "Didn't Sword Macken tell you? I'm surprised. I'd like to travel down to the surface."

Radyn looked around and stretched his senses for anyone nearby, but as near as he could tell, they were alone.

"Expecting a trap?" she asked.

He imagined her finding a way to kill him down below, then leaving his body for the predators to devour. "I can't think of another reason why you'd request me, specifically, to take you down to the surface. Nor can I imagine how you wrangled the permission to make this happen."

"It's the benefits of having so many friends in high places. But you can rest assured, all I want is to show you something."

Radyn weighed his choices. He had a direct order from the Swords, as well as an assignment from Jyn. Traveling to the surface with this woman was about as safe as stepping into a hungry dragon's open mouth, but it was what the clan demanded of him. More than that, though, it was what Firestone's safety required. What good was all his effort if he shied away from conflict?

"I hope it's interesting," he said.

"I think you'll find it very much so."

When he'd first met her, she'd manipulated the attention of the crowd with ease, but her draw was no less with an audience of one.

"What's your name?" he asked.

"You can call me Melanie," she said.

"Your real name?"

She shrugged. "I'm sure you'll figure it out. Everyone says you're such a clever young man."

Radyn hated that he was pleased by her flattery. He made himself sound as stern as possible. "Normally, passengers wait closer to the edge. There's a loading area where you should wait."

She tucked a loose strand of hair behind her ear and grinned. "No. I want to watch you work."

Radyn knew it was a pointless fight he wouldn't win, so he focused on the task at hand. He pushed the mysterious woman from his thoughts as he approached Tanwen. "A distracted rider is a dead rider" was the common refrain among veteran riders. Radyn first connected with the shardstone in his band. Dragons refused to submit to anyone without a shardstone, but were surprisingly cooperative otherwise.

Radyn bowed, and Tanwen dipped his head in response. Radyn took the gesture as permission and climbed on top of the dragon's muscular neck. Riding had lost some of the sharp edge he'd first experienced when he dropped toward Whitehawk, but his appreciation for dragons and for flight had only grown. Feeling their incredible power underneath him always humbled him.

Once he was secure, he motioned for Melanie to climb on. Normally, he would have offered instructions, but he decided not to today. As he'd suspected, she climbed up with the grace of a frequent rider. She knew exactly where to place her hands and feet so precisely that it wouldn't have surprised him to learn she'd ridden Tanwen before.

Then she was behind him, her arms wrapped tightly around his waist, and Tanwen was moving forward.

Riding a dragon was one part focus, one part will, and one part surrender. Radyn focused his will and asked Tanwen to walk toward the edge of the city. The dragon obeyed. Usually, Radyn would have checked on a passenger, but he figured he would test Melanie's preparedness. He told Tanwen to jump, and Radyn, dragon, and passenger plummeted off the edge of the city.

Melanie didn't so much as gasp. She didn't tighten her grip even as the wind pulled her hair straight back.

Tanwen leveled off, and Radyn asked Melanie about their destination.

"Head northwest," was all she said.

He followed her directions, impressed by her grasp of the land. Firestone had detailed maps of the surface, used by the Singers to guide the city toward its various destinations, but few outside Singers and riders ever set eyes on them. It soon became clear, though, that Melanie knew both exactly where she was and where she wanted to go.

Their destination was something between a mound and a hill, though it seemed too symmetrical to be natural. Radyn had Tanwen swoop around the mound twice, keeping his eyes open for danger, though he wasn't sure exactly what he should be looking for. He tried to dig up lessons from his training, but against the endless backdrop of grass, his attention waned.

He didn't see anything immediately dangerous, though, so he asked Tanwen to land on top of the mound. The dragon seemed reluctant, but eventually, it spread its wings and settled to a gentle stop where Radyn had requested. He and Melanie climbed down, and then Tanwen swept his wings and took off to search for a meal.

Radyn considered Macken's warning and almost urged Tanwen to be cautious, but he didn't. For Tanwen, even the predators that might hunt Radyn and Melanie were prey, and the dragon was certainly more comfortable around the surface than Radyn was.

Radyn looked around. He'd always thought the surface of Firestone impressive, but he realized now just how small it was. He was less than an ant here, a speck of dust on an infinite land. The open sky had always comforted him, but something about seeing it from the surface made it seem so much bigger.

"It's your first time, isn't it?" Melanie asked.

She spoke as though she already knew the answer. He glanced at her and saw that the little hint of a smile had returned, as if she was laughing at him.

"You can always tell when it's someone's first time," she explained.

Radyn didn't have a suitable response. The vastness

of the land overwhelmed thought, leaving him in a lasting state of awe-inspired silence.

Eventually, reason returned. Impressive as the sight was, he couldn't guess why Melanie had brought him to this place. "Why did you want to come here?"

She answered his question with another question. "Tell me, Radyn, how much do you trust the Singers and the clan?"

Radyn knew he wasn't much of a liar, so he told the truth. "I owe an enormous debt to the clan. My father was killed in Whitehawk's raid several years back, and the city and clan cared for me after. Since then, Elora has taught me more about the world, and more about myself, than I ever thought I would learn."

She listened with rapidly fading patience. "I didn't ask how much you owed the clan. I asked you how much you trusted them."

It was a troublesome question, and Radyn didn't have to fake his discomfort. "I'm not sure. They haven't always been honest, even among their own ranks. I would say that I still trust them, but that trust is more conditional than it once was."

"What if I told you they were lying about more than Whitehawk? What if I told you they were lying about *everything*?"

Radyn crossed his arms, Jyn's words from the interrogation room echoing loudly in his memories. Though it felt petulant, he gave the same answer he had then. "I wouldn't believe you."

"And that, my new friend, is why we're here. Words alone will never sway you, so I've brought you here."

Radyn looked around. "I'm unconvinced."

Melanie's smile was wide. "Are you connected to your shardstone?"

Radyn frowned. Normally, the answer would be yes, especially with the shardstones now scattered throughout his body. But a rider always disconnected from their shard after dismounting from a dragon, and he'd done the same. Since then, he'd been distracted by the sights.

He reconnected, and his eyes went wide.

He heard a song, unfamiliar to his ears, but recognizable all the same. His eyes traveled down to the mound they were standing on. The song was faint, but it didn't seem that it was due to distance. It was simply weak, a sputtering candle near the end of its wick.

Melanie spread her arms out to encompass the mound. "Whitehawk's Engine isn't the first that died," she said, "and there's one right below us."

19

Radyn squatted and pressed his palm to the earth. His hands were no strangers to digging in dirt, but there was something about this soil that seemed remarkable. He wasn't sure if he was sensing something real or if his romantic notions of the surface were simply coloring his perceptions.

The soil didn't consume more than a fraction of his attention, though. What he felt more clearly than soil was the song of an Engine buried under countless tons of grass and clay. He looked up at Melanie, all feelings of doubt and skepticism wiped away by the wonder and impossibility of what he sensed. "What happened here?"

"I could tell you, or I could show you."

"Show me."

They descended the mound together. Melanie walked with the sure steps of someone who had explored this area before. She led him to a small depression near the bottom of the mound that Radyn had seen from the air but hadn't thought much of. Now that they were closer, he saw that the depression was some sort of entrance that had been covered with wooden planks and brush.

Melanie started to clear the brush away, and without being asked, Radyn lent his strength to the effort. Between the two of them, it took only a minute. They stacked the planks neatly to the side, and Radyn stared into the darkness. Someone had dug a cave, but the marks of shovels and picks made it clear that this was entirely man-made.

He turned to Melanie. "How did you find this place?"

"It wasn't me, but a Singer from long ago who heard a second song where there shouldn't have been one. I believe, though I'm not certain, that this Engine's song was stronger then."

Radyn shook his head, wondering at the implications. Melanie led him in, and within a dozen paces, she found a lantern and pulled it off of its hook. She held it up toward him. "Will you do the honors?" Radyn reached out and touched the lantern, understanding instinctively what she asked.

It wasn't anything like the lamps around Firestone. He channeled a bit of the Engine's strength into the lantern and it lit, illuminating the cavern for a dozen paces in both directions.

Melanie bowed her head in thanks and led the way deeper into the cave. It didn't take long for them to reach a metal hatch that reminded Radyn eerily of the hatches used to secure the important parts of Firestone. Melanie gestured for him to open the door, so he did. He expected the latches to be stiff and unyielding, but the wheel turned smoothly, and the latch disengaged with a nearly silent *click*. He pulled the door open without a problem, revealing darkness within.

When he hesitated to enter, Melanie stepped in front of him. He shook his head and followed. Before they'd gone even a hundred feet into the rooms, Radyn had noted the obvious. "These hallways look exactly like Firestone's."

Radyn was convinced that they didn't just appear to be the same, but that they were the same. This dim hallway brought back memories of his rescue in Whitehawk, and how strange it had felt to be walking the twisted hallways of the fallen city that were so eerily similar. It was the same here, and he had to remind himself that he was on the surface, buried underground.

"When the Makers built the great cities, they were mostly built to the same design. But this tells us they used the design on the surface, too," Melanie said.

As had always been the case, since the moment they'd left Firestone, Melanie seemed to know exactly where she was going. Before long, Radyn did, too. The twists and turns became familiar, and although the doors and warnings didn't exist here, he would have known they neared the Engine, even without the weak song growing stronger in his head.

There wasn't even a door to the Engine room. The hallway led straight there without interruption. This Engine didn't glow with the familiar pale blue light, but there was no mistaking the enormous stone. The tubes and wires that connected it were the same as in Firestone, though here they'd been pulled taut as the stone fell.

"Do you know what happened here?" Radyn asked.

"We don't. A proper excavation and examination

would require not just all of Firestone's effort, but likely a friendly city's, too. Needless to say, such cooperation isn't coming soon."

Radyn shook his head. From where he was standing, nothing seemed more important than seeking the answers to the questions these ruins raised. If they understood their past better, if they understood the Makers better, perhaps they could once again live on the surface without fear.

It was the silent dream they all clung to. The one Melanie had spoken out loud during the meeting.

He understood the sentiment was unpopular, at least among those who led the cities. The refrain had been the same for as long as he had been alive. Not only was survival enough, but survival was something they should be grateful for.

This changed his mind. They'd passed no signs of violence on the way in. No predators roamed the sealed hallways. There were no corpses, no blood-spattered rooms like there had been in Whitehawk. This city, or this shelter, hadn't been overrun. It had been abandoned, which meant people had lived here, at least for a time, successfully.

Humans had lived on the surface.

It changed everything, and Radyn's knees felt weak as he contemplated the possibilities.

Melanie interrupted his wondering when she gestured toward the broken Engine. "Do you want to touch it?"

Radyn started. Though he stood right next to the nearly inert Engine, its discordant song was still powerful. Back in Firestone, initiates feared simply approaching the

Engine. Touching it seemed the height of hubris and foolishness, and he remembered Jelrik warning him about encountering the song of the Engine alone.

But standing before this was nothing like standing before the active Engine of Firestone. He wasn't even sure if there would be a reaction.

"Is it safe?"

"No one has died yet."

It was hardly the reassurance he craved, but it was enough.

Radyn stretched out his awareness, and he listened to the song of the ancient Engine and noticed how, when it was at its strongest, it harmonized with the song of his own shardstone. He reached out and placed his hand against the stone.

The result was instantaneous. As soon as his fingertips pressed against the smooth surface, it flared to life, filling the chamber with a shimmering blue light. Strength like he had never experienced filled his body to the degree he feared that his skin would burst, like a cow's intestine stuffed too full.

The song of the Engine became his whole world, a pulsating beat and soft melody. He relaxed into the song the way Elora had taught him to relax into the strength of additional shardstones. He allowed the power to pass through him without resistance, without trying to grasp it and hold it as his own. Some strength was simply too much for a human to carry.

He pulled his hand away from the stone and looked at it in wonder. The experience was nearly indescribable, but he was left with a lingering feeling of unity, a feeling that somehow he and the Engine were two parts of a much larger whole.

To his surprise, the Engine continued to glow even after pulling away. Melanie answered his unasked question.

"When others have touched it, it has come alive for anywhere from a few minutes to a few hours. But then it fades again."

"Has a Singer ever tried singing to it?"

Melanie nodded. "The results are little different. Their maintenance seems to last for longer than the touch of a lesser manirah, but the effect still fades."

Radyn continued to stare at the Engine. "Why did you really bring me here?"

"It is one thing to know that those in charge of Firestone have lied. But this was the only way I could think of to show you how extensive those lies actually are. These are not well-intentioned lies told under the guise of the greater good. These are fundamental lies about our city and our history that prevent us from moving forward."

Radyn couldn't deny what he saw in front of him. Nor could he deny that this was another lie to add to all the others. But he resisted the idea that the lie was malevolent in purpose.

"What if the defense is the same? What if the reason we don't know about all of this is that it is better for us if we don't?"

Melanie inclined her head. "I would turn the question back on you. Do you believe, having seen all of this, that there is any explanation that justifies this lie?

That justifies withholding this much of our past from us?"

Radyn grimaced but didn't answer. Yes, there might be chaos if the people knew what lay buried beneath the surface, but there were materials down here, entire Engines that might still be repaired.

They might once again live on the surface, if only they knew.

The truth needed to be told, but he wasn't convinced Melanie was the one to tell it. "What would make you better than those who have kept us alive for centuries?"

"I would have us stop running. Whitehawk taught us that the cities won't last forever. We need to start fighting again, not against each other with these petty raids but against the predators that have overrun the surface. Our future isn't in the sky but spread out across the land."

Radyn thought back to the meeting and made an intuitive leap. "That's always been the goal, hasn't it? When you told the others we might heal the Engine, it was to distract them from your true purpose."

Mysteries unraveled as he tugged at the end of the thread. "You're preparing a group to return to the surface. But how? The clan knows what you know but is hiding the truth. You might have enough influence to get yourself down here, but how would you ever bring down enough to start a settlement?"

"Eventually, the clan will have to be convinced. That's where you come in."

"What do you want from me?"

"I want your loyalty and your strength. I want to know that when I challenge the Blade, there are at least a handful of respected warriors inside of the clan who will back my claim."

Radyn felt like he was attempting to ride a dragon through the heart of an enormous storm, buffeted this way and that by winds he barely understood. All he knew was what he believed: eventually, for the safety of all, they needed to spread beyond Firestone. So long as all he knew and loved was in the city, it would be at risk of the Engine failing. He couldn't imagine putting Aria through such a disaster again.

If this got them closer, it was worth whatever personal risk he incurred.

He bowed to Melanie. "My first duty will always be to Firestone. So long as I believe that your way is best, you have my word that I will support you. But if I believe, even for a moment, that's untrue, I will turn my sword upon you without a moment's hesitation."

Melanie bowed. "I would ask for no less."

She looked around the room. "Come, there is much more to show you."

Radyn followed, wondering what would be here that wasn't in Firestone. They hadn't made it far before Melanie swore under her breath.

"What?" Radyn asked.

"I'd expected we would have much more time, but I was wrong. I'd hoped to keep you here longer, to show you the wonders of this place. But now, it would be best if we were going. The monsters of the wild lands have ways of sensing our presence we do not yet understand, and I sense that some are already approaching."

Radyn pushed out his own senses but felt nothing. "How do you know?"

"A story for another day. For now, we must be on our way."

Radyn reluctantly agreed, though he wanted to spend more time inside the mound. The two of them made their way out of the ruins. Once they left the cave, Radyn helped Melanie replace the boards and cover them with brush until the entrance was nearly invisible. Then he called for Tanwen, and the dragon swooped down. Through their connection, Radyn felt a deep sense of contentment emanating from the dragon. The hunting, it seemed, had been good.

They climbed on, and Tanwen barely needed a suggestion from Radyn before he took off and beat his mighty wings. They lifted into the sky, and Radyn banked the dragon in a wide circle around the mound. Off in the distance, he saw dark shapes approaching. There was no smell that could travel so far, yet somehow, the beasts of this land always knew when humans dared set foot.

And yet Melanie had known of their approach. From the moment he'd first laid eyes on her, he'd suspected there was more to her than he knew, but now that curiosity had only increased. As soon as they returned to Firestone, he'd question her until she answered.

Their departure created a sudden and new longing in Radyn's heart. He didn't think often about the surface, at least not more than anyone else he knew of. But now, the idea of leaving and returning to Firestone seemed anathema to him. His true home was down there, except that even with all of his strength, he wouldn't last a day. If this new dream was to come true, he'd have to become much stronger than he was.

He gave the area around the mound one last look,

then told Tanwen to head for home. The dragon, with its belly full of food, happily agreed. They were most of the way home when Melanie tapped on his shoulder and spoke into his ear. "Look east," she said.

Radyn did and swore to himself. Off in the distance, little more than a speck, was another city. It looked the same as Firestone, but Radyn had given Tanwen the order to return home, and the dragon could always find his way, so that wasn't Firestone.

"Is there supposed to be a Gathering?" Melanie asked.

"No." Radyn tightened his grip on Tanwen. Only one reason remained for why a city would be so close to Firestone.

Firestone was about to get raided again.

20

Radyn urged Tanwen to hurry, and the dragon needed little encouragement. It sped forward, slicing through the air with its enormous wings and a strength Radyn didn't fully understand. Wind pulled his hair away from his face and made his eyes water.

From this distance, it was unlikely that the city could spot them, but Radyn kept searching the sky for other specks. The raiding city would send out scouts ahead, both to clear the sky of Firestone's scouts and keep an eye out for Firestone itself. A small part of Radyn, drunk on childhood stories of clan heroes, was tempted to bank Tanwen toward the raiding city and attack its scouts alone.

He didn't succumb to the temptation, though. Such heroics might have made wonderful stories for him at night after a long day spent in school and in the fields, but it would accomplish little here. Maybe he got lucky and took one or two dragons out of the sky, but he'd be swarmed and killed eventually and Firestone would lose one of its best chances at a warning.

So he leaned forward and urged Tanwen on, grateful the dragon had fed well while he'd visited the surface. It wasn't long before Firestone appeared, a dark speck against a background of clouds. It grew rapidly. Their arrival didn't go unnoticed. A few scouts came close, then pulled away when they recognized Tanwen.

Radyn and Tanwen made straight for the landing zone. The dragon spread its wings out wide and angled them to catch the wind, bringing them to a sudden stop in the air. Tanwen dropped the last few feet to the ground, absorbing the landing with its massive legs. Radyn leaped off the neck and ran for the staging office. "Raid!" he shouted.

The reaction to the news was close to instantaneous. The call was picked up by others in the area, spreading throughout the landing zone in moments. People went running, shouting themselves hoarse as they sprinted to their stations. One Dagger tugged on a rope connected to a bell, ringing the alarm that was picked up by other bells across the surface. Nervous tension spread across the farmlands like a fire across dry kindling.

Farmers ran to the nearest shelter, and it wouldn't be long before Daggers and Swords started climbing to the surface. Radyn found Macken shouting orders to Daggers who ran to obey.

After Macken sent a group of Daggers to seal up the dragon's nests, he turned to Radyn. "Good to see you back. Is Tanwen hurt?"

"No. We're the ones who reported the raid. There's a city inbound, maybe thirty or forty miles to the east."

"Did you get close enough to identify it?" Macken asked.

Radyn shook his head. "You're the closest Sword. What are my orders?"

The stout commander bit his lower lip. "The Blade claims you've got some promise. Is that true?"

Radyn wasn't sure how to answer that question. "I don't lose many sparring matches, but I've never fought in actual combat."

Macken cursed under his breath. "I need dragons in the air, but most of my best riders are down near the recyclers on some assignment today. You're already connected to Tanwen, and he likes you, anyway. Get up in the sky and keep us safe."

Radyn's eyes went wide, but he didn't question the order. He bowed quickly, then turned and ran back to Tanwen. Only then did he realize he hadn't seen Melanie since they'd landed. He looked around for her but saw no sign.

He let the matter drop. There would be time enough to track her down later. Tanwen was still where they'd landed, his head raised and searching the sky. "They want us up there," Radyn said.

Tanwen lowered his head and Radyn climbed up. Once he was secure, Tanwen walked over to the edge of the city and dropped off. Radyn grinned as they fell. His first raid as a Dagger, and he'd been given a dragon! His heart pounded and his fingers tingled. Through their connection, Radyn felt Tanwen's pleasure, too.

The dragon extended his wings and shot them into the sky. Tanwen rose faster than the beating of his wings justified. Radyn felt as though his body was melting, his consciousness merging with that of the great beast. Their emotions were two harmonies that slowly merged into one soaring melody.

Academics liked to argue why the dragons were so willing to cooperate with humans. The arrangement certainly served them, but there was no need on their part. They could survive well enough on their own.

Now, for the first time, Radyn thought he understood. Dragons were creatures of muscle and power that humans could barely comprehend. But humans were creatures of senses and reason, and together, they became something more than the sum of their parts.

Tanwen spotted the advancing dragons first, far above them, and soared upward. Radyn watched the enemy dragons for a moment, then urged caution. He convinced Tanwen to bank and fly in the opposite direction, toward the raiding city. After a mile, he glanced up and behind them, pleased to see none of the attacking dragons had broken off to hunt him.

At a thought, Tanwen launched them straight into the sky. Radyn bit back the urge to shout, his blood pounding through his veins. He'd trained as a rider, but there'd always been a sense of caution between him and the dragons. Tanwen abandoned any such caution, and Radyn had never flown half as fast. They rose above the level of the attacking dragons and approached from their flank, keeping the sun behind them.

Attacks from underneath weren't uncommon, as the underside of a dragon's throat was typically vulnerable, but dragons were also more aware of what happened below them. They spent most of their lives searching the ground for prey, so successful surprise attacks from below were rare.

The odds of a lethal attack from above were less, given the thick scales along the dorsal side of the dragon, but Radyn hoped to catch the other riders by surprise. If he could take down one or two dragons before they reached Firestone, it would be an incredible success.

They caught up to the other dragons quickly. As Radyn expected, each of the attacking beasts was carrying a large steel basket in their claws, each holding at least a dozen warriors. Now that he was close enough to the dragons, he could see the markings that identified them as Nightkeep's.

That fact gave him pause. Nightkeep wasn't one city, but a collection of three that had banded together. They were some of the most dangerous cities in the sky, but they rarely made use of that strength. They kept to themselves and often served as mediators between lesser cities.

He held Tanwen back, a feat that consumed most of his focus for almost a minute. The dragons were coming close to Firestone, and so far, Firestone's response was lackluster. Radyn had seen half a dozen dragons waiting for riders, but none were in the sky yet. He looked again for any sign of peace from the dragons but saw none.

When a city wanted to communicate with another city, the accepted practice was to send one or maybe two riders as messengers. The riders attached white flags to their backs and were cautiously welcomed at their destination. Today, Radyn saw no white flags. That, combined with the troop carriers, convinced him they were raiders.

Still, he hesitated. He'd seen no fighting yet, and if he inadvertently started a battle that didn't need to happen, the consequences for Firestone would be terrible.

Then, off in the distance, he saw two dragons attacking one another. One of Firestone's scouts had engaged the enemy. Confident he wasn't wrong, Radyn urged Tanwen forward. He was grateful the dragon didn't roar and give away their approach, but the surge of pleasure that ran through both rider and dragon made it clear Tanwen wanted to.

Radyn reached back and grabbed his hilt. It was a basic design, a one-shard hilt that was given by the clan to new Daggers as their first weapon. Normally, it wouldn't be capable of doing more than creating a short sword.

But Radyn had the shards in his body, and for the first time, he was allowed to use them. Light flared from the base of the hilt, first to the length of a sword, then much longer. He pushed his thought to Tanwen, and the dragon rumbled with its approval. Tanwen sped forward one last time, watching the dragons below as if they were prey trying to flee.

When the dragon judged the moment was right, he folded in his wings and dropped. Radyn thought he'd understood Tanwen's limits before, but he was once again humbled by the dragon. They fell far faster than a dropped boulder, Tanwen speeding down. Radyn gripped Tanwen's scales and dug in with the toes of his boots, fighting simply to remain attached. The enemy dragon grew bigger. It was an elder, almost twice the size of Tanwen, but it never saw the danger that approached from above.

Radyn pressed his thighs against Tanwen as he raised his maniblade. There was nothing for him to do except hold on and trust Tanwen.

They passed the dragon from Nightkeep in the blink of an eye. Tanwen dropped them in the space between the dragon's neck and the leading edge of its wing, and Radyn's enormous maniblade cut cleanly through three-quarters of the dragon's neck. He barely felt any resistance at all. Tanwen unleashed his long-withheld roar.

Then they were past and it was done. Radyn pressed his torso close to Tanwen's neck and risked a glance back. The other two dragons in the formation continued toward Firestone, but the elder in the middle tumbled from the sky. It had let go of the basket, and from Radyn's distant vantage point, it looked as though the falling dragon was surrounded by a handful of specks of dust.

It was easier to think of them that way.

Tanwen slowly spread his wings, bleeding off some of the speed of their murderous descent. Before long, his wings were wide and they fought for altitude once again. Radyn directed Tanwen toward the other two dragons. Loaded with passengers as they were, there was less they could do to avoid Radyn's blade and Tanwen's jaws. This time, they approached from below, Tanwen eager to close his jaws around the throat of an enemy dragon.

A rapidly growing shadow caught Radyn's attention. Another dragon had split from a distant formation and approached. Radyn urged Tanwen to hurry, but it soon became clear they were in a race they were destined to lose. He watched for a moment longer, then had Tanwen break away from his attack run.

As they banked away, Radyn got his first real glance inside the baskets the dragons carried. They were stuffed full of passengers, but few wore the uniforms of Nightkeep's clan. Most were dressed as common farmers.

Radyn didn't have the time to wonder why. The dragon and rider from Nightkeep weren't satisfied with merely driving him away from the passenger-laden dragons. They pursued, and they were fast. Radyn let Tanwen have free rein, trusting the dragon's instincts more than his own. He disconnected from the hilt and returned it to the sheath at his hip so he could hold on to Tanwen with both hands.

It was good that he did. Tanwen banked and swooped, twisting in the air to gain any meager advantage over his pursuer. Radyn was pressed tight against the dragon's neck, then fought to hold on as the dragon dropped out from under him. He grunted when Tanwen spread out his wings and stopped with impossible suddenness, slamming Radyn into his neck.

The violent maneuvers worked, and the other dragon sped by in a flash of tooth and claw. Tanwen became the eager pursuer, and the dragon from Nightkeep twisted to avoid snapping jaws. Tanwen bled speed, then dropped straight at the enemy dragon.

It caught both riders and the enemy dragon by surprise. Radyn almost slipped when the two dragons collided in midair. Tanwen and the enemy dragon snapped and clawed at one another, each seeking some decisive leverage over the other. They twisted and spun as they fell, clouds and the earth below twirling around Radyn so quickly they blended one into the other. His stomach did somersaults, and it was all he could do to hold on.

The neck under Radyn twisted suddenly, and Radyn found himself face-to-face with the enemy dragon. Its massive jaws closed on Tanwen's neck, barely missing taking off Radyn's right arm. The teeth by Radyn's arm ground against the heavy scales, finding meager purchase. The teeth below locked into Tanwen's neck with a meaty *thunk* Radyn felt throughout his body. Tanwen roared in pain. Dark, warm blood sprayed and spun in the air as the enemy dragon worked its teeth in deeper. Tanwen tried to fight the other dragon off, but his strength faded as he lost blood.

Radyn reached to grab his hilt. He formed a blade the length of a sword and stabbed it straight into the dragon's snout.

In an instant, the enemy dragon let go and reared its head back.

Tanwen seized the momentary advantage, digging his teeth into the newly exposed neck of his enemy. His jaws closed and ripped a chunk of dragon flesh away. The dragon from Nightkeep let out a gargled half-roar, then went silent and limp. Radyn caught one last glimpse of the dragon's rider, who held on to his dead beast with a look of grim determination.

For a moment, Radyn worried he would share the same fate. Tanwen slowly tumbled, the ground racing ever closer. But then Tanwen spread his weary wings and they leveled off. Radyn pushed some of the strength of the Engine through his shardstones into Tanwen's body, and the dragon used the gift to close the open wounds. It wasn't the full healing the dragon required, but it would stop the bleeding and keep Tanwen in the air.

He didn't have much fight left in him, though. Radyn searched the sky. The battle had intensified as the dragons closed in on Firestone, but it looked like several had landed.

Radyn pressed his forehead against Tanwen's neck. "Bring me home, friend, and then you should drift off someplace safe until this battle is over. You've done enough."

Tanwen's exhaustion and wounds carried through their connection, but the dragon lifted Radyn higher into the air without complaint. They came up on Firestone from the east, away from most of the fighting. Radyn circled once, studying the scene before descending. Several dragons from Nightkeep had successfully landed in the fields, and the surface was chaotic. He cursed when he saw several of Firestone's dragons still huddled in their nests. The warriors from Nightkeep didn't seem interested in the landing zone, though, so the dragons were safe for the moment.

The raid couldn't have come at a worse time. Most of Firestone's defenders hadn't even been able to get into the air.

Light flashed as the swords of Firestone's clan clashed with those of Nightkeep's. For the number of warriors that had landed, though, the amount of duels being fought seemed low. Radyn feared Nightkeep had simply overwhelmed Firestone's defenders. Even worse, it looked like not all the farmers had found shelter yet, exposing them to the dangers of the raid. Radyn spotted a pair of Nightkeep Daggers wandering the fields unopposed and figured it was as good a place as any. He asked Tanwen to drop him, and the dragon complied. Instead of landing, Radyn jumped off, falling nearly a dozen feet to the surface. He rolled when he hit the ground, then watched Tanwen to ensure the dragon safely escaped the battlefield.

By the time Tanwen was safe, the two Nightkeep Daggers had found him. The blades emanating from their hilts were the length of short swords, but both moved toward him with confidence. Like them, he wore the uniform of a Dagger. He was glad they didn't give him time to think about the battle to come. He treated it like any of his training duels, except this time, he was allowed to connect to all his shardstones. The hilt in his hand came alive, his blade sword-length.

That caused the pair to hesitate, but only for a moment. Their numbers and recent success made them confident. They came at him together, displaying a coordination that spoke of days of hard cooperative training.

But after the fights Elora had fought with him, it didn't matter. They didn't bother to hide the shifts in their weight, and their eyes openly stared at their targets. His senses gathered the information without thought, and instinct guided his body through the spaces in their attack. He cut through the opponent on his right with a single pass, then leaned back as his partner attacked wildly. The second Dagger fell a moment later, and Radyn looked down at his hilt, glowing with the brightness of the Engine.

He rarely won against Elora, and when he did, it was more often a fluke than anything he'd excelled at.

He'd never considered the possibility his first real duel might end so quickly.

The victory didn't have time to go to his head. Screams came from his left, and he hurried through the wheat to the source of the sound.

He emerged on a path between fields, about thirty paces from where a Firestone Dagger had just lost an arm to a Nightkeep Sword. He sprinted toward the duel, but the Sword cut once and put the Dagger of his misery. She looked up at Radyn with a resigned expression. For a moment, she reminded him of Elora. Smaller than average, with thin, wiry muscles that possessed a strength so many underestimated. She kicked up dirt as she sprinted at Radyn.

The difference between her and the Daggers he'd just defeated was immense. Her shard-assisted speed and strength were greater, but her technique and experience put her in a different class. Radyn still saw the path of her first cut, which he avoided easily, but her weight and eyes told him different stories when she attacked again. He trusted in the shift of her weight, but the tip of her sword cut a shallow gash across his forearm.

He responded with a combination that pushed her back. Her expression changed, changing from boredom to interest.

They passed again and again, and Radyn felt very much like he was training against Elora. The Nightkeep Sword's senses weren't as sharp, but her experience seemed greater than Elora's, negating the slight advantage Radyn had.

She couldn't fool the sharp awareness Elora had instilled in him, though, and that proved to be the difference that mattered. She couldn't land a decisive blow, and eventually, he slipped one past her. His first cut opened her up from shoulder to stomach, and she fell to her knees.

She looked up at him and grunted. "Impressive."

Radyn gave her a quick nod, and she bowed, exposing the back of her neck. Radyn took her head with a clean cut.

He looked up, finally able to spare a moment of awareness for the surrounding battle.

Except it wasn't much of a battle anymore. The Nightkeep dragons were taking off, enormous baskets in their mighty grip. Firestone, beaten and bloody, didn't send any dragons in pursuit. A few small fires burned in the fields, but fire teams were already being directed toward them.

Radyn took a deep breath for the first time in what felt like a full day. He let the blade fade from his hilt and he sheathed it.

Hurried footsteps made Radyn turn around. His body felt impossibly heavy all of a sudden, but he wrapped his hand around his hilt.

The pair of Swords that came around the corner wore Firestone uniforms, though, and Radyn vaguely recognized them. They took him in, standing over the corpse, and then their eyes went wide. "Did you kill her?" one asked, pointing at the corpse.

Radyn looked down at his defeated enemy. "I did. She was strong."

The Sword scoffed. "Strong? That's Amaya. She was one of their best Swords. She'd been carving a bloody path through the fields."

They looked like they wanted an explanation, but Radyn had none to give. Their expressions danced between skepticism and awe, but Radyn's mind had already turned elsewhere.

Nightkeep had dedicated an enormous amount of dragons and warriors to this raid, but it hadn't lasted all that long. He'd lost track of time during his duels, but they couldn't have been on the surface for more than twenty minutes.

He turned away from the Swords to examine the surface. Something more had happened here, and he intended to find out what.

21

The aftermath of the battle faded, leaving Radyn with more questions than answers. The longer he considered what he'd witnessed, the less sense it made. Raids on major cities were rare, simply because the odds of them producing meaningful gain were slim. To Radyn's knowledge, none of the cities had been built with raids in mind, but hundreds of years had given every surviving city plenty of opportunity to adapt. Those adaptations, as well as the fact that attacking a flying city was already a tactical challenge, made raids increasingly uncommon.

When a raid was launched, it was typically for one of two reasons. Either the attacker hoped to attack during harvest, stealing bushels of much-needed food in a lean year, or the raid targeted the dragons that each city cooperated with. Losing too many dragons could cripple a city and could sometimes result in dramatic concessions.

This raid did neither. They'd completely ignored the

Nest, and it was nowhere close to harvest. So, what did they hope to accomplish by landing so many people?

He stood still and considered. He flipped through his memories, looking for a clue he'd missed.

The enemies he'd fought had been strong, and Nightkeep had lost several dragons in the raid. It had been a costly effort, so not one made lightly.

He stretched his memories back farther, then cursed.

The warriors of Nightkeep in the basket hadn't all been dressed in clan uniforms. Many had been dressed as farmers. What did that enable? He somehow doubted Nightkeep had gone to all that trouble to surreptitiously lend them a hand with the fields.

He closed his eyes and remembered where he'd seen the dragons landing when he and Tanwen had circled above the city. Most had gathered farther to the north, so he went in that direction. He found one entrance to the city below, guarded as it should be by two Daggers. He and the guards exchanged quick bows.

"What was the evacuation like?" Radyn asked.

"A mess," one Dagger responded. From her tone, she was salty about it, too. "Not sure if there were just a lot of farmers napping in the fields or if they'd gotten turned around, but they were streaming in even after the first dragons landed."

Radyn's stomach dropped like a stone. "How many would you say came through late?"

The guards shared a look. "Maybe a dozen."

"You recognized them?"

The woman shook her head. "No, but I haven't been assigned surface duty for a long time. The whole schedule got shifted because of the training exercise the

Swords are doing down below this week. But everyone either knew this week's password or had the appropriate band on."

Radyn's blood went cold. "Who is in command of the aftermath?"

"Senior Sword Jyn. He set up command just outside the Nest."

"Thank you." Radyn bowed and hurried away, running to find Jyn.

The Senior Sword's command area was a study in practiced efficiency. A ring of high-ranked Swords surrounded Jyn, accepting messages and problems as they came in. The Swords handled most problems on their own, but when something required a decision beyond their authority, they turned to Jyn.

While Radyn was forced to wait in line, he watched the process unfold with awe. Decisions were made in the shortest possible time, and he advanced through the queue faster than he would have believed possible. There was something about Jyn's presence that proclaimed his authority. He never hesitated, he deliberated. He spoke with calm confidence despite the blow that had just landed against his beloved city.

When Radyn finally had his turn, he didn't bother with the Sword that greeted him. "I need to speak to Senior Sword Jyn," he said.

The Sword was unperturbed, and Radyn realized he'd probably heard the same line several times already today. "That's a decision that's up to me, Dagger. Now, what is it?"

Behind the Sword, Jyn finished with a decision, and Radyn shouted his name. Jyn looked up, and the Sword raised his hand to slap Radyn across the face for his insubordination.

"It's fine," Jyn said, halting the slap before it landed. "Let him through."

The Sword growled but let Radyn through.

"What is it?" Jyn asked.

"I believe the purpose of the raid was to insert saboteurs within our ranks. People dressed as farmers went below. They had the appropriate bands and passwords."

Jyn's stare was hard, but Radyn didn't wilt under the weight of it.

He didn't even ask any questions. He just nodded once. "That would explain a lot."

Jyn barked an order, and a few moments later, the ring of protective Swords had closed around him. Jyn spoke quickly, but quietly. "Everything else stops. Radyn here has brought the information we've been wondering about. Several groups of Nightkeep warriors have infiltrated Firestone for reasons unknown, dressed as farmers. They have the appropriate bands and passwords to get them into the city. Each of you is to descend into the city through separate entrances. Take as many Swords and Daggers as you can find as you go. Ensure all farmers are in their proper raid shelter. If anyone isn't, pursue them and apprehend them. If you can spare the strength, send a messenger back here with news, and I'll send reinforcements as they arrive on the surface."

Jyn spread out a map of the surface. He assigned each of the Swords an entrance, assigning one to Radyn as well.

"Sir, I'm only a junior Dagger. People won't listen to my orders."

Jyn ripped the senior Sword insignia off his uniform and handed it over. "It's not an advancement, so don't let it get to your head, but at least everyone will listen to you."

With that, the Swords spread out, leaving Jyn alone to address the remaining problems on the surface.

Radyn had been assigned one of the farthest away entrances, which had certainly been a deliberate choice on Jyn's part. He didn't see another soul until he reached the entrance, guarded by a single young Dagger. Radyn didn't recognize him, but he looked about ready to wet his pants.

"Did many farmers come through here during the raid?" Radyn asked.

The Dagger took in Radyn's new insignia and nodded quickly. "Yes, sir."

"Come with me. It's fine to leave the entrance unguarded for a bit.

The Dagger didn't hesitate for a moment, and Radyn wondered if it was because he just wanted to be off the surface or if he was cowed by the insignia. Either way, Radyn appreciated not having to explain himself.

The two descended the ladder into the darkness below. Once Radyn reached the bottom, he froze as his memory flung him into the past. Less than three years had passed since the last raid, but joining the clan had been a dividing line in his life. Before, he'd been a child cowering from the raiders, and now, for a moment, he was that child again.

He stuffed the memories down with an angry shake

of his head. Firestone needed him to be as strong as Viktor had been on that day. He needed strength to spare, to spread among those who couldn't defend themselves.

He led the junior Dagger through a door and into the connecting hallway. Radyn allowed his hearing to sharpen, and he caught the quiet whispers coming from a few rooms down. He walked down the hall slowly, each step landing toe-heel-toe to avoid making any noise against the deck.

As he approached closer, the whispers resolved into conversations he could catch snippets of, and he relaxed. The hushed tones weren't those of invaders planning on springing an ambush but a group of farmers caught in the raid. He recognized the fear in their voices as echoes of his own so long ago.

He allowed his footsteps to land heavily so as not to surprise them, and when he turned the corner, he held his hands up and away from the hilt at his hip. His precautions didn't stop two of the women from screaming when they saw him, though.

He was confused until the Dagger explained. "You're covered in blood, sir."

Radyn hadn't even noticed, but when he looked down, he saw just how true the observation was. Dragon and human blood both stained his clothes, and he imagined he presented a terrifying visage. He bowed, hoping the gesture would calm some of their nerves. "I apologize for frightening you, but we're here to help. Is anyone here hurt?"

One man claimed that he'd sprained an ankle descending the ladder too quickly, but otherwise, they were fine. Radyn focused on them each in turn, seeking some sign of betrayal, but he saw none.

"We fear that a group of enemy manirahs might have disguised themselves as farmers to cause trouble. Has anyone else passed this way since the raid began?" he asked.

Everyone in the room nodded. After a moment of speaking over one another, one woman said they'd seen a separate group of farmers hurrying inward, possibly ten or fifteen minutes prior. The farmers had offered to share their shelter, as there was space for more, but the other group had declined.

In the chaos and confusion of the moment, none of the farmers had thought much of it, but now that they'd been prompted by Radyn, they agreed the entire situation was odd.

Radyn left the farmers to hide. He figured they were safe enough from whatever the raiders planned, and he didn't have the time to waste. The Dagger ran after him as he raced down the hallway to the nearest stairwell. Radyn took the stairs three at a time, using the rails to slingshot him around corners and down additional flights.

Most levels were guarded by Shields, and at each one, Radyn stopped to ask if a group of farmers had passed that way. Each Shield said no, and Radyn would charge down another flight of stairs.

At the bottom of the stair, seven levels beneath the surface, he received a confirmation of all his fears. A Shield had been guarding the door, and it ended up being the last service she performed for Firestone. Radyn squatted next to the body and turned it over.

The weapon had cut through bone and flesh with ease, opening her from shoulder to hip. The Dagger behind Radyn gagged and turned away.

Radyn stood. Only a maniblade left a cut like that, which meant the pretend farmers had indeed been manirahs. Bloody footprints led further inward.

Radyn forced himself to think like his enemies. Unlike Whitehawk, this group didn't seem interested in Firestone's Singers, and why should they? Nightkeep had dozens more Singers than Firestone and a much larger population to draw from. Besides, their path had already dropped them below the majority of the residential and command areas of Firestone. Both the academy, the Singer's wing, and the High Council headquarters were above. It was possible this group was a diversion or sought a roundabout route to their destination, but neither idea felt true.

Raids happened quickly, and Nightkeep's dragons had already fled. Whatever these manirahs were after, they'd move quickly.

Except they wouldn't have to, Radyn realized. They were dressed as farmers, and thanks to the raid, almost every citizen of Firestone had sealed themselves in shelter, waiting for the all-clear. They could melt into the city, spreading out like a disease ravaging a body, and they'd be almost impossible to root out.

The sinking feeling in Radyn's stomach grew. He ordered the Dagger back to the surface to report to Jyn while he followed the group. After seeing the Shield's fate, the Dagger didn't argue.

Radyn followed the trail, though it didn't last for long.

He tried a few stairwells, asking Shields if they'd seen anything suspicious. None had.

He swore and pressed his forehead against the cold steel of a wall. The group had either vanished or dispersed, and he didn't know how he'd track them.

Nightkeep had successfully infiltrated Firestone.

22

Radyn wiped his hands on his pants, though there was nothing to wipe off. He wanted to stand and pace, but he feared the consequences that would result, so he remained firmly seated on the bench. He considered connecting to his shardstone and listening to the conversation happening behind closed doors, but he couldn't bring himself to do it. The clan might have violated his trust, but that didn't mean he had to break his own word.

Better to be true in a sea of lies than to blindly follow a coward.

Magni had tried to strike up a friendly conversation earlier, and Radyn had tried to speak freely, but other thoughts were too heavy in his mind and he kept trailing off. Eventually, Magni gave him a sympathetic smile and let him be.

If they were alone in the hallway, Radyn might have acted differently, but he didn't know the other Dagger guarding Jyn's study. The senior Sword had doubled his protection after the infiltration, and Radyn figured it was a wise decision. Losing Jyn would be a disaster for Firestone's clan.

Right now, though, he was wondering if a travesty wasn't exactly what they needed. Elora had thought the clan less tradition-bound than the Singers, but Radyn wondered if it wasn't the other way around. The clan's traditions were simply buried deeper.

The door opened and Macken stepped out. He stopped briefly before Radyn. "Tanwen returned and is being healed. Some of the wounds on his neck are deep, but I saw how you attempted to help him. Your efforts might very well have saved his life."

Macken bowed, then turned sideways to slide around Magni. The sight was almost enough to make Radyn smile. There wasn't a hallway in Firestone big enough to allow those two to pass shoulder to shoulder.

Jyn appeared at his door a moment later and gestured to Radyn. He stood up and followed the senior Sword into the study.

The senior Sword settled into the chair on the other side of the desk and gazed at Radyn through lidded eyes. He looked exhausted, but that was befitting one of the clan's most important Swords in the days following a raid. Radyn had only slept for a few hours last night, waking up every time someone walked past his room.

And he slept in the middle of the academy, one of the safest places in Firestone.

"Your last message said you needed to speak with me urgently, and luckily for you, your heroics yesterday gave me a reason to invite you here. What's so damn important?"

"Yesterday, before the raid, I was given orders to escort a citizen down to the surface."

"So Macken told me. He's furious, and I can see why. Luckily for us, though, because of it, we received a warning several minutes before we would have otherwise. I'll investigate the matter, but what's your point?"

Radyn connected with his shardstones and focused his full attention on Jyn. If the Sword noticed, he gave no sign. "The woman who I escorted was the same one who led the meeting I attended. She called herself Melanie."

Jyn perked up at that. "Do you know what happened to her?"

"No. After I landed at the Nest and sounded the alarm, I lost her."

"She's got friends who are powerful enough to issue orders for the surface, though. That's useful information, but you could have written it in a letter. As you well know, I've got bigger problems on my hands at the moment."

"She brought me to an underground structure, designed the same as Firestone, that used to be powered by an Engine just like ours."

Jyn's reactions were subtle, perhaps even invisible to most, but to Radyn, he might as well have written a declaration in large symbols. His tired gaze focused on Radyn and his heart slowed. Radyn witnessed Firestone's greatest predator prepare for combat. He formed a maniblade in his mind, ready to flare it into life at a moment's notice.

Jyn didn't move a muscle, as though he recognized the danger.

His answer was low and filled with menace. "And?"

"People lived on the surface. There were no signs of violence. I don't know what happened, but they *lived* down there. Melanie claims her mission is to return humanity to their rightful place on the surface."

Radyn swore that Jyn had stopped blinking, but after last night, he refused to back down. Jyn might be stronger than Amaya was, but Radyn was confident he could make it a fight. The silence stretched between them, and Radyn's muscles grew tired from being ready to spring into action.

"You're sympathetic to her cause, aren't you?" Jyn asked.

The Sword leaned back an inch in his chair and relaxed. Radyn let out a slow breath and did the same. It felt like the moment of greatest danger had passed. "I am. This was her argument, but it's one I agree with. So long as we are limited to the cities, we risk the same failure that brought Whitehawk down, and unless I misunderstand, there's little we can do to control that failure. I don't doubt the difficulty of returning to the world, but at some point, we'll need to."

Jyn studied him for a moment more, but it appeared he'd already decided, back when he relaxed in his chair. "We have tried many times before."

"What?"

Jyn nodded. He stood, walked over to his bookshelf, pulled an old, slim volume from it, and returned to the desk. He placed it gently between them. "A record of each of Firestone's attempts to establish another city on the surface. You may borrow it, so long as you realize it is one of the three remaining copies and is extremely valuable. But I can summarize it quickly."

Radyn indicated he should.

"The years after the exodus were troublesome for all the cities. Our ancestors had grown up on the surface and known nothing else and then, within the space of a few years, were driven from it for good. The great cities are wonders, but those who were fortunate enough to escape the slaughter sometimes didn't recognize the extent of their good fortune. They couldn't stand living in these hallways, only seeing the surface occasionally. They hadn't adapted, and the plague of monsters wasn't as thick as it is today. Firestone's leaders, driven both by their desire to return to the surface and by the demands of a vocal few, attempted to establish cities on the surface. The great cities could never linger long, afraid to attract one of the enormous nuddu, but they provided all the support they could."

Jyn pushed the book closer to Radyn. "Every attempt failed and rarely were there any survivors. Sometimes, the reasons were mundane. Monsters broke through the established defenses and killed everyone. Disease wiped one settlement out. In others, we still don't know what happened. People just...vanished."

Radyn shook his head. He couldn't imagine an entire settlement full of people vanishing without a trace.

"The attempts continued for three generations, but eventually, people adapted to living in the great cities. Now, the clan has to mandate everyone goes to the surface for their health, but you know there are those who would never go up top if they didn't have to. All they know are the hallways and lamps of Firestone, and the very idea of the sky terrifies them. They take their surface time under an umbrella, so they pretend they're still surrounded by stone and steel. Between that and the knowledge that any attempt to live on the surface was doomed, the attempts stopped."

"Why not just tell us the truth?" Radyn demanded.

"We never lied, although I understand why you feel that way. A hundred years ago, schools still taught what had happened, but the need disappeared. We found that the less we taught about the surface, the less people thought about it. Now it is a silent truth, one only revealed to the senior Swords who rise to leadership positions within the clan. We keep the truth alive, so that we are prepared when cults like this rise. We don't teach the history anymore because most people don't care."

"They would now," Radyn argued, "now that the Engines are failing, the surface will seem much more appealing."

"I think you dramatically underestimate how scared people are of the surface." Jyn sighed, then said, "But for now, we have more important matters to attend to."

"Finding and capturing the manirahs from Nightkeep," Radyn agreed.

"Celebrating your heroism and granting you the rank of junior Sword," Jyn said.

Radyn sat, slack-jawed, as he stared at Jyn. "What?"

"The last few months have been difficult ones for Firestone. We need something positive we can focus on, something that reminds people we are still stronger than we've been in years."

"We can't celebrate, not with enemies in our midst!"

"Sit down and think, Radyn. We've already spread the word throughout the city. Every citizen knows they're supposed to report strange faces in their neighborhoods and markets. Shields are tearing the city apart from top to bottom, and we've got every critical hallway stuffed with Swords and Daggers. What else would you do to find them?"

Radyn thought for a moment, then admitted Firestone was already doing all that it could. It might take some time, but they couldn't hide for long. "It still doesn't feel right to celebrate, and certainly not celebrate me."

"To the contrary, there's no better time. People are rightfully uncertain, and it's in those times that it's vital they have people they can look up to, and you're more than deserving. Your actions against Nightkeep saved countless lives, and there are still plenty of people who remember how much blood and sweat you spilled helping after the Little Fall. On top of all of that, you defeated Amaya, who was well-regarded. She might have been Nightkeep's third or fourth strongest Sword, which is no small feat considering the size of the city. You're even making me curious what it would be like to duel."

Radyn didn't know what to say. He supposed he couldn't argue with any one point, but it all felt very sudden.

Jyn's mood shifted, and it felt as though a sudden storm had blown through the room. "While I have you, there is one more matter I would bring to your attention. Perhaps you or Elora can get to the bottom of it."

"Sir?"

"I suspect Firestone's clan has a traitor in its midst."

"Sir?" Radyn couldn't wrap his head around the thought. He'd already been asked to accept too much, and all he wanted was to return to his room, close his eyes, and think about everything he'd learned over the past two days.

"I became suspicious after Whitehawk's raid a couple of years ago. Their timing seemed too perfect to be a coincidence, and I feel the same about Nightkeep's raid. Most of our riders were down near the Engine when the alarm rang, which meant we lost several valuable minutes when they could have been in the air defending us. Once, I'm willing to attribute to bad luck. Twice, and I start to think there's something else going on. They also had the proper bands and passcodes, which meant they were uncommonly prepared. A traitor is the simplest explanation."

Jyn's accusations bugged Radyn, but it took him a few seconds to figure out why. "Sir, when Melanie and I were down below, exploring the ruins of the city, Melanie said something about wanting to keep me longer. I thought little of it then, because I assumed she just wanted me to see more, but now I'm wondering if she had something else in mind entirely."

"It's possible. I know it doesn't need to be said, but I'll say it anyway: be careful. If this 'Melanie' was coordinating with Nightkeep so that you were away from the raid, it means you've really drawn quite a bit of attention. Stay sharp."

"Yes, sir."

Radyn stood to leave.

"And Radyn?"

"Yes, sir?"

"Get yourself a new dress uniform tailored. I want you looking your best for the celebration."

23

Radyn knocked on the door and tugged on his clothes. They were new and stiff and made him feel like even more of an imposter. The new junior Sword patch on his shoulder did nothing to ease the feeling.

Elora opened the door. She was attired in a dress that clashed with how he normally thought of her. "I didn't think we'd see you so soon," she said.

"I left the moment Jyn let me out of his sight."

Elora laughed. "You'll pay for that tomorrow. I think he would have paraded you around for another few hours if he could."

"It's a cost I'm gladly willing to pay."

She let him in and called out, "Jelrik, our guest of honor has arrived!"

Then she turned to Radyn and spoke quieter. "Aria is already here, and Jelrik has been more than happy to show her the extent of our library."

Radyn imagined the scene, and it brought the first genuine smile to his face that evening. "If you're not careful, your library is going to be a few volumes slimmer when she leaves."

"I expect I'll have to search her before she takes off for the night," Elora agreed.

"You know I'd be happy to." He paused and let the weight of the last few hours fall off his shoulders. Here, he could finally just be himself. "Thanks for this."

Elora shrugged as though it was nothing. "You deserve a celebration."

Before he could say he'd just escaped one, she said, "A real one, with friends."

His arrival pulled Aria and Jelrik from the study, and from the way Aria looked back at the room, his prediction of a few of the books going missing was close to coming true. Like Radyn and Elora, Aria had acquired new clothes for the occasion, and her dress looked about as uncomfortable for her as Radyn's clothes felt to him.

It took him a moment to realize he was staring. Aria's dress lacked any of the frills and ornamentation that had surrounded Radyn during the official ceremonies, but it made more of an impact because of that lack.

"I see you survived," Aria said.

"I wasn't certain for a while, but knowing you would be here gave me the strength to endure."

Jelrik rolled his eyes and shook his head. Of the four, he was the only one who looked at home in fancier attire, but as a Singer, he was more used to the need. He gestured to the chairs in the living room. "Please, take a seat. I'll pour the drinks."

Elora led them to the living room and took a seat. Radyn and Aria sat on the couch next to one another.

"You did well," Elora said.

Radyn shook his head, finally able to release some of his pent-up frustration. "It still doesn't feel right, celebrating when Nightkeep has manirahs just waiting around somewhere."

Radyn waved away Elora's look. He'd argued with her about this at Jyn's celebration, and she hadn't been too patient with him. "I know, I know. Everything that can be done is being done, it just feels wrong."

In the spirit of the evening, Radyn let his complaints go. There was another question that had been bothering him that he hadn't asked. "Elora, just how strong are you?"

Jelrik returned with four glasses. Each was filled with a light brown liquid. Radyn had heard of whiskey, but he'd never sought any out. Firestone didn't allow its production, and the stronger liquors Radyn had sampled from the illegal stills had never impressed. But Jelrik had apparently bought a bottle, from Nightkeep of all places, during a Gathering ten years ago. He saved it for only special occasions, and tonight had been deemed sufficient reason.

Radyn was honored and accepted his glass with a quick bow.

Jelrik answered the question Elora pretended to ignore. "She's strong enough to go toe-to-toe with Jyn, but neither of them will admit it."

"Actually, Jyn told me once that Elora was the only Sword in Firestone he couldn't always beat," Radyn said.

Jelrik took Elora's hand. "Leadership has changed him, if he's finally willing to admit it."

"Why do you want to know?" Elora asked.

Radyn shrugged. "Everyone is always telling me

about how Amaya was so strong, but I don't think she was any stronger than you. Had the two of you dueled, I think you would have won."

Radyn had meant it as a compliment, but Jelrik looked disgruntled. His face fell, just for a moment, before he raised his glass in a toast. "To Radyn, Firestone's youngest Sword."

Everyone raised their glasses, and Elora and Aria echoed Jelrik's toast.

They sipped their drinks together, and Radyn's eyes went wide as the whiskey coated his tongue and warmed his throat.

Jelrik had been watching and grinned at Radyn's reaction. "Good, isn't it?"

"It's incredible. Thank you again for your generosity."

"It's nothing. We're glad to have you here, and I don't think I've seen Elora as happy as she is when she's training you."

Radyn's cheeks flushed, and he didn't think it was just the whiskey.

"I'm grateful to be training under her. I don't think I'd be anywhere near as strong as I am today if it wasn't for her."

Jelrik's face fell for a moment, but he hid it quickly. Radyn changed the subject to something he thought was safe. "How long have you been a Singer, Jelrik?"

He seemed happy to change the topic. "Nearly two decades now. I didn't set any records for becoming the youngest Singer, but I became one early in life. I've been very fortunate. There's nothing else I'd rather do."

"Do you hope to become Master of the Song someday?" Aria asked.

Jelrik laughed and shook his head. "Never, so long as I can help it. Becoming Master of the Song means less time singing, and that's where my heart is. There are others more interested in the position."

Jelrik turned the conversation back to Radyn. "How about you? Now that you're a hero for warning us about the raid and have become the youngest Sword in Firestone history, are you thinking of becoming the next Blade?"

"I'm sure I have less interest in becoming the Blade than you do in becoming Master of the Song," Radyn said.

Jelrik didn't look convinced. "Really? The way Jyn was looking at you tonight, it's clear he wants you to help him lead the clan when he gets the chance. You're young, but after a few years serving under Jyn, the position would be yours for the taking."

Radyn scoffed. "The only thing I want from Jyn is for him to acknowledge that I'm stronger than him."

Elora laughed loudly before covering her mouth. "Good luck with that."

The strength of Jelrik's reaction caught Radyn by surprise. He downed the rest of his whiskey in one gulp, then stood and left the room in a huff.

The room was silent in the wake of his departure.

Aria was the first to speak. "What was that about?"

Jelrik returned a moment later, his anger mostly mastered, and sat down heavily on the chair. He glanced over to Elora, who'd seemed surprised neither by his departure nor his return. She tilted her head, giving him permission to say whatever it was he was going to say.

He bowed toward them. "I'm sorry for the outburst.

My feelings about the clan are complicated, but I tend not to share them with anyone but Elora."

Jelrik turned the full force of his gaze toward Radyn. "Isn't there anything you want more than strength?" He glanced meaningfully toward Aria, as if hoping to prompt an answer in that direction.

"Jelrik, has Elora ever told you about how my father died?"

The Singer nodded.

"After he died, I was furious at him. Some reasons were justified, and others, perhaps, were not. I know how many lives he saved that day, and that's just the ones that were in the stairwell. If Whitehawk had kidnapped our Singers, who knows what might have happened? He died a hero, but there were days when that didn't matter to me. I was furious because he didn't come back to me."

Radyn took a deep breath. "I've let go of most of that. Now I'm more interested in honoring my father's last act than I am in hating it. But there's a part of me that still wishes he'd been stronger, so that he could have fought out of that crowd and back to me."

Radyn turned to Aria. "I'll never leave anyone behind because I couldn't fight my way back to them."

Jelrik looked like a commander who'd just realized he'd stepped onto a battlefield he had no chance of conquering. He sighed, leaned back in his chair, and looked longingly at the half-empty glass in his wife's hands. "It doesn't feel right for me to tell you what to do, Radyn, but would you accept one piece of wisdom I've learned since becoming a Singer?"

"Of course." Radyn might disagree with Jelrik, but he

liked Elora's husband well enough, and if his master loved the Singer, his wisdom was worth hearing.

"No one can sing to the Engine by themselves," Jelrik said.

"Really?" both Aria and Radyn asked in unison.

Radyn had known that the Singers always worked in groups, but he'd never realized that cooperation was a necessity.

Jelrik nodded. "The Engine's power is beyond the control of any individual Singer, including the Master of the Song. But when we sing together, it listens and responds."

The Singer interlaced his fingers, then squeezed them together. "I know you've heard the song of the Engine before, and I know that you've come to many of the same conclusions we Singers have—that the power of the Engine reflects some much greater power, something fundamental in our world we don't yet understand. If you accept that's true, you'll understand something of the meaning of what it is to be a Singer."

Radyn didn't have any trouble connecting the dots. "You think cooperation is somehow fundamental to our world?"

It was a laughable idea, but Jelrik shook his head. "Not cooperation, connection. It can't be that foreign of an idea. You even use the language when describing your use of the shardstones."

Radyn wasn't sure what he made of the Singer's claim. It almost sounded ludicrous, but after hearing the song for himself, Radyn wasn't so sure it could be easily dismissed. "What advice would you give, then?"

"The type of strength you pursue is a lonely one. I

won't be trite and tell you we're all stronger together, but there is a strength in connection. Though you two might not admit it, it's what makes you better Swords than most. It's not your physical strength or your speed, but the depth of your connection with both the shardstones and your enemies. You know how they'll move almost before they do."

Jelrik's words stuck like a lump in Radyn's throat, but it was clear the Singer had said his piece and had no more to share. After an awkward silence, Elora asked Aria about her most recent projects, and the tide of the conversation flowed into gentler waters.

The rest of the evening was pleasant, but Radyn couldn't shake Jelrik's advice from his thoughts. When he and Aria left, walking hand in hand down the hallway, Radyn's pace was slow. Aria had spent enough time with him to know the rough direction of his thoughts. "What he said really got to you, didn't it?"

Radyn grunted. "That obvious?"

"It seemed to bother you more than anything else tonight, and that was after surviving the celebration Jyn prepared for you."

"Do you think he's right?"

Aria shrugged. "Does it even matter? I'm less concerned with your reasons for becoming strong and more interested in what you decide to do with your abilities. Everything I've seen tells me that you want to use what you've learned to protect Firestone and help others. That's enough for me."

Radyn squeezed her hand. "Thank you."

"Any time. Now, unless you've got something more important planned, I think we should return to your place tonight and celebrate your ascension to Sword properly."

She grinned, and the last of Radyn's worries slipped away. He knew they'd return in force in the morning, but for now, he had more important matters to attend to.

24

The next morning came too early, and Radyn spent a few minutes wondering if he should just return to sleep. Aria was curled up against his side, her breathing soft and regular. It was the sort of moment he wished he could capture and return to upon demand. His memory was good, but like all memories, it was subject to the ravages of time, and he wanted something that would last, as perfect as it was right now.

Duty pulled him out of bed, though. He wanted to see if the Shields had turned anything up in the search for the Nightkeep manirahs, and he'd promised Elora that he would train with her later this morning. She'd been vague about it when they'd spoken last night, which made him think she had something unique lined up for the day. There was no expectation he would continue to train with Elora, but he couldn't imagine allowing their relationship to change. Strong as Firestone claimed he was, he still had more to learn from her.

He took one last look at Aria before he left for the day.

They'd grown closer over the past few months than he'd dared to hope, and it still seemed unreal. He smiled and closed the bedroom door softly.

From his small apartment, he climbed one flight of stairs and made his way to the clan headquarters. If the Shields had found anything, the clan would know. He asked the Dagger working the welcome desk if any word had come in, but he shook his head. The Shields had searched through most of the city but hadn't found a trace of the intruders.

Radyn was disappointed but not surprised. It wasn't as if the Shields could identify every person in the city. If the Nightkeep manirahs were prepared, they could easily pass for Firestone residents.

He held out more hope that an observant citizen would report strangers in their neighborhood, but Jyn's warning about a possible traitor worried him. The Shields would have no chance of finding the raiders if they had inside help. Still, there was nothing more he could think of doing, so he made his way down two levels to the training rooms where Swords dutifully trained their initiates. He found the room Elora had reserved, knocked, and entered. He was early, but as he'd expected, Elora was already there waiting for him. She ran through one of the clan's basic forms while she waited, gracefully flowing from one position to the next.

She didn't stop when he entered. "I wasn't entirely sure you would make it today."

"I told you I would."

"True, but yesterday was a long day, and from the way Aria was looking at you, I'm not sure you got much sleep."

Radyn blushed and cast his eyes down. Eager to change the subject, he said, "I got the sense you had something special for me today."

She finished the execution of her form. "You think I'll give you special treatment just because Jyn wanted to raise you to Sword?"

Radyn snorted. "I hope not, but no, I was thinking more that you had something specific in mind when you asked if I would train with you today."

Elora gestured for him to sit on one of the two cushions in the room. Radyn noted they were pushed closer together than usual. He took one as Elora took the other.

"Something is happening in Firestone, and I can't put my finger on it," Elora said. "Jelrik isn't being allowed much time with the Engine, Nightkeep hopes to accomplish *something* by flooding our hallways with manirahs, and we still haven't found the mysterious woman of yours. They've got more guards in more places than ever, but something still feels off, doesn't it?"

Radyn nodded. He'd felt much the same, though he'd failed to articulate it so clearly.

"So, we're going to get to the bottom of it, starting with the one problem I know we can explore on our own."

"What's that?"

"We can find out what's happening with the Engine."

"How?"

"You heard my husband last night. There's a reason the Singers always work together." Elora held out her hands. "You survived the song before, and if we combine our strength, we should be able to dive deep enough to find out what's wrong."

"What can we find out that Jelrik hasn't felt?"

Elora shook her head. "If Jelrik was less of a stickler for rules, I think he would have found out already. But singing is an active process—he wouldn't necessarily feel anything unless something was distinctly wrong with the Engine. And he still hasn't had that much time with the Engine with the new schedules. We're going to listen."

Radyn stared into her eyes. How many times had he sat here while she'd cautioned him against doing this very thing? It was too easy to lose oneself in the song. Extricating oneself from the song was one of the greatest skills that separated a Singer from the Sword.

As usual, she understood the direction of his thoughts. "You forget, I've been taught the basics of singing, and you've separated yourself from the song once before. I won't sit here and tell you it's without risk, but I believe that by working together, we'll be strong enough to learn what the Master of the Song is hiding from us."

"What does it matter? We know something is wrong, and that our Engine isn't healthy. Is learning more worth the risk?"

"A healer can't heal unless they know exactly what's wrong. We can't help the Engine unless we know the same. Jelrik will be furious, but if nothing else, we can pass along what we learn to him, and maybe he'll do something with it."

In the end, Radyn's curiosity got the best of him. He nodded and took her hands.

"Listen for the song. Dive deep with me, and let me lead," Elora said.

Radyn closed his eyes and took a deep breath. Then he connected with every shardstone both in and on his body. The silence of the training room filled with the beats of their hearts and the flow of blood through arteries and veins. Beneath that, the song whispered its promises.

He focused his awareness on the song, and it grew louder than he'd heard it before. He sensed Elora's influence, pulling him closer. It was still the most beautiful melody he'd ever heard, and it brought forth the memories he treasured most. His first night with Aria. The day he first formed a maniblade in his hand. Eating supper with Father in the fields. It was the song of all those memories and more, and he understood how one could lose their awareness in the soaring crescendos of the song. Of all the ways to find one's way to the gate, it felt like one of the most peaceful.

A harmony was added on top of the song, and the song shifted in response. The harmony was plain compared to the song, empty of deeper meaning. It was like someone was playing the right notes, but without the proper feeling behind them, a song without soul. He'd not heard this song before, but he was certain it was the Singers directing the Engine to their next destination.

Radyn couldn't help but think the Singer's song crude, like giving a child a drum set and inviting them to play with Firestone's best band.

His awareness was pulled deeper until the song of the Engine drowned out all other sounds.

Then he heard it. A discordant note, faint but

unmistakable. Elora yanked his awareness toward that note, which played only occasionally. Radyn didn't know how long they spent with that note, but it felt like ages. He grimaced every time it sounded, but Elora seemed content to sit with the sound until she understood what it represented.

When she pulled them away, it was with surprising suddenness. Radyn gasped as his awareness returned to the training room. He disconnected as well as he was able from his shardstones, grateful for the numbness that spread across his senses.

"What was that?"

Elora shook her head. "I'm not sure, exactly, but it wasn't coming from outside the Engine. It came from within, and I fear it means the Engine truly is failing. To me, it felt as though the Engine is missing something, or it's lacking something it once had."

"How can it be lacking something? It's the Engine!"

"I don't know. I'm sorry."

Radyn would have asked her more about the Engine, but it was clear she didn't know more than she'd said, so he asked, "Why did you pull us out so suddenly?"

"My husband is coming."

Radyn turned around, but the training door was closed and he'd heard no one approaching on the other side. When he shot Elora a questioning look, she shrugged. "The Singers are sensitive. He noticed us. When he arrives, let me do the talking. He'll be upset."

Radyn's next question was cut off by the sound of heavy footsteps in the hallway. A moment later, the door flew open and Jelrik stormed through. He slammed the door closed so hard that Radyn thought it might crack.

Jelrik stopped a few feet short of Radyn. His nostrils flared, and Radyn wondered if they were in any danger.

Ever since he'd joined the clan, Radyn had heard persistent rumors that Singers kept secret techniques that allowed them to defend against attack. He'd never seen any evidence of such techniques, but he thought he might soon. He'd eaten supper with Jelrik, spent countless nights in their home, and spoken with him often about the life of a Singer, but he'd never once seen the Singer's face so twisted with anger before.

Jelrik controlled himself, if barely. "You told me you'd never."

He left the rest unspoken, but Radyn could guess.

"It needed to be done," Elora said.

Jelrik's fists clenched until they were white. "The Master of the Song ordered us—"

"Who cares?" Elora interrupted.

Jelrik's eyes bulged, but Elora plowed forward. "Firestone is in danger, and the Master of the Song isn't letting you investigate."

"Because he's decided it's too dangerous!"

"Which was why Radyn and I assumed the risk on your behalf."

He turned to leave, but Elora was on her feet and in front of him before he reached the door. She'd moved so quickly, Radyn was sure she'd used her shardstones. She was fast, and he wondered if there were depths to her skill she hadn't revealed to him yet.

No wonder Jyn thought she was a decent match for him.

Elora spoke softly. "The Engine is lacking something. I don't know what it is, but I'm sure of it."

Something flickered in Jelrik's gaze, but he couldn't hide it from Radyn or Elora. "You knew," Radyn said.

Jelrik swore and sighed. "You two are obnoxious sometimes. Yes, I knew. We just found out this morning in a report from the Master of the Song. *He's* been investigating and coordinating with Nuela, looking through old documents to see if the Makers left us any clues. You two risked your lives for nothing."

Elora didn't care about that. "Did they find a solution?"

"We think so. We got word from Nuela's desk this morning with new coordinates. This morning's song directed the Engine there."

"What's at the coordinates?" Radyn asked.

"We're not sure. Nuela claims it is someplace that might have Makers' technology. Someplace we might find whatever it is the Engine is lacking. There's even been some rumors it's where the great cities were built."

"I thought we didn't know that," Radyn said.

"Until today, I didn't think we did, either, but Nuela claims the location has come from ancient texts only she's had access to."

"Why haven't we flown over it before? That seems like a place that would be incredibly useful."

Jelrik ran a hand through his hair. "It's because the coordinates are a hundred miles within a forbidden zone."

Elora and Radyn cursed together, and for the first time, Radyn wondered if Firestone had any chance of surviving at all.

25

Radyn floated high in the sky, mounted atop Tanwen and using every sense both he and the dragon possessed to watch air and land. The long night was about to end, and Radyn felt the exhaustion deep in his bones. He and the other Swords had been in the air constantly since yesterday, taking only a few hours a day to rest before launching skyward again.

Even Tanwen, strong Tanwen, was weary. His wings moved only as much as was necessary, and Radyn felt the dragon's tiredness as his own. What he wanted was to return to Firestone, crawl into his bed, and sleep for a day.

Before long, he'd be able to. Daylight didn't eliminate their risks, but the dangers were easier to spot, meaning fewer Swords needed to be in the air.

Unfortunately, there was no telling how much longer the Swords would need to pull additional duty. They were to arrive at the coordinates sometime around midday, but what happened once they arrived was a matter of some debate. Nuela, in her announcements, hadn't been clear on the point.

From his altitude, it was almost hard to believe they were flying over the forbidden zone, the land of the Makers. He'd learned about it in school, of course, but he'd never thought he'd be visiting, much less with the entire city behind him. It was a sign of how desperate Nuela must have felt the situation was.

The forbidden zones stretched in a rough line, usually several hundred miles wide, that extended across the continent. They were typically centered on the old cities of the Makers, now hollowed-out shells overgrown with vegetation and wildlife. They were forbidden because the nuddu roamed there, the only creatures large enough and dangerous enough to threaten a great city.

Radyn's duty, shared by the dozens of other Swords in the sky, was to make sure none of the nuddu came close to Firestone. They were described as shadowy, shapeshifting creatures, which gave Radyn little to go on. However, the few older Swords who'd seen one told him he'd recognize one when he saw one.

Fortunately, the dual moons of the planet had been bright last night, and the sky was cloudless. Nothing had approached, and Firestone now neared its destination.

Despite the danger, the view was incredible. Snowy mountain peaks rose in the distance, cast in hues of purple and blue as the last of the night faded away. The ground below was becoming increasingly rugged, and the Singers directed the Engine to pull Firestone higher as the ground rose to meet it.

Finally, the sun broke over the horizon, and Radyn directed Tanwen to return to Firestone. The weary dragon did so without complaint, and when they landed at the Nest, Tanwen went straight to sleep. Radyn wished him well, then stumbled down the stairs to his own apartment.

He was surprised to find Aria there waiting for him. She was sitting in a chair, reading through the book Jyn had given him. "I was wondering if you were going to make it back in time," she said.

He stifled his yawn. "For?"

"Nuela's announcement. She's summoned the head of every family to the auditorium at the beginning of prime shift."

Radyn's exhaustion vanished. "How much do you think she's going to say?"

"Only way to find out is to go. She's got a reckoning on her hands, though. The clan hasn't said anything, but people are worried. The markets are quiet and the hallways are almost empty after supper. They know something is going on, and it's only the weight of tradition holding everything together right now."

Prime shift wasn't far away, so they descended through the levels until they reached the auditorium. A sizeable crowd had already gathered, and Radyn figured it wouldn't be long before they squeezed everyone in shoulder to shoulder. He and Aria found seats near the back and watched as more people piled in. By the time Nuela took the stage, the place was standing-room only, and there wasn't much of that left.

The room went silent as Nuela bowed to the crowd. In a way, she reminded Radyn of Melanie, capable of pulling attention toward her as though it were as natural as breathing. He wondered how much of the ability was because of her position, how much of it was because of her legend, and how much of it was something innate. There was no doubting she had the complete focus of the entire city.

She looked every inch the leader the city needed. She stood tall, and though she wore a simple clan uniform, looked resplendent. The lights on the stage seemed to emphasize the scar running down the side of her face, reminding everyone of the sacrifices she'd already made for the city.

Nuela took a deep, slow breath, then said, "Our Engine is sick."

Had the announcement come from anyone else, or had it been delivered in any other way, Radyn was sure a riot would have broken out in the auditorium and quickly spread throughout the city. The tension in the room thickened. Radyn swore under his breath and wondered what Nuela planned. Why tell the truth now, after lying for so long?

She held up a hand. "I know there will be many questions and concerns. Bear with me for a while, and I hope that many will be answered."

She bowed again, and the weight of her authority was such that the assembled citizens remained largely silent. "The story begins with The Little Fall. At that time, our most senior Singers discovered that the song of the Engine had changed, in such a way they believed a hostile party had carried out an attack. When we discovered the ruins of Whitehawk and studied its Engine, we believed our suspicions were confirmed."

She studied the crowd, then continued. "Here, the hero of our story is Haden, our Master of the Song. While he believed someone had attacked us, he wanted to understand how this new weapon worked and how we could protect ourselves. He created a song that eliminated the Engine's problems and was convinced it would protect us from future attacks. He wasn't content with this, though, and continued his study. The process was long, and I'm not sure any Singer besides Haden could have discovered the truth."

Nuela paused again, letting the tension build. Right before it erupted, she said, "Just in the last few days, he discovered that our Engine isn't well. It lacks the strength it once had, and if something isn't done, the day will come when Firestone will fall, just as Whitehawk did."

The long-awaited outbursts came. Several voices demanded answers, some cried out, and others were angry at not being told sooner.

Nuela endured the barrage without flinching, her presence as commanding as ever. She held up a hand, and after a few moments, the crowd quieted again.

"I hear those among you who are upset. I understand, but remember that it's only recently we've been sure of this problem. Though I've heard the whispered speculations since the Little Fall, it's only in the past few days that Haden has found conclusive evidence of the Engine's illness."

Nuela's claim addressed one complaint, but Radyn saw plenty of unsatisfied faces. If Nuela wasn't careful, she'd still have that riot on her hands. She didn't seem concerned, though, and she continued without hesitation.

"My master once taught me that most of the difficulty in life comes from not knowing exactly what problems you're trying to solve. He claimed that if I could define the problem, the answer would be clear, and never has that proven more true than today. Thanks to Haden's diligence and skill, we've found the problem, and because we know the problem, I know the answer."

Those who had been muttering quieted.

"There is a set of numbers that has been passed down from Blade to Blade since Firestone's Engine first lifted us into the sky, a secret more closely guarded than any other. Those numbers are coordinates—the exact place where Firestone was built by the Makers—the exact place where the Makers left the materials to repair the Engine. Thanks again to Haden, we've caught the problem before it became too late."

Radyn looked around the expansive auditorium. He saw relief on some faces, but doubt on plenty of others. The office of the Blade commanded tremendous respect and obedience, but Nuela pushed the boundaries nearly as far as they would go.

The times called for nothing less, though.

"I have already ordered Firestone toward the coordinates, and we shall be there before the end of prime shift. I will not lie to you and say that this task is without risk. We're passing over forbidden airspace, which is why our Swords have been pushing themselves to breaking the last few days. They've been keeping us safe from danger. Soon, though, we'll come to the area where Firestone was launched. Once there, I will need volunteers to travel down to the surface."

Nuela held up a hand to stop the inevitable objections. "The place where Firestone was built and launched is one of the few places in this world that is safe. It was one of the last bastions of the Makers and was never overrun by the monsters on the surface. Time on the surface will be brief, but we'll need as many volunteers as possible to make our time there as short as possible. Shields are gathered outside to take your names and give further directions."

Nuela bowed once more to the crowd. "I realize this is a lot to take in, and I'm sure there are those among you who will say I should have done something differently. That is fine. What is important today is that Firestone is in danger. Our Engine is ill, we're flying over dangerous territory, and Nightkeep still has infiltrators hiding somewhere in the city. But the answers are right before us, and if all of us work together, I believe we will come out of this stronger than ever. I will travel to the surface myself with the first group of volunteers, eager to help in every way I can."

With that, she turned on a heel and left the stage, the crowd speechless behind her.

Her sudden departure left the crowd stunned, and scattered muttering soon became a deafening din. Neighbors spoke with one another, debating their interpretation of what had just happened. Radyn wanted to do just that with Aria. They left the auditorium, and Radyn noticed no small number of citizens were lined up to volunteer with the Shields.

Once they were beyond the worst of the noise, Radyn asked, "What do you think?"

"I'm not sure what I think, but if Nuela has an answer, I'm glad I'm here. Once things have quieted down, I might sneak down to the observation deck to glimpse everything. I never imagined I would see a Maker city."

"Me either," Radyn said.

"What about you?" she asked.

"I'm too tired to think straight, but I hope she's right, though."

They made it back to Radyn's apartment, and Radyn climbed straight into bed after he extracted a promise from Aria that she would wake him up in a couple of hours. Tanwen would be rested enough to fly and could return to keeping an eye on the city.

He fell asleep a few moments after his head hit the pillow, cautiously optimistic for the first time in days.

26

Aknock at his door woke Radyn. Aria answered it, then let Elora in. Radyn shuffled out of his bedroom, wishing he'd had an hour or two more to sleep. "What is it?"

Elora looked little better than he did. "Direct orders from Nuela. We're approaching the coordinates, and she wants us up in the air."

Radyn rubbed his eyes, gave Aria a quick kiss, and followed Elora toward the stairs. Before long, they were at the Nest, connecting with their dragons. Tanwen looked a little more rested, but wasn't excited by the idea of flying Radyn around again. His displeasure was clear through their connection.

"I know, but we're almost there, and with any luck, we won't be there long. We need to keep Firestone safe."

Tanwen grumbled a weary acknowledgment and let Radyn climb on his neck. They met Elora and her dragon and were surprised to see Jyn there, too. At Radyn's look, Jyn shrugged. "I think Nuela's worried, though she's trying not to show it. The greatest dangers will be from the surface, so it makes sense to have the best riders in Firestone protecting the area."

Radyn supposed that was true, though he didn't like how thin circumstances had pushed them. If Nightkeep was looking for the perfect time to strike, he didn't think they'd find a better one than now. The only fact that kept him from panicking was that if they did attempt to cripple Firestone, they'd be stuck in a forbidden zone with the citizens they'd attacked. He couldn't imagine anyone being quite so foolish.

On the other side of the Nest, farmers and riders were working together to prepare the baskets the dragons would ferry down to the surface. The operation would be even more intensive than Whitehawk's rescue operations, and Radyn predicted a long stretch of short flights to and from the surface.

At a thought, Tanwen leaped into the sky, and Radyn got his first glance at a Maker city.

It impressed him less than he'd hoped. At one point, almost forgotten by their descendants, the Makers might have built a majestic city, but most of what Radyn saw was rubble. A few enormous foundations hinted at the size of buildings, but nothing stood. The creatures that sought to remove humanity from the world had torn every building that reached for the sky down.

Radyn tried to imagine what the city had been like, but his imagination fell short of the task. The ruins were miles in diameter, a city larger than anything he could dream of, but also one stuck to the ground. One that could easily be overrun.

As he flew over the ruins, he looked for dangers, but

nothing moved below. He and Tanwen flew closer to the mountains, pulling ahead of Firestone and scouting for danger.

They didn't find danger, but Radyn spotted their destination. He was glad he had been holding on tightly to Tanwen. If not, he might have fallen to his demise.

Firestone's birthplace.

It could be nothing else.

To call it a hole in the ground didn't even come close to the truth. It was a chasm, an endless pit. The hole by itself was a marvel of engineering.

He knew well the size of Firestone. He'd lived there his entire life and been fortunate enough to fly around it with Tanwen. But seeing it in this context was something entirely different. It made him realize just how large Firestone was and reminded him of the skill of the Makers. The hole looked as though it could fit a mountain within it, and at one point, it might have.

Awe-inspiring structures lined the bottom of the hole, fulfilling purposes Radyn couldn't begin to guess at. Some looked like a hand of impossible dimensions, ready to catch Firestone if it were to drop from the sky.

Firestone's progress across the land slowed as it neared the hole. Radyn banked and fell in close to Elora. "Do you think the coordinates lead there?"

Elora looked between the city and the hole. "If what Nuela said is true, it makes sense. It has to be the birthplace of the city."

They flew together, dragon and rider alike, searching for potential dangers. The ruined city still appeared dead, though. Radyn had halfway expected to find the ruins inhabited by the various wildlife that safely called the surface home, but he didn't see so much as a bird's nest.

As they neared the hole, Radyn studied the massive steel wall that surrounded it. The wall was gouged, burnt, and dented, but as they flew around, Radyn could see no places where the creatures had entered. It protected the hole and for several hundred feet beyond.

The refuge Nuela had spoken of. It didn't seem as absolute as Radyn had imagined, but the squat structures protected by the wall remained intact, so it had done its job.

Radyn hoped it didn't need to repeat the feat today, but he was encouraged by the fact that it had succeeded in the past.

By the time Firestone's shadow passed over the hole, it was barely moving. Radyn said a quick, silent thanks to the Singers, who'd become experts at navigating the city through the generations. Any change in motion was so subtle the citizens within the city rarely noticed when it started or stopped, which spoke volumes about the Singers' skill. The last quarter mile took as long as the three miles before had. Radyn and Elora continued to circle, gaining altitude so they could see farther.

A sudden queasiness ran through his stomach, and Radyn grunted.

It passed a heartbeat later, but he hadn't imagined it. The discomfort had been sudden and strong. Radyn felt his discomfort echoed in Tanwen's senses, where the sensation held a sharper edge. "Did you feel that?" he shouted over to Elora.

She nodded.

Radyn searched for the source of the sensation, and it

didn't take him long to find it. The moment he listened to the song of the Engine, he heard the discordant note, loud and jarring. The Singers were singing, too, and as Radyn listened, he swore.

Elora realized it a moment before he did. "The Singers are hurting the Engine!"

Radyn agreed. He couldn't say why, but it was happening. He turned his attention from the surroundings to Firestone. At first, he saw nothing of note, but as he watched, his eyes went wide.

Before he could turn Tanwen toward the city, a shadow passed overhead and Radyn flinched.

Jyn and his dragon placed themselves between Radyn and Elora. "What was that?" he asked.

"The Singers are hurting the Engine," Elora shouted.

Jyn shook his head. "That can't be. Nuela and Haden are both down there, keeping it safe during the retrieval."

"That's not all," Radyn added.

Both Jyn and Elora turned to him, and he pointed down. "The city is falling."

They followed his finger and watched closely. The fall wasn't dramatic. It was controlled, no doubt part of the complex song the Singers stabbed the Engine with. Most likely, the people within Firestone hadn't even noticed. Those on the surface, if they were paying attention to the world beyond Firestone, might realize, but Radyn didn't hear any alarms pealing from the bells.

Jyn was the first to acknowledge that Radyn was right. "We need to get back to Firestone, but we need all the Swords. Radyn, circle around and order the other Swords to return to the Nest. I'll set up—"

Radyn wasn't listening. He banked Tanwen hard

toward Firestone, Jyn's shouts chasing him down. Aria was down there, and he'd sworn that never again would she be trapped in a city on the surface. Tanwen folded his wings and they plummeted, slowing down at the last possible moment.

Tanwen landed hard, strong legs flexing as he absorbed the impact on Radyn's behalf. Radyn jumped off and spared a moment for a quick bow. "Take care of yourself, friend."

He turned to run but stopped when another dragon landed hard right in front of him. Elora leaped off, her eyes blazing with fury. "What in the hell do you think you're doing?" she shouted.

On any other day, seeing her angry would have caused him to flinch away, but today he stood strong. She was in his way, and there was work to be done. "Firestone will never touch the ground," he said.

"Jyn is collecting the other Swords, because *you* decided you were too important to help. We wait here, and once the Swords are assembled, we'll make our way down to the Engine Room and fix whatever is broken."

"We don't have time."

"You're just one—"

"*They're breaking the Engine.*" Radyn moved to step past her, but she slid so that she was in his way.

"You're wrong," he said. "We don't have the time to wait."

He saw the doubt lurking in her eyes, and for the briefest of moments, she glanced to the sky as she thought, probably calculating the time it would take Jyn to return with the rest of the Swords currently out on patrol. Radyn connected to all his shardstones and struck, punching her hard in the stomach. She caught the movement, but too late. His blow landed clean and she dropped to her knees. She'd be up on her feet in less than a minute, but that was all the time Radyn needed.

"Sorry, but I have to stop them," Radyn said.

She tried to say something, but he'd knocked the breath out of her, and her voice failed.

Radyn ran for the nearest stairwell.

He stopped as soon as alarm bells started ringing. He feared they were for him, but when he followed the source of the sound, he saw that it was coming from a lookout tower near the edge of the Nest. The Dagger on duty was pointing back in the direction Firestone had just come from.

Radyn stopped and stared.

He'd never seen such a creature, but he knew exactly what it was. As the veterans had said, there was no confusing it with anything else. Closer in height to a mountain than a tree and darker than a shadow, it maintained a vaguely human-like shape, though it melted, bent, and reformed at will. At times, Radyn thought he saw stars within that inky darkness.

A nuddu was on the horizon, and it lumbered toward Firestone.

27

Radyn rushed down stairs and leaped down ladders. He ran through crowds, causing no small number of citizens to yell after him, but he couldn't be bothered. He took one set of stairs four at a time, slamming into walls to stop his momentum, then pushing off them to run down the next flight.

Despite his hurry, Elora caught up to him within a few levels. He was almost surprised that she'd been able to follow him until he remembered he'd left quite a trail of unhappy citizens behind him.

"I'm not stopping," he said.

"I know. That's why I'm going with you."

His heart leaped at the declaration. He'd hated arguing with Elora and hated even more what he'd done to get past her. He couldn't imagine doing anything different, but knowing that didn't take his shame away. "Sorry I hit you."

"You'll pay for it once we're sure Firestone is safe."

Radyn jumped down another ladder. Only two levels

remained between them and the Engine, though they still had farther inward to go. "Did you see the nuddu?"

"I did."

There wasn't much else to say. Perhaps the beast had even been what convinced Elora to help instead of wait. Their time grew short.

Radyn found a stairwell that led down the last two levels, and he took the stairs as fast as his body could carry him. He slammed through the opening on the Engine level, then sprinted inward. The area was familiar, and he knew he was getting close. Before long, they'd see the pale blue glow of the Engine.

He bounced around a corner and finally found the Swords guarding the Engine Room. Radyn had expected four, but there were ten instead. Nuela must have been very panicked about protecting the Engine. A wise call.

He called out to the Swords. "The Singers within are betraying us! Firestone is dropping."

The Swords glanced at one another, and Radyn slowed a dozen paces away. Their reactions bothered him.

All he wanted to do was charge through, but he forced himself to take a deep breath and tear his attention away from his body and emotions. It drifted through the hallway, absorbing details.

They wore the uniform of Firestone's Swords, but Radyn didn't recognize their faces. That could be true for a few—he didn't know everyone in the clan by sight, but in a group of ten? He would have known at least one. He sniffed a hint of blood. The uniforms looked wrong, too, though it took him a second to understand why. They were all clean, without a patch, stain, or rip to be found.

No Sword had a uniform that pristine, not unless they'd just ordered one.

"Radyn," Elora whispered.

"I know," he responded.

He kept walking, closing the gap between him and the imposters. Their stances changed. The two closest to him smiled, but the subtle shift of their weight told another truer story.

Nothing he saw would have convicted the imposters before a clan tribunal, but he didn't care. The city was dropping and a nuddu approached. He knew, and that was enough.

He didn't even reach for his hilt. Why bother wasting an extra second of surprise? Maniblades appeared in both hands as he launched himself down the hallway. He cut through the first two before they realized they were in danger, and the two behind barely had time to form their swords before they were brought low.

The third pair was ready, and maniblade clashed against maniblade as they met Radyn's charge. He let the maniblade in his left hand disappear as the Nightkeep Sword on his left sliced at him. Expecting resistance where there was none, the warrior lost his balance. The maniblade reappeared in Radyn's left hand, and he stabbed the off-balance Sword in the throat.

Then Elora was beside him. Radyn retreated a pace, let the maniblades vanish, then grabbed his hilt and formed a maniblade with it. Most of his experience was only with the one weapon, and the hilt was more reliable in battle. He rejoined Elora, who'd already cut through the last of the third rank of swords. Only four Swords remained, but they were fast, and the hallway to the Engine was no wider than any other in Firestone.

One of the enemy Swords came at Radyn while staying close to the wall. Radyn wondered at the approach, as it kept the Sword's right hand too close to the wall to use.

He cursed himself for his foolishness a moment later. A maniblade appeared in the warrior's hand, slicing through the wall without a problem. The Nightkeep Sword cut at him and he misjudged where the maniblade was. He blocked the cut with his own weapon, but it knocked him back several steps, away from the battle forming around Elora.

Radyn swore. They never used the walls to mask their movements in training, because why would they want to tear up Firestone? The enemy Sword revealed a weakness in Radyn's training, and he hoped there weren't many more surprises where that came from. He shifted to the center of the hallway, carefully placing his feet to avoid bodies.

The Sword attacked again, his maniblade darting out like a snake's tongue, flickering toward Radyn's vitals. He sensed the shifting of weight that indicated an attack. But tracking that and his footing stretched his awareness, and his blocks were slower than they should have been. One of his feet slipped in blood. He caught his balance quickly, but it put him on the defensive.

The Nightkeep Sword smelled his victory and redoubled his efforts. Technique faded as his wild speed increased, pushing Radyn backward ever faster. Finally, the Sword knocked Radyn's hilt from his tired hands with a tremendous blow. He grinned viciously as he brought his maniblade up for the last cut.

Radyn formed his two maniblades without the hilt, stabbing them deep into the Sword.

In answer, the infiltrator growled and stepped forward, impaling himself deeper on the maniblades. Radyn moved them up and across, cutting the Sword into pieces before he could do the same to Radyn. The Sword's weapon died as he did, and Radyn stumbled back and out of the way of the falling body parts.

He gagged at the sight of so many bodies. Barely any room remained for him to place his feet, and exhaustion made his limbs heavy. His maniblades vanished, not because he let them go, but because he lost focus. Elora fought the two remaining Swords up ahead. Beyond that duel was the Engine room, where the pale blue glow of the Engine was flickering.

He thought of Aria, waiting for him to return. Of her quiet confidence in his ability.

He'd made a promise.

Radyn connected with every shardstone both in and on his body, filling himself with strength. Tired muscles screamed as he forced them into motion. Shardstones might provide unlimited strength, but a body could only endure so long. He reached down, found his hilt, and sprinted forward.

Elora heard him coming and shifted to the right. Radyn went left, lashing out at the nearest sword with a dagger-length maniblade. The imposter blocked it, but the cut knocked him off balance.

Radyn left the fight behind. He trusted Elora to finish

what he'd started, and all that mattered was getting to the Engine and stopping the Singers from killing them all.

Radyn threw his weight against the door, but it didn't budge. He tried the latch, but it was locked tight, jammed by something on the other side. He peered through the window, but a piece of fabric covered it. The light of the Engine was visible, and shadows swayed as the light danced. He slammed against the door again, but all he earned was a sore shoulder.

He cursed. They didn't have time for this. He took a step back, channeled his strength into the hilt, and stabbed it into the door, cutting through the latch. Then he kicked the door open and stepped through.

The song of the Engine stuttered and moaned. All around the Engine, Singers were clustered on the walkway. No voices echoed in the room, but their song screeched in his mind. Radyn winced against the assault, instinctively dampening his senses to deal with the onslaught.

He raised his maniblade and stumbled toward the first Singer on his right, but before he'd made it two steps, a light flashed from across the room and leaped at him.

Radyn threw himself backward as an enormous maniblade cut through the space before him. It cut through the wall and the walkway. He stopped and spun as the light flashed up, cutting beside him as he retreated. His assailant landed on the walkway's railing right next to him. Metal screamed and tore. Radyn looked down and realized a wedge had been cut from the walkway and he stood in its center.

He didn't react fast enough to leap to safety. Walkway, assailant, and one very confused Radyn tumbled to the bottom of the smooth, spherical room. He fell off the walkway and crashed, end over end, to the bottom. When he stood, he saw his assailant clearly for the first time, waiting patiently.

Nuela stood across from him, a maniblade in her hands and murder in her eyes.

28

"If I'd known you were going to be so much trouble, I would have tossed you off the edge of Firestone the day you were born," Nuela said.

"What?" Radyn's head was still spinning from a combination of the fall, the discordant song of the chorus, and exhaustion. Now his Blade stood before him, threatening him with her maniblade. New experiences had piled up, robbing him of the ability to think his way through any of them.

"Andre was so proud that day. The man had the possibility to be one of the greatest warriors Firestone had ever known, and he drew people to him the way a corpse does flies. But your mother would have none of it. She wasn't going to lose her husband to any of the clan's foolishness. It had been one thing when it was just the two of them, but when he became a father, she would hear no arguments. I hated you for that. Andre was one of my closest friends, and maybe one of the few people who truly understood. I thought he'd be by my side until the day I traveled to the gate."

Nuela's gaze traveled to the past, but the second Radyn flinched, she was back, maniblade leveled. The tip didn't waver.

"It never even occurred to me he would be on the surface that day. He'd been out of my mind so long, and then there he was, a hero one last time."

She shook her head. "He always was infuriating like that."

Pieces clicked together in Radyn's tired head. "You cooperated with Whitehawk. That's why the clan response was so slow that day."

Nuela barely nodded her head. "It was such a simple plan. I gave the clan an excuse to keep most of their warriors on the lower levels, so there should have been minimal casualties. They would have taken the best of our Singers, including Haden, and I would have negotiated to have them returned without further bloodshed. The cost would have been minor, but the potential benefit so great."

She gave a bitter snort. "I think it would have worked, except your father held them off for too long, giving the rest of the clan time to respond."

"They already knew their Engine was sick, didn't they?"

"It was dying, and their Singers were at a loss. But I was a new Blade, and even though I saw the wisdom in sending our Singers to them, I couldn't send all of our most talented Singers to another city. All confidence in my leadership would have been lost. This way, we could study the Engines' failures, and Firestone would have received tribute in recompense."

Her eyes turned hard. "Because I honor the friendship of your father, I will give you one chance. Take off your band, drop your hilt, and kick them both to me. My project is almost finished. There's no need for additional blood to be shed."

Radyn summoned all the strength remaining to him and leaped at her, cutting at her faster than a dragon could snatch a running deer from a hillside. There was a flash of light and heat, and then he was past her. Had he cut her so easily?

He twisted around to look, but she was unharmed. She turned slowly, not a hair out of place, and shook her head. "Your father, at least back when he was clan, through and through, would have been proud. That was a beautiful cut."

Radyn lifted his maniblade to strike again, but there was no glowing blade. He tilted his wrists. The hilt had been cut right above where he held it. He stumbled backward. He hadn't even seen her attack. What kind of speed did she possess?

The corner of Nuela's mouth turned up in a smile. "You really thought you could challenge me, didn't you? Did Jyn fill your head with possibilities? I'm guessing he did. You're probably almost as good as him, but there's so, so very much left for you to learn."

She raised her maniblade again. "Last chance. I'm well aware you've mastered the old forms. Take off your band, and show me your ankles. The only way you live through this is if you convince me you don't have a shardstone anywhere near you."

Radyn's thoughts raced, but he quickly realized there wasn't anything to think about. He couldn't beat Nuela in a duel. The last pass had proven that definitively. He unstrapped his band and tossed it at her feet. Then he showed her his ankles, rolled up his sleeves, and pulled his pockets inside out. As he did, he figured out most of the rest. Nuela was clearly cooperating with Nightkeep the same way she had Whitehawk, but why harm their Engine? Why bring them down in the forbidden zones?

"Why?" he asked.

"You haven't figured it out yet? I'm a little disappointed, after all the good things Elora and Jyn have had to say about you."

Radyn fought the urge to roll his eyes. The longer he kept Nuela talking, the more of a chance Elora had of coming to help. Truthfully, he was worried that she hadn't shown up yet. He'd expected her to take care of the two Swords remaining in the hallway with little difficulty.

He closed his eyes and took a deep breath, considering what he'd learned from Nuela. She'd cooperated with both Whitehawk and Nightkeep. Both cities had been willing to expend considerable resources, too. Firestone's Engine was having its own problems, and within this all, Melanie was creating a group, made up of willing Firestone leaders, to settle on the surface.

The realization struck like a bolt of lightning and he staggered backward. "All the Engines are failing, aren't they?"

"Clever boy. I don't know if there is something happening to the Engines that could be fixed if we had more knowledge, or if the Makers only designed the cities to last for so long. There's so much we don't know. I don't know if our Engine will fail today or in five years, but we can't stay in the sky."

Her last line struck like a hammer blow, as it revealed another devastating truth. "There's nothing down here for us."

"We have the walls the Makers built, never breached."

"There's a nuddu coming. The walls won't do anything."

"The walls were never breached, not even by the nuddu. I don't know how, but they repel the creatures. Humanity needs to return to the surface, and I've volunteered Firestone to lead the way."

Nuela took a step toward him, bringing her maniblade an inch from his neck. "A new age begins today. I'm not delusional. I know it'll be the hardest transition humanity has ever made, but it's the only way we survive. Strength like yours is more valuable than food, more valuable than steel, and even more valuable than the dragons. You swore an oath to protect Firestone when you became a Dagger, and that applies just as much when it's on the ground as when it's in the sky. Will you help the city, or do I have to kill you here?"

Radyn anguished over the answer. He sensed no falsehood from her, nor even a hint of madness. And although he cursed her, he understood. The citizens were, on average, terrified of the surface. *He* was terrified of the surface, and he was among the strongest Swords in the city. Never in a dozen years would she convince them it was better to try their luck on the surface. The transition could only be forced.

He understood, but he didn't know if she was right. He assumed Haden had tried everything in his power to repair the Engine, but what if the solution lay with one of the other Singers?

The nuddu loomed large in his memories. How could they trust Maker machinery they understood even less than their own city?

He saw both sides, and he couldn't decide.

She brought her maniblade closer to his neck. "Your father would have understood."

Radyn's doubt hardened into certainty. He already had his hand in position, and he was connected to the shardstones embedded in his body. The maniblade appeared in his hand, thrusting through the bottom of Nucla's chin and up through the top of her head. Her maniblade winked out and she crumpled at his feet.

"Father died defending Firestone from you."

He looked up. The song of the chorus continued unabated, grating against his senses. Until he stopped that song, Firestone was as good as doomed.

Perhaps it was already too late.

He reached down and picked up his band, returning it to his wrist. What he really wanted was to lie down, cover his head with a pile of pillows, and go to sleep.

For a week.

One last time, he let the shardstones fill his limbs with strength. His muscles burned and his bones felt brittle, but his body just had to hold out a little longer. He ran up the side of the spherical room, thrusting dagger-length maniblades into the wall to help him climb back to the walkway. When he reached the cut section, he launched himself up, let his maniblades vanish, and pulled himself onto the walkway. He lay there for a moment, the cool grate pressed against his cheek.

"Radyn," said Elora. Her voice was weak.

He pushed himself to his feet and stumbled into the hallway. Elora was leaning against the wall, holding her side. Blood leaked freely through her fingers. He rushed to her. "What happened?"

"That last Sword was good. Better than Jyn, I think." She offered a bloody grin. "Killed him, though. Next time I convince Jyn to duel, I think I'm going to have some surprises for him."

Radyn wasn't so sure. The wound looked too big for even the best healers to close up, but he said nothing about it. His vision blurred as tears sprang to his eyes. "Hang in there for a few more minutes. I've got to stop the Singers."

"Do what you need to. I'll be right behind you. Just need to gather my strength for a minute."

Radyn didn't want to leave her, but the work wasn't over. "I'll be back as soon as I can. I'm sure help is on the way, too."

Leaving his master behind was harder even than leaving his father on the surface. Fury washed over him, and maniblades appeared in his hands. He stepped back onto the walkway, snarled, and ran.

Singing took complete focus from the chorus. They only noticed as the first Singer fell, but they were too deep in their song to react. He gave them no chance. His swords bit through neck after neck, and he ran the perimeter of the walkway as fast as his tired legs would carry him. Eight Singers died in seconds, and Radyn stopped again in the hallway, a few steps from Elora.

He let the maniblades fade for what he hoped was the last time that day. The song of the chorus had ended, but the light of the Engine still flickered. He reached out to the Engine, listening to its song for a moment before disconnecting.

He leaned against the wall next to Elora. He'd done everything he could, and it still wasn't enough. Firestone would fall, and the nuddu would arrive. He swore.

"What's wrong?" Elora asked. Her eyes were open, but it didn't look like she was aware of her surroundings.

"The Singers did something to the Engine. I killed them all, but the Song of the Engine is still wrong."

She was so still for a moment he worried she'd already gone to the gate. Then she pushed against the wall and tried to stand up. She failed, hitting the wall hard.

"What are you doing?" he asked.

"I'm going to heal the Engine."

"Have you lost your wits? You're not a Singer, and even if you were, you're alone! There's nothing you can do."

"Watch me."

Elora pushed herself up again, but again lost her balance and fell back against the wall.

"You'll need to help me. Take me to the Engine, to where the walkway juts out," she said.

"That's suicide!"

"I've done it once before, and in case all my training has failed you, you might notice I'm not doing so well, anyway."

He was about to argue again, but she grabbed his wrist. "Radyn."

He closed his eyes, understanding everything she'd meant to say. "Fine."

Radyn guided her over to the cut-out section of the walkway. Her sight seemed poor, and she put so much weight on him that he felt like he might as well be carrying her. The journey to the Engine stretched on forever, but it was still completed all too soon.

She clutched tightly at his upper arm. "I'm proud of you."

Then, without any more warning or preparation, she reached out and touched the Engine.

29

The moment Elora touched the Engine, it lit the room with a blinding light. Radyn flinched away and covered his eyes, but he couldn't escape the song. It swelled to a deafening crescendo. Blood trickled from Radyn's eyes, nose, and ears. The song filled him from heel to crown, a monstrous power barely controlled.

He felt as though he was battered by turbulent winds of pure energy. He was about to fall when a hand reached out and took his. It was slippery and covered in blood, but the storm faded and he swam in an ocean of limitless power.

Elora held onto him for a moment more, and his curiosity got the better of him. He stretched his awareness through her so he could seek some understanding of what she was doing. What he found defied easy description. Hundreds, maybe thousands, of connections ran between Elora and the Engine. Songs danced along the web of connections.

How are you doing this?

He received no answer. The amount of strength rushing through her was more than was meant for any human, but for one beat of the song after another, she contained it and distributed the power where it needed to go.

He pushed his awareness deeper, slowly becoming aware of another presence that resonated with the Song of the Engine. It was deeper, though, and almost infinitely more vast. For all the power of the Engine, the Engine was a drop of water in a holding tank compared to this. Power filled from this even deeper well, spreading throughout the Engine.

Radyn started to explore deeper, but a force gently stopped him.

This isn't yet for you.

With surprising gentleness, Elora thrust him away, and for the first time since the shardstones had been inserted within his body, he couldn't feel a connection with the Engine at all. He stumbled back into the wall and slid down it. His legs couldn't even support his weight anymore.

He couldn't hear the song now, but he could see the Engine, and it was more beautiful than it had ever been, glowing brighter than the sun.

Elora had a wide grin, and it looked like she was a child again, without a care in the world. Her hand slipped off the Engine. She wobbled for a moment, then collapsed to the ground and was still. Radyn reached toward her, and the last thing he saw before his world went black was the peaceful, contented look on her features.

When he woke, he was in a familiar room.

Or at least, it looked the same as the interrogation room he'd been in before. His wrists and ankles were bound with steel and chain, and this time, they'd searched him and removed his band. He searched for the shardstones within his body and breathed a slow sigh of relief.

They remained hidden, and he could connect with them. Whatever had happened in the Engine room hadn't broken him for good.

With his sharpened senses, he could hear the commotion on the other side. Now that he was awake, he expected to have visitors soon. He looked down at his chained wrists.

It wasn't quite the hero's celebration he would have liked.

He wished they would have at least put him in a bed, though if they'd given him the chance, he would have been asleep again within a minute.

Eventually, the door opened. Jyn stepped in, shut the door behind him, covered the window in the door, and took the seat opposite Radyn. He said nothing. He just sat and stared.

"Congratulations on the promotion," Radyn croaked. He needed water, but Jyn didn't look inclined to go get him any.

Jyn wore the uniform of the Blade. In the time Radyn had been unconscious, he'd become the 13th Blade of Firestone.

Of Firestone. If Jyn had time to become the Blade, it

meant Firestone had survived. "What happened?" Radyn asked.

"That's what you can tell me first." Jyn's voice was as sharp as the edge of a maniblade. "The last time I saw you, you were disobeying a direct order, and Elora was following you. The next time I see you, there are enough dead bodies to make me think Firestone is at war. Nuela is dead, and lying next to her body is your broken hilt."

"And Elora?" Radyn asked, though the answer seemed obvious enough.

"Dead, too. The only person with a pulse anywhere near the Engine was you, and it took our best healers days to figure out how to bring you back from a coma. So right now, I need answers."

Radyn wondered if he needed to lie, but he was too tired.

Truth was always simpler. And he didn't care about the consequences. Firestone was safe.

So he told Jyn everything, starting from his decision to disobey the order to the moment he watched Elora sing to the Engine by herself. Every word was true, except he didn't reveal the existence of his embedded shardstones. That, he felt, was too valuable a secret to share. He said instead that he'd taken a hilt from one of the Nightkeep Swords and tucked it in his belt. It was a weak lie, but Jyn didn't seem too concerned with how he'd killed Nuela.

When it was over, Radyn leaned back in his chair. He was tired.

Jyn stared at him for a moment, then stood up with such force his chair went tumbling backward. He swore so loud the walls shook, and then he started pacing the room. After a minute, he stopped and pointed at the door.

"Do you have any idea the amount of tension there is out there? Nuela makes her big announcement, and then nothing happens except dozens of dead people suddenly appear near the Engine room, including the hero of Firestone, the 12th Blade. I'm one bad day from having riots on every level of this city, and you're here telling me that *Nuela* was going to crash us into the ground? What am I supposed to say?"

"Do you believe me?"

"I wish I didn't, but I do. The pieces fit, and it matches with what I've been able to find out on my own."

"What happened, after?"

Jyn picked up his chair and slumped down into it. "I don't know how long the battle was over before we arrived. We found the bodies and quickly identified them as the Nightkeep infiltrators. Some among the Singers were our own, including Haden."

Radyn hadn't even noticed. He'd been so exhausted, they'd been nothing more than targets. They'd all been traitors.

"Our loyal Singers took over, led by Jelrik. They raised Firestone back into the sky and sent us straight north, following the quickest route out of the Forbidden Zone. The nuddu quickly lost interest once we were moving fast. The Singers tell me they can't hear any discordant notes in the Engine, no matter how deep they dive. According to them, it's stronger than it has been in any of their lifetimes."

"Elora did it all," Radyn said. "She figured something out, even if the cost was her life. Can I see Jelrik?"

Jyn shook his head. "He's broken with grief, and he's made it clear he wants nothing to do with you. In his mind, Elora followed you, disobeying my orders. He blames you for her death."

Radyn closed his eyes, trying to keep tears from coming again. Days might have passed, but it only felt like minutes since he'd watched Elora sacrifice herself. She'd only been there because of him. "He's not wrong to do so."

He breathed out slowly, trying to consider some of the implications of a new idea. Talk of Jelrik had sparked a solution, though it wasn't a pleasant one. He thought it worked, though.

"Tell them the truth about Elora. She deserves to be a hero for what she did. She *is* a hero for what she did. The reason we're all in the air right now is because of her. But for all the rest of it, blame everyone but Nuela. Blame Nightkeep, reveal Haden's treachery, and make me a fool. There's enough truth there; it won't be hard. I disobeyed orders, and eventually, Nuela herself had to come and save me from the traitors, but in the process, died. I can become the villain so she can remain the hero."

This time, it was Jyn's turn to lean back in his chair. He considered, carefully, for several minutes. Radyn almost fell asleep.

"They'll hate you. Nuela was well-loved," Jyn said.

"I don't care. So long as I can tell Aria the truth."

"I can't guarantee your safety, and there will have to be a public tribunal. I can keep you from death, but you'll be banished from the clan for negligence."

"I know, and you don't need to protect me."

Jyn stood slowly. "I didn't want to start my time as Blade this way."

"The lie is better than the alternative. If you lead the city well, it won't matter how it started."

Jyn shook his head. "I would have liked to have had you around to advise me."

Radyn snorted at that. "You say that now, but after a week of my advice, I think you'd change your mind."

"Probably."

Jyn looked around the room, but there was nothing for him to look at. He sighed. "This might be the last time you and I have a chance to speak together. You'll be exiled from the clan and reviled by all who loved Nuela. Your name will likely be crossed out in blood from our ranks. So I want to take this opportunity."

With that, Jyn got to his knees and pressed his forehead to the floor, honoring his prisoner.

When he rose, he pulled a hilt from behind his back. He handed it to Radyn. "It was Elora's. Jelrik wanted nothing to do with it, and I think Elora would have wanted you to have it. She loved you like a son."

Radyn wished it was easier to wipe the tears from his eyes, but his chains didn't have enough give in them. "Thank you, Jyn, truly."

Jyn gave him one last brief bow. "Farewell, Radyn. I'll make sure you're released today, though I think it would be best if you stayed at Aria's place until the tribunal. There are already demands that I bloody your name, and Nuela's greatest admirers might try to take revenge into their own hands."

Radyn nodded, and Jyn left the room.

He stared at the ceiling, and his thoughts kept turning

to Nuela talking about his father. When they'd first met, she'd told him she would help him understand Father better. Though it hadn't happened the way she'd expected, it had happened.

He'd grown strong like his father and joined the clan. His youthful boasts of wanting to become stronger echoed painfully loud in his memories. And in the end, it had brought him nothing but heartbreak. He was glad he'd been able to help Firestone, but he didn't want to pay such a high price ever again.

If Jyn's predictions came true, and Radyn had little doubt they would, his days with the clan were numbered. It would be months, if not years, before he could walk freely without having to look over his back.

The thought didn't bother him much at all. Like his father, he'd leave the clan behind for good, no matter how long it took. He would propose to Aria soon, and he would return to the surface to farm. He smiled at the thought, and imagined Father would be proud. After all this time, he was going to trade his maniblade for a hoe.

THE ADVENTURES CONTINUE!

Top of the morning!

I hope that wherever you are in the world, this finds you doing well. Thanks for reading, and I hope you enjoyed the story. In an age of endless entertainment options, the choice to spend your time in these pages means the world to me.

These Fallen Swords was an absolute pleasure to write, and I'm excited to share more of Radyn's journey and his world with you. Look for book 2 to arrive in January 2024!

Ryan

October 2023

ABOUT THE AUTHOR

Ryan Kirk is the award-winning and internationally bestselling author of over thirty fantasy novels spanning nearly a dozen worlds. He lives in Minnesota with his family, where he enjoys long, meandering walks outside even when the snow is high enough to cover his legs. When he isn't glued to his keyboard, he's usually in the woods, either on foot or on a bike.

RyanKirkAuthor.com
contact@waterstonemedia.net

facebook.com/waterstonemedia
x.com/waterstonebooks
instagram.com/waterstonebooks